STORIES FROM OTHER PLACES

Nicholas Shakespeare

STORIES FROM
OTHER PLACES

Harvill *Secker*
LONDON

1 3 5 7 9 10 8 6 4 2

Harvill Secker, an imprint of Vintage,
20 Vauxhall Bridge Road,
London SW1V 2SA

Harvill Secker is part of the Penguin Random House group
of companies whose addresses can be found at
global.penguinrandomhouse.com.

Penguin
Random House
UK

First published by Harvill Secker in 2015

www.vintage-books.co.uk

A CIP catalogue record for this book is available from the British Library

ISBN 9781846559747 (hardback)
ISBN 9781473521728 (ebook)

Typeset in ITC Galliard Std by Palimpsest Book Production Limited,
Falkirk, Stirlingshire
Printed and bound in Great Britain by Clays Ltd, St Ives plc

Penguin Random House is committed to a sustainable future
for our business, our readers and our planet. This book is made
from Forest Stewardship Council® certified paper.

To M.B.

I have in my face
the faces of everyone I have loved.

How can you say I am ugly?

Vyacheslav Kupriyanov

Contents

Oddfellows   1

The White Hole of Bombay   102

The Princess of the Pampas   122

Freshwater Fishing   156

The Death of Marat   175

The Castle Morton Jerry   215

The Statue   227

The Orange-bellied Parrot   265

Acknowledgements   276

Oddfellows

It's a little before 10 a.m. on New Year's Day 1915, and the sun strikes broadside the picnickers waiting at Sulphide Street station. Hats and parasols give faint protection to the 1,239 men, women and children who sit or stand in the open ore-wagons, clutching spiky handles of wicker hampers, mopping temples, pointing.

The thermometer registers 101 in the shade.

Since August, many of the same faces have been seeing off volunteers to join the Commonwealth Expeditionary Forces. Now it's their turn to board a train from this station, with 'Broken Hill' painted in black on a white board.

Dressed in freshly laundered summer clothes, the last passengers hurry along the platform and clamber into the trucks which the Silverton Tramway Company has hosed out for them.

Four trucks away from the locomotive that is being stoked up, Mrs Rasp, a podgy, flat-faced woman whose masculine features remind some of the Prime Minister, tells Mrs Kneeshaw in a breathless voice about the letter she has received from her son Reginald.

His infantry squad has arrived in Egypt!

'He says the canal is only a hundred yards wide . . . and there's hardly a tree for miles. You'd think you were outside Broken Hill . . .' She wipes a trickle of sweat from the bridge of her big nose, and resumes, fanning her face. 'They are near the place where the Children of Israel were supposed to have crossed the Red Sea.' Her straw hat shimmers at the news; she has bought it for the picnic outing at her favourite drapery store in Argent Street.

Mrs Rasp is floury white, large and shapeless, like her thoughts and the shapeless things she says. A captain of the League of the Helping Hand, she has that inattention to the opinions of others that one often associates with a double-barrelled name. Her round head cranes forward beneath its halo of cream straw. 'He wants me to send him a balaclava sleeping cap, as he's likely to be exposed to severe cold during the European winter.' She is anxious not to lose Mrs Kneeshaw's attention.

Seated quietly opposite in a rose silk dress, Mrs Kneeshaw shields her screwed-up eyes with a flattened hand and says nothing.

Since September, Winifred Kneeshaw has been in charge of the Red Cross Society tea-room in Argent Street. She is an elegant woman who has completed her training with the newly established Australian Branch of the British Red Cross and has gained her certificate for proficiency in ambulance work – afterwards, she will say that she didn't expect to be called upon so soon to use her knowledge. She finds it hard in this heat to focus on Reginald Rasp in Egypt.

This is a day to forget absent ones. To set aside unwelcome thoughts of war. In a moment, the whistle will shriek, and the train will steam out of the station, ferrying its cheerful cargo not to Adelaide and from there across the Indian Ocean to Suez – but fourteen miles north-west, along the narrow-gauge line to Silverton.

New Year's Day is Manchester Unity Day, and the friendly society's picnic, organised by the Manchester Unity Independent Order of Oddfellows, the greatest gathering of the year in Broken Hill. Today is for those left behind, so far as Mrs Kneeshaw behind her screening fingers is concerned. An opportunity for everyone to draw together and to show their sense of communality after one of the most testing periods in the town's history.

For sixteen years, the metals mined from Broken Hill have been railroaded to Port Pirie and shipped to the Saxon city of Freiberg, 'the Mecca of ores', to make bullets for the Kaiser's guns. But Australia is at war with Germany. For the fifth successive month, the conical heaps of zinc and lead concentrates have piled up untouched. Abandoned, like the German Club in Delamore Street.

'I just wish we could borrow some of Reggie's cool weather,' Mrs Kneeshaw murmurs, and pulls up the corner of her dress and wipes her eye, revealing to Mr Dowter, sitting straight as in a pew beside Mrs Rasp, a flash of white petticoat.

Not wishing to draw attention by averting his gaze too immediately, Clarence Dowter goes on staring with pursed lips and a wooden expression in the direction of Mrs Kneeshaw's exposed underclothes. He is the town's Sanitary Inspector, and has agreed to officiate this afternoon as umpire in the women's seventy-five-yard race at the picnic ground. He is a short, mournful-looking Irishman with a downturned mouth, a forehead dented like his homburg hat, a mop of blue-black hair that competes oddly with his sparse, much fairer beard, and small grey eyes that miss nothing. In the raging sun, his hollowed-out face seems on the verge of melting. Head cocked at an angle, he taps his oval cigarette on a silver case, and after an interval which he decides is long enough shifts his glance to Mrs Lakovsky's latest baby.

'Don't go tiring yourself, mate!'

Mrs Rasp twists with her mouth open to see who it is that Roy Sleath, the policeman's son, is trying to grab the attention of.

It's not hard to recognise the young man who leaps agilely aboard, clasping a bulging brown paper bag: he is of the more athletic type of Broken Hill miner, all elbows, with sandy hair and sharp nose.

'Hey, Ollie, over here!'

Waving down Roy's incitements, he stops in front of Lizzie Filwell, a pale fourteen-year-old with dark brown hair and a prematurely corrugated forehead, and opens her hand. To the girl's obvious delight, he drops a yellow peach into it. He chats with her parents, sitting on either side of her, glances quickly around, and vanishes from view, then reappears, erect, in front of Roy, and chucks him under the chin, before moving on.

For Lizzie's elder sister Rosalind, seated in the same wagon, the day promises something momentous.

Rosalind Filwell wears a white skirt to her ankles, which, like her hands and feet, she wants to be more dainty than they are, and a pomegranate-pink felt hat fringed with a muslin veil to fend off the sun and the flies. Her abundant black hair is twisted into a French knot above her oval face. Her deep-set hazel eyes cast their own shadow, so that according to the angle of her face she can seem attractive or plain. When they fix on Oliver Goodmore, the man pushing his way towards her, she looks tired.

One month shy of her twenty-second birthday, Rosalind is certain that Oliver intends to use the pretext of the afternoon's events – the picnics under the pepper trees, the distribution of dolls and lollies, the running events (where he is expected to shine) to escort her at some point along the dried creek-bed, there being no strong breeze or dust, and propose.

She knows this because her best friend Mary Brodribb, who waved to her just now from the adjacent truck, personally helped Oliver to select the engagement ring in Harvey's jewellery store.

But is this what Rosalind wants?

She looks up at him in his low-neck flannel shirt and narrow-brimmed hat, with the sun striking his unprotected chin, and his squinting face smiles down at her. His ticket says second class, but from everything in his manner he feels in first.

He throws a leg over the wooden plank which Mrs Rasp has earlier dusted with her fan, and holds out his paper bag. 'Hey, Ros, put these in your hamper, will you, because I'll probably drop them knowing me.'

Her hands occupied in packing away his peaches and apples, he reaches out to touch Rosalind's cheek with a thick index finger, which has a crescent of dirt she cannot avoid observing.

'Did you sort out Tom's motorbike?'

He doesn't answer her, still puzzled by something.

'I was looking for you over there,' and squeezes in beside her on the temporary wooden bench. 'I reckoned you'd be with Lizzie.'

2

Rosalind had risen early that morning, woken by a dog. She lay in bed and listened to the howl rising and falling. A harmless noise by day, the cry swept through her like the phantom of her brother's voice, and in the small hot bedroom whipped her thoughts into a mob of skittish anxieties that gathered her off on drumming hooves.

She threw back the sheet and slipped out of bed. Her shadow followed her across the floorboards as she felt her way past the chamber pot which her father had bought at auction when Alderman Turbill moved to Adelaide, around the side table that she had decorated with ribbons and fabrics and her own mirror – egg-shaped with a silver border from which dangled a spare handbag, inherited from her grandmother – to the window. Her first impulse after widening the latch – to gulp in the air. It had the whiff of saltbush, and was a reminder of how the night's smells were stranger than the day's, and had more in common with the baying that challenged her from beyond the mullock.

Every time Rosalind looked out of the bedroom which she had shared with William until his death three years ago, and since then with her younger sister Lizzie – burbling to herself in her sleep in the parallel narrow bed – there, 600 yards away, loomed the mullock. It hung over the town like an enormous slouch hat, throwing out a long, unwelcome shadow.

Ordinarily, the gigantic heap of tippings would have been a barrier to check Rosalind's roving thoughts. But her thoughts were not obedient. She peered into the black shape that it cast, and felt a dizzying tug. As if the mullock was clutching out to unite her shadow with its own.

Rosalind had climbed it often enough in daylight – with Oliver, and before that with William. From the top, Broken Hill could clearly be seen in miniature below.

She saw herself gazing down through the smoking shaft heads: onto her parents' bungalow in Rakow Street, the yard with the dairy cows and wrecked buggy, over the galvanised rooftops and humpies of North Broken Hill, over the water tanks perched on angle-iron towers as if ready to stride off, over the dust cloud raised by a string of camels, across a red sandy loam covered with saltbush and bluebush, mile after mile, to Silverton. This was the extent and limit of her world, sandwiched between the Umberumberka Creek in Silverton, where dawn was appearing over the dry and dreary tableland in – what had he called it? – two bullock hides of light, and the slag heap that frowned over every street.

Her idea of the universe was indeed wretched. The only break in the drip-drip of the days was the train.

Sydney was a distance of 1,446 miles by railway, and it cost as much to travel there by train – on a roundabout route through Adelaide, Melbourne and Albury – as to London by ship. Most likely, she would live to see the ocean only in a mirage.

Rosalind's shadow on the striped wallpaper showed the nightdress pulling tight across her breasts.

She had felt rebellious since William was taken away. His death made her afraid of everything and nothing.

· Her fingers squeezed the latch till they hurt. All these

stupid questions about who she was going to marry. Come to your senses, Rosalind. And her whispered words in the dark produced a shudder in the bed behind.

Suddenly, she wanted to vanish. Not to be here, in this room, with her shadow on the wall and Lizzie moaning, as she always did when her bladder was full – Rosalind had already woken her sister twice and helped her onto the chamber pot.

In their grief, their parents seemed to have forgotten Lizzie's complications. She had become Rosalind's responsibility. But however much Rosalind loved her little sister, she longed to leave.

If she could change place with one of those stars.

Like them, Rosalind felt fully formed. She knew her mind. She knew everything came hard, what the price of everything was in Stack & Tyndall's drapery store, where she stood behind the counter. She could envisage her future with Oliver. It did not need much imagining. Even Lizzie could have drawn it in one of her episodes of normality.

She moved and her shadow moved. Other women kept telling her that she had a good figure. Rosalind dared not contemplate what that meant.

Still gripping the latch, she leaned forward, tossed by another thought: his body thudding into her every night, his rough fingers touching her.

Her thoughts bucked and she held on tight. It was terrible to be in this state of disarray.

The stars glittered in the water trough outside the Freiberg Arms Hotel and on the railway behind. Her eyes picked out the iron tracks and followed them – past the garden fences, towards the Picton sale yard. The rails curved beside the trench containing the wooden stave water pipe to Silverton.

The train was the only way out. Either that, or you plunged into the earth.

In William's day, she would have expected to see a long line of men walking as all miners do in the world, heads lowered, ready to descend into darkness. This morning, Rakow Street stretched deserted and silent. The mines had been working half-time since August. The presence on the pavements, and in the bars and boarding houses, of so many unemployed single men with no hope of work, save as soldiers, was unsettling. Miss Pollock had taught that the Aborigines named the district Willyama, meaning Youth. Once upon a time, this was a town of prospectors looking for lodes, and finding them. Now, there was nothing for a young person to do in Broken Hill, except die or leave. Or sail to Suez.

Oliver was one of the fortunate ones, earning twenty-six shillings for three shifts a week. He was twenty-seven and had come from Melbourne ten years before, at the urging of his uncle, Clarence Dowter, to assist him in the laying of the water pipe. He had stayed on, doing various jobs, until he was offered a position in the South Mine, working in the same team as her brother.

Soon, he would be climbing out of bed in his rented room in Piper Street. Rosalind saw him soaping his nose and face, washing the smoke and fumes off him and his musty carbide smell, and putting on his suit for the Oddfellows' picnic. And before he locked his door and strolled over to Tom Blows's garage and then to Alf Fiddaman's grocery store, he'd slip that gold-bound garnet into the pocket of his flannel shirt.

She felt a hostage to her parents' expectations. Oliver was the life they wished for her. Rosalind's mother in particular.

Rosalind was lucky to have attracted an admirer, was her mother's opinion. Emmy Filwell had lost her son to the mine; her youngest daughter to the water on her brain. With more girls than boys in Broken Hill, she wanted Rosalind settled.

Encouraged by Mrs Filwell, steadily and persistently Oliver had been at her, trying to get her to say yes.

What would William have thought?

Oliver was with her brother in the South Mine on that November night, three years ago. They were popping rocks 825 feet below the surface, when William crawled away on his hands and knees, and Oliver heard him say, 'I can't find it along here,' then heard a sound like something falling, and on crawling after him discovered that his mate had tumbled down a winze sixty feet deep, fracturing his skull.

Oliver had helped to compose the lines they had put in the *Barrier Miner*:

Do not ask us if we miss him,
There is such a vacant place;
Can we e'er forget his footsteps,
And his dear, familiar face?

He had never been able to explain to her what, precisely, William had been looking for, in the dark, on his hands and knees.

Oliver, called Ollie by all who knew him (but not by Rosalind), had her brother's hands and fingernails. A practical man, with a box of second-hand tools, he could repair an electric motor with his eyes shut, or a radiator hose, or a blocked pipe beneath the sink, and in his spare time was vice-captain of the Broken Hill rugby team and secretary of the local rifle club.

Who never hid his delight when he saw Rosalind.

She enjoyed her power over him. Under pressure from her mother, she had started to put aside money that she earned from the drapery store towards their future together. Oliver Goodmore at least offered an escape from the morbidity of the Filwell household and the nagging responsibility of her sister.

Oliver was good with Lizzie. He was natural with her, and patient, and never laughed when she was silly. Rosalind liked that.

Then she saw in him a kindness that pleased her.

He was not like his friends, who always had one too many. He had flashes of intelligence and tenderness, and was ready to help others. He was quite authoritarian, although he could hold that in check if he wanted to be nice. When he wanted to be nice, he gave her the full battery of his attention.

Rosalind was thinking about this when there was a movement at the corner of Garnet Street. The street was not empty after all. She watched a thin horse lumber out of the mullock's shadow, drawing behind it a white cart.

The cart glistened like a patch of silver as it came creaking down the far side of the road. She craned forward. Two men were seated side by side under the canopy. They were dark-skinned, and beneath their open khaki coats wore red jackets, and on their heads clean white turbans. The tails of the turbans trailed over their shoulders.

They made a strange contrast in the starlight. The old man, short and fat, sitting with his arms folded; the younger, slim, also clean-shaven but taller, slapping the reins. And above them, the pyramidical shape of the mullock.

The configurations of the night were inexplicable as her sister's madness. The old man seemed to have twinkling rings on his fingers and toes.

As if Rosalind had murmured 'Stop!' the horse pulled over and started drinking from the water trough opposite. Only then did she recognise the younger man – Gül Mehmet. She had never seen Gül in a turban.

The portly old man seemed familiar, too, except that he had shaved off the grey beard which she recalled scrolling over his pot belly.

Rosalind tilted her head. But their conversation was inaudible above whatever Lizzie was now tittering about in her sleep, like the giggles that other children burst into on seeing her.

With reluctance, Rosalind turned from the window. She would have to wake up her sister so that she didn't wet her bed.

The two men had ridden out that morning from the North Camel Camp at the extreme end of Williams Street. The camp consisted of a few galvanised sheds surrounded by a loose wire fence. There was a small brick building with a tin roof that served as a mosque, and two struggling rows of date palms. Here lived thirty or so camel drivers, mostly Afghans and Indians, with their families and animals.

The settlement had been there since 1890 and was resented by a minority in Broken Hill, who nicknamed it 'Ghantown'. Their prejudice found its mouthpiece in a former editor of the *Barrier Miner*, Ralph Axtell, who though he had been living for some years in Melbourne had returned to Broken Hill a fortnight before to visit a sick cousin. The Benevolent Society, on hearing that Axtell planned to remain in town until after Christmas, had invited him to give an end-of-the-year address. This had taken place the night before the picnic outing, at the Trades Hall on Blende Street.

It being New Year's Eve, many Benelovent Society

members chose to remain at home with their families. But the poor size of the audience, patchily spread out over the three front rows, failed to douse Axtell or the fervour of his delivery. Those who attended his talk, including a reporter from his old newspaper, listened intently to what he had to say.

A nuggety socialist with a high forehead and a thick ginger moustache, Axtell transformed when on stage into a dynamic orator. He was a skilled agitator against Afghans and other 'Turkey lollies', as he called them. His fiery lecture was a get-together of his old saws, and calculated to fan the anti-Turk feeling which had re-emerged since the outbreak of war. The target of his scorn was the posturing German Kaiser, but Axtell went further to include the Ottoman Sultan and Caliph, Mehmet V, who that summer had signed a treaty with the Germans; then to encompass all Muslims, who were said to regard the Sultan as their leader; before homing in on those who lived just up the road, 'in that smellful spot known as Ghantown'.

Axtell reminded his listeners that he had nothing against the foreigner – provided he joined a union and was a white man. Axtell's particular gripe was with the Afghans, as many in the room might recall. Ten years earlier, he had stood in this very hall and warned that if the citizens of Broken Hill did not crush the Afghan, the Afghan would crush them. Nothing since had induced Axtell to alter his opinion. These 'Ram Chundahs' and 'Hooshtas' were dangerous. They were bound by their faith to respond to the call to jihad that the Sultan had announced in November – being sympathetically disposed towards those whom Broken Hill's sons, husbands and brothers were, he said, 'even at this moment battling with their lives'.

Axtell looked around. He saw a history of fear overlaid with hate in the faces below. Gazing up at him were snow-bearded veterans who had fought in the Boer War, as well as anti-war miners who marched in protest to the Sulphide Street station, their band playing 'The Internationale' while they themselves hooted and booed recruits departing for the Ascot Park training camp in Adelaide.

In a quiet, suddenly insinuating voice, Axtell reassured his small audience: 'Self-preservation is the first law of nature.' Whatever one's opinions on the conflict in Europe – as a good socialist Axtell had plenty – the entire sympathy of the nation ought to be with the White Australia policy.

At this, several aldermen in the front row muttered 'Hear, hear', and Clarence Dowter, seated beside his nephew, began nodding.

'The Afghans have taken our jobs,' Axtell went on. They were brutal and depraved. And filthy in their daily habits. Even the Aboriginals found them unacceptable! In only the short time that Axtell had been back in Broken Hill, he had learned that it was almost impossible for residents to live near the camel camp, due to the nause-ating stench from the decomposing entrails of dead animals thrown out by the inhabitants.

Axtell concluded by suggesting that the time had come to expel the Afghans and that a new Citizen Vigilance Committee be formed against this Asiatic canker, of which the Afghan presented the most visible sign – 'with that diabolical grin of dissimulation which of all people he possesses to perfection'. He called for a show of hands.

Next to Oliver, his uncle's arm flew up, as did the arms of Oliver's mates in the rifle club – young men like Roy Sleath, the policeman's son; Alf Fiddaman, the grocer; and Tom Blows, a friendly, round-faced lad with jug ears who worked for the Water Pipe Company. Even old Ern Pilkinghorne, though deaf, raised his hand after a moment. Eyes sunk in his narrow head, and with his white beard neatly trimmed, Ern had not heard a word, but he liked to attend these meetings; the sight of so many enthralled faces was a solace.

Emboldened by their example, Oliver, who had come here at the last moment at Tom Blows's request, lifted his hand into the air. Even so, Axtell's speech made him feel uncomfortable. It untethered emotions, suspicions and latent jealousies which he would have preferred to stay unaroused.

To meet the cost of his engagement ring, Oliver had put his name down for the half-shift on New Year's Eve; he was not due at the mine until 10 p.m. Instead of going back to Cobalt Street with Tom Blows, who wanted him to take a look at his motorbike – he complained it was backfiring – Oliver had called at Rosalind's house. He had decided to ask her to marry him at the Oddfellows' picnic next day. But he had to act quickly. Before he could propose, he first needed to secure Mr Filwell's permission – something that Oliver had been planning to do earlier in the week, until some camels intervened.

The sun was growing stale in the sky, the last sunset of the year. Oliver walked in a loping gait up Blende Street and slowed as he approached the Filwell bungalow. Perhaps to calm himself, he started singing a music-hall song that he had learned from William.

Rosalind was with her mother in the kitchen, slicing tomatoes, when she heard him.

'Listen . . .' said her mother, straightening her matronly body. She was still waiting for William to return, and he didn't.

Instead, it was Oliver's baritone which competed with the chop of steel on wood.

> *In her little handsome bonnet, and her cotton dress,*
> *She's as fine as any lass of high degree . . .*

From his chair in the green-papered living room, her father called out, 'Open the door for Ollie.' His voice travelled easily through the house.

A pink-faced man with a grey moustache, Albert Filwell always looked angry, even when he was laughing. Yet William's death had crushed him. Soon after his son's accident, he had given up mines for cows; and twice a week he taught the Broken Hill Brigade boys how to shoot. But his self-esteem had rotted.

Towards Oliver, he behaved with a complicated hostility. He knew that he should support the young man's court-ship of his daughter. It was a link to his son, like the song.

Rosalind wiped her hands on her apron and went to let Oliver in.

'Get us something to drink, would you, Ros?' her father said, after she had ushered Oliver into the living room.

She brought in two glasses and a bottle of ginger beer, and returned to the kitchen, promising to be back once she'd finished preparing the picnic. She and her mother were making hogget sandwiches with tomatoes and lettuce, and a lamington cake. Oliver had already volun-teered to bring fruit.

With exaggerated care, Oliver poured out the ginger beer. He felt doubly grateful to be left alone with Rosalind's father. Quite apart from the matter they needed to discuss, Albert Filwell would be a dependable sounding board for the turbulent feelings that Ralph Axtell had stirred up.

Filwell winced as he raised his elbow to take the glass. 'Rosalind tell you what happened?'

Oliver sat down and slapped his pockets for his pipe. 'Your horse went berserk, right?'

'I'll say she did.'

His right arm swaying in a sling, Filwell was eager to go over it again, how his horse broke its tackling when it encountered a camel string heading back towards Ghantown. His milk buggy – damaged beyond even Oliver's capacity to repair it – had overturned, and he was jolted from his seat, falling heavily to the ground.

Through the thin partition, Rosalind could hear him saying, 'I was howling the place down. I tell you, I was groaning worse than a foundered mule. Dr Large sent me off to the bloody hospital. On Boxing Day!'

She opened the oven and peered in at the sponge. Her father never talked to her like this. Her thoughts were to be confined to the kitchen, patted and kneaded into the same standard shapes, and put into the oven and baked.

In the next room, Filwell continued to air his grievance. His mare had every right to go berserk. Camels were evil creatures, with their agonising bray. Eating the bush and polluting the waterholes. 'I'd like to put a bullet in the lot of them!'

Rosalind took this in, grimly, as she pressed into the sponge to see if it would spring back: *A horse goes berserk at the sight of a camel. A camel goes berserk at the sound of a cockatoo. We all go mad at something*, and slid back the pan. *Even a rabbit bouncing past can start off the cows.*

'Now, Rosalind, a kitchen isn't for standing in.' Grief had made her mother snappy. She held her dimpled arms around a bundle of clothes. 'Why don't you wash that lettuce while you're waiting?' and opened the door and went out.

Oliver's voice came through the wall. She could hear every word. 'Do you know the owner?'

'Oh, I reckon,' said Rosalind's father. The chair creaked as he rocked back. 'It's that butcher fella. The one your uncle keeps taking to court.'

'Those Afghans and their bloody oonts.'

And Rosalind pictured Oliver scowling as he excavated with a thick index finger the scorched bowl of his pipe.

Before he found work in the South Mine, Oliver had earned his living as a woodcutter. Then the Afghans had arrived and raided all the firewood for fifty miles around. Just as they'd moved in on the striking shearers and displaced the bullock and horse teamsters. If his uncle didn't make a stand to defend the butchers, it wouldn't be long before the Afghans took all the butchers' jobs too.

'You know what the trouble is, Mr Filwell?' For a moment, Oliver assumed the union-leader's tone of his uncle. 'People don't speak up. When I don't like someone, I say what I think, and I don't like the Afghans.' He read the papers, but he never read anything that had an explanation for why they should be here. 'All I know is that I don't cadge, Mr Filwell. And I claim the right to object to cadgers in any shape.'

Rosalind's father tilted forward on the chair-scratched lino, fighting his slight aversion to Oliver. 'I'm with you there,' raising his glass with his unaffected arm. His lips clamped down on his mouthful of ginger beer, and there was a loud noise as he swallowed it.

To Rosalind, all her father's restraint and fortitude seemed to have disappeared at the memory of his collision with Molla Abdullah's camel train – Oliver's as well. She had never before heard Oliver speak with such spite. Was this what he believed in his heart?

She picked up the lettuce that Alf Fiddaman had let her have cheap, and peered at it for dirt.

But Oliver had not finished. What upset him more was the way that Afghans looked at white women. Exactly as Afghan competition had killed off the woodcutters, the teamsters, and other white jobs, so were white women in danger, Oliver believed.

Rosalind felt her heart speed up. A slug was wiggling its way deep into the lettuce. She picked it out and flicked it into the sink – only to be trapped by a recent memory of looking on hypnotised at Oliver's big, stumpy, confident, grease-covered hands as he sorted out the blockage in the pipe beneath.

'I'm not just talking about Sukey.'

Rosalind inclined her head until it touched the weatherboard partition. Back in March, Mary Brodribb had told her about Sukey, a tall, bony girl who rode in on a grey horse and charged ten shillings for twenty minutes behind a blanket that she draped over a branch.

'Other white women, too, get involved with them.'

Did Oliver have Gül in mind? Did he have *her* in mind? She wondered with panic if Mary might have spoken to him.

Oliver laid it out like Axtell. Young Australian women who should know better stood hanging about the camel camp. Something attracted them. And some could end up getting into trouble, married even . . .

So Oliver and her father peddled stories of disease, dirt and depravity. To Rosalind, overhearing and unable to pull away, it was dreadful what they said in their low ridiculing voices. It was as if something about the uncivilised and disgusting Afghan provoked a fear that ran deeper than any shaft in the South Mine. She wished they'd stop it.

Through the partition, she listened as Oliver said in a different voice, 'Something else I'd like to talk to you about.'

Her pulse was beating as she angled her ear against the wall to hear more, but her mother was calling from the yard for Rosalind to take the sponge out of the oven.

Making cakes was all her mother knew how to do after William died, and she had not discovered how to stop. William had appreciated her cakes – more so than Rosalind. Of his sisters, only Lizzie shared his sweet tooth.

The door opened.

'Should I use jam for the icing?' Her mother in a clay-coloured cardigan stood staring at Rosalind.

'You know I don't like jam,' said Rosalind. '*Or* cake.'

'This cake isn't for you.'

'Who's it for, then?'

Stout with depression and with shoulders sunk, her mother walked slowly across the floor of the kitchen to the cupboard, holding her arms away from her side, as if carrying two heavy metal pails filled with the washing that she took in to earn extra money.

Suddenly, Rosalind was all directness. 'It's not going to bring him back, Mother. He's gone. He'll never eat another of your cakes.'

'Well, Ollie likes jam.' Her face defiant.

Rosalind gave a harsh laugh. 'He's called Oliver. You're not his mother. You're not his mother-in-law, either,' and untied her apron and flung it onto the kitchen table.

Seconds later, Rosalind strode into the living room. 'What have you two been gabbing about?' looking from her father, who had a strange embarrassed expression as if he wanted to let her into a secret, to Oliver, who stood with his back to the fireplace, smiling.

'If it's not Rosalind –' said Oliver, concentrating on his pipe, as on the occasion when he came home late with William, eyes not meeting hers but proud of something he had seen or done. (It turned out he had been scrawling 'scab' on a grave.)

She crossed the room in a perversely springy walk and spread her hands on the back of her father's chair. She breathed heavily. 'Aren't you going to tell me?'

Oliver was silent. In the kitchen, the jam cupboard opened and closed. Her father seemed compressed into his twitching arm. The only sound, the helpless clock on the papered wall.

Oliver tapped out his pipe against the empty hearth.

'Well, goodnight, Mr Filwell. I'm pleased we've got that sorted. I'd better get down to the poppet head.' And in the hallway – 'Goodnight, Mrs Filwell! I hope that sink's still behaving itself!' And in a voice that he tried to make softer to Rosalind, who had opened the front door for him, 'Goodnight, you.'

He stood under the fluted-glass lily shade and looked into her eyes, as if she was now available to him and he had some sway over her. 'I'll see you at the train station at ten, then,' touching her arm. 'Tom's asked me to take a squiz at his motorbike. If I'm late . . .'

Rosalind found her smile and kissed him quickly on the cheek. 'I'll keep a place for you.' Her arm was all tense, waiting for him to leave.

He tried to slam the door shut from the outside, but she was still holding the handle.

Rosalind listened to him walking off. He was singing to himself, the only song he knew.

She's a pretty liddle girl from nowhere . . .

One slow step at a time, she made her way back to the living room.

Her father sat looking at her.

She brushed a grey wisp of hair away from his ear. Picked up the bottle. 'More?'

'I'm doing very well,' draining his glass and handing it to her.

She held the empty glass against her chest.

His face had taken on a weight, as if charged with some mineral. 'You been arguing with your mother again?' And when she didn't reply, 'Ros . . . I don't . . . Is something wrong?' suddenly intimate, as though he had a vision of Oliver Goodmore prising the glass from her fingers. Then of Oliver unbuttoning her pale blue blouse. Touching her high young breasts . . .

He raised his injured arm, and stretched out to Rosalind, so that she smelled the Chamberlain's Pain Balm which she had rubbed into his bruised elbow two hours earlier.

His sling was beginning to smell, too.

'I can't describe it,' she said, resisting his invitation to hug her. 'It's just . . .' And wriggled her shoulders as if something was crawling there.

Opposite Rosalind's window, the horse finished drinking. The cart clopped on, following the railway line towards the Picton sale yard. She could see the two men still engaged in conversation. They must be up this early in order to reach Silverton in time for the picnic. Gül would need to be selling his ice creams before the sun grew too angry.

Rosalind had last encountered Gül eight days earlier, at the town's Christmas Eve dance in the Trades Hall. He stood inside the vestibule with two other dark-skinned young men.

Lizzie stared back at him through eyes lazy and

narrowed. Her face in her oversized head had the energy of an unformed sentence.

'Ros,' she rejoiced, 'look what I see.'

Rosalind remembered the way Oliver turned his long nose in the men's direction, his annihilating glance.

'Camel-li-as,' he said. He pronounced the word with a lilt before the third and fourth syllables, as if he could already sniff the strong camel odour.

'What?' It was Rosalind's turn to say something, indignant over that 'Camel-li-as'.

'From Ghantown.'

Rosalind knew where they were from. She concentrated again. She wanted to ask Gül about the injury to his hand. But he was being restrained from entering by a suddenly superior-looking Roy Sleath.

Something in Gül's expression continued to hold Rosalind. He wore European clothes, and stood straight and tall.

'Strike me pink,' said Oliver, puffing up his cheeks like a bugler. 'Isn't that Lakovsky's Turkey lolly?'

But she was not revolted by him as Oliver seemed to demand.

Nor Lizzie.

Her sister was chewing her knuckles and looking into his hurt dark eyes. He was refusing to budge.

'Alf will help see them off,' Oliver decided, and called over to a stoutish young man with a wart on his eyebrow.

'Shall I ask him to dance?' Lizzie enquired, and kicked

out her legs in a crude jig. She had no sense of her effect on others.

'No,' ordained Oliver in a cavalierish voice, 'you will dance with me.'

Arm in arm, he escorted Lizzie through the packed hall towards the stage where a brass band was beginning to play.

Leaving Rosalind standing there.

Meanwhile, Alf Fiddaman, who could be a bit of a hothead, was aping the Germans' marching style and thrusting the three Afghans back towards the entrance with Roy Sleath's assistance. 'Sorry, camel lips!'

Rosalind was conscious of a savage intensification of feeling. Gül seemed to look at her, before raising his hand – still wrapped in her handkerchief. It was a small gesture, but remembered to exaggeration by Rosalind as some sort of farewell.

Then, without resistance, he turned and walked out.

She thought of Gül next day when her father shooed away a small group of Afghan children who stood hopefully on the doorstep in their best clothes, asking to be allowed to join in the family's Christmas celebrations.

One girl, braver than the rest, with paler skin, stood her ground. 'Please, mister.'

'You please yourself what you do, but if you ever come round here again you won't walk away from the place.'

The choppy pitch of his voice upset Rosalind, and she

made the mistake of saying so in front of her sister. 'After all, local European children are welcome at the Ramadan feast.'

'How do you know?' said Lizzie, stepping out of her slow churn of thought. She unwound her glance from the drawing she was doing of the crocodile she had always believed lived under her bed, and looked up at Rosalind. 'Ros, you haven't been hanging about there, have you?'

She had, but she did not reveal this to Lizzie. Her younger sister was the last person she would have told.

A loud explosion eight months earlier had drawn Rosalind to the settlement. A shot in the camp that brought out all the cats and dogs in Williams Street, returning at a run with bits of offal dangling from their jaws. Evidently, they knew when a sick camel was slaughtered.

She had been on her way to the Brodribbs' house, to lend Mary a novel she had borrowed from the free lending library, and was already in a restless mood. Moments before, she had experienced an awkward encounter with her former teacher.

An engagement broken off, a Greek-sounding name. Miss Pollock had recently come back to Broken Hill with an orange dress and not much else, after things had not worked out in Adelaide. ('He promised her the earth,' confided Mary, who believed in the infallibility of everything she overheard in Harvey's, even when the speaker was

Mrs Rasp, 'then treated her like dirt.') And though Miss Pollock professed chirpily there was no place like home, she hadn't truly returned.

They had stopped on the side of the road. Miss Pollock, who was never at her best in public, started off politely, but soon became oddly inquisitive, asking Rosalind about her life since the last time they had met, almost four years ago, when Rosalind was about to leave school.

'Mrs Stack offered me a position.'

Miss Pollock nodded. A job at 'The People's Drapery' wasn't to be sniffed at, with everyone at the front or being laid off; seventy-five per cent of the population were on half-time.

But her smile was congested.

'And you'll get married,' she said out of her unusually lined face. 'And live here. With your grandchildren.'

Rosalind remembered her grandmother swishing around town in her moss-coloured dress, muttering to herself.

She wanted to say 'I expect you are right,' but altered this into 'I would like something more.' She looked surprised by the words that blurted from her mouth, as if put there by someone else.

'Something more?'

'Yes. Something more.' Rosalind's voice sounded steely in its surround of politeness.

Miss Pollock gazed at Rosalind. 'There's nothing more,' she said matter-of-factly, and her expression turned to pity.

'You must realise this is an egotistical town, Rosalind. It makes you think of yourself only.'

BANG.

At the sound of the shot, Miss Pollock broke off their conversation, and hurried away.

Rosalind couldn't help being infected by her teacher's mood. She continued along Williams Street, and was less than 100 yards from the Brodribbs' house when she saw a little grey dog, too small for what it had snatched, lie down in the shade and lick its tongue around something large and shiny. As if tugged by an invisible rope, she decided to turn right, towards Ghantown, and see for herself this much-talked-about place.

If you don't behave, the Afghans will get you, her father used to joke.

Provoked by her father, and by the picture painted by one or two of Oliver's mates, but most of all by her unsatisfactory exchange with Miss Pollock, Rosalind walked along the perimeter until she entered the camel camp. She did not know what she would find, or even what she was looking for. Her brother in the dark groped for something he could not see.

And what had she seen?

Square wool bales like wombat dung.

Children returning in a line from school, the boys in turbans, clean white trousers and black waistcoats with large buttons.

A sockless man at the top of a ladder pollinating the date palms.

From under the trees came a strong, latrine-like stench.

Cross-legged on a tarpaulin, a black-haired young man sat repairing a broken saddle with a packing needle. He did not move his head as she passed.

Further in, camels lay on their stomachs on the flat ground, swinging their lower lips back and forth as they chewed. They looked jittery and somehow different from the creatures that meandered in placid columns beside the road to Silverton. His arm around a camel's neck, fondling its ear, a boy talked soothingly in a foreign language – in Pushtu? – calming them.

The transition exhilarated Rosalind. One moment she was wandering along Williams Street, saying a stilted good afternoon to her old teacher; the next, she could have been standing on the banks of the Nile. It was hardly possible for her two eyes to take it all in.

Bent over under the bough of a white gum, a bare-headed man with a protruding belly sawed noisily at a carcass. Patriarchal, thick, and divided in two, his grey beard seemed to brush the ground.

Rosalind stood there uncertain, her eyes on this small, stocky butcher who was cutting up the dead camel, in between fending off a pack of darting dogs and cats – until a woman in a veil hurried over and motioned her into a skillion-roofed shed with a hessian partition, no windows but open one end. Patched-up clothes and dried dingo scalps dangled from bent wires, like the hooks that held up her father's horse harness. On a table constructed from packing cases was a jam tin filled with dripping, and a slush lamp with a strip of trouser cloth for wick.

The veiled woman scrubbed out a plate with wet sand, put onto it something plucked from a box suspended by wires, and indicated that she should eat. Rosalind thanked her. She examined the doughy offering, the depressions with thumbprints, and took a tiny polite bite. The tart, peppery flavour was invigoratingly unlike her mother's johnnycakes.

Rolled out on the ground was a brilliant-coloured rug, embroidered with unfamiliar patterns and motifs. Invited to sit down, Rosalind knelt and looked outside at the camels. She was conscious of the tinkling of bells and of muscles relaxing on arched necks. Also, of the odd way the animals examined her. Miss Pollock had taught that the camel had a membrane like a black film, which in desert storms shut across the eye while the lid remained wide open, to protect it from stinging sand. So Rosalind chewed on her curry-flavoured chapatti and gazed back.

'Without the camel,' Miss Pollock had told her class in Gypsum Street, 'the empty places would never have been opened up at all.'

A goat came in at the entrance and stood and eyed Rosalind, the sand bubbling and darkening around its hind legs. Under the white gum, the long-bearded figure went on sawing. She thought of Sukey, who lived wherever night overtook her, and wondered if it was over that branch that Sukey tossed her blanket.

Rosalind had visited the camp once more, at the end of June. A holy man from Sinde was touring the bush mosques. It was Ramadan, and camel men from miles around had gathered to be within the emanation of this travelling imam whom everyone was talking about.

She was intensely curious to see what a holy man looked like. He was twice descended from the Prophet, the papers said.

When she reached the camel camp: the noise. The braying and bleating was louder than the town's brass band tuning up. Rosalind was again made welcome. She was given a glass of tea and invited to take her place on a bench where a slender young man who had arrived late was removing his sandals, adding them to a heap. Also milling about were children whose faces she recognised – Prisks, Rutts, Spanglers, Deebles. Their families lived in the neighbouring streets.

Figures bustled past dressed in white flowing clothes. What Rosalind saw mocked the stories she had heard. These people weren't unclean. She was surprised by how exceptionally clean, in fact, they were. Her mother couldn't have laundered their clothes to this standard.

It was made clear to Rosalind that she couldn't join in the prayers, but she managed to eavesdrop. So many worshippers had assembled at the mosque that its door had been wedged open in order for those outside to hear. She peered over their backs into a room about twenty feet long by fifteen feet wide, heavily carpeted, and lit by two lamps. In successive flashes, she catalogued a driftwood stand with an open book resting on it. A bunch of emu feathers on the wall. Two pictures – Mecca? Bethlehem? And lying on the carpet, face up, a circular wood-framed clock that might have come from the railway station.

Glancing from time to time at the clock, the holy man stood leading the prayers. Rosalind's only yardstick for holiness was the Reverend Cornelius Hayball, and the imam did not look like him. He was under average height, sandy-complexioned with a white beard, and on his head a bright white turban. He bent and kissed the Koran, then turned the pages from the end, reading passages aloud.

Transfixed, Rosalind watched the lines of worshippers kneel on the prayer mats, touch the ground with their foreheads, then sit back, chanting in unison, '*La-ilaha-illa-Allah wa ashhadu anna Muhammadan abduhu wa rasuluh.*'

A balding assistant with a divided grey beard limped after the imam. Rosalind recognised the sawing figure from under the gum tree. And then it came to her where on another occasion she had seen this man: he had helped shovel away the sand after the dust storm in January.

That storm was one of the most violent anyone could remember, announced by dark specks tumbling high overhead – twigs, bones and other detritus blown by currents of wind into the upper atmosphere, and far in advance of the angry tube of grey smoke that rolled across the horizon from east to west. She and Lizzie had raced inside to block all keyholes, windows and fireplaces. For four days, red-brown dust and gravel had rattled down on the iron roof in Rakow Street, blocking out the sun. By the time the storm passed on to the Mallee, their house was buried up to its bargeboards. The cameleers had had to bring along the scoop which they used for excavating water catchments. They had worked for hours. And this short fat man with the long forked beard and a limp had been their foreman.

Otherwise, she looked around at men who were physically imposing and graceful in their movements. Rosalind also saw one white woman with four children.

All this occurred in June. She met Gül nearly five months later, in the second week of November. She had finished her afternoon shift at the drapery store and was walking home when she heard a clang.

The white-painted cart on which he sat shaking a cowbell caught her attention more than Gül. It was hitched to a thin bay horse with its head in a nosebag, and was low-sided like her grandmother's four-poster bed – so that Rosalind's first thought was of her grandmother, stalking through the dust in a tattered dress, after losing her savings to a lanky hawker of bogus mine shares that she had purchased under the balcony of the Denver City Hotel.

Rosalind waited until the steam tram had passed, then stepped closer. The four barley-sugar posts supported a dark green tarpaulin to shade the ice-cream chest in the back.

She read the words italicised on the side of the cart.

Lakovsky's Delicious ITALIAN ICE CREAM. A Food fit for Children and Invalids.

She was about to cross the street when he called out in surprisingly good English, 'Warn your children against inferior vendors!'

'I don't have children,' and looked at him. Dressed in waistcoat and watch.

Was he one of those sitting back on his heels outside the mosque? He had given her the excuse to stare, at least. He wore loose blue dungarees tied at the ankle and under his waistcoat an oversize bushman's shirt that hung down over his trousers. One of his boots had no lace.

She felt her face colouring. 'Are you new to Broken Hill?' for something to say. She had never before seen this two-wheeled cart.

But he was not to be pinned down so easily. 'Prompt delivery and general satisfaction is my motto.'

At this, Rosalind couldn't help smiling. She recognised his manager's words.

'Does that mean Mr Lakovsky's freezer is working again?'

Leo Lakovsky was a Russian Jew from Odessa who advertised himself as 'Broken Hill's No. 1 champion ice-cream manufacturer'. He recently had imported an expensive freezer from America, powered by electric motor. But less than a week after he installed it at his premises in Blende Street, the famous electric motor had broken down. Distraught, Lakovsky had summoned Oliver Goodmore. The machine needed to be mended if he wasn't to have his licence taken away by the town's overzealous Sanitary Inspector, Oliver's uncle, Clarence Dowter.

'Oh, it bin working very well.' The bell was put down and he swivelled. From one of the tubs inside the chest, he scraped out a spoonful of ice cream.

He turned back, lifting it for her to taste.

'Buttermilk ice. Only four per cent fat. Most delicious.'

The sun was shining. His hands, she saw, were clean.

Shyness prevented her from knowing what to do.

'I'm . . .' ruffled by a gust that no one else in Argent Street seemed to be feeling.

She knew the person who had repaired the freezer. She could tell him that. Or that Oliver was twisting Lakovsky's arm to favour Rosalind's father as the chief supplier of his milk, in place of that larrikin Beek who wasn't a member of the Milk Vendors' Association.

'Go on, taste.'

The ice cream was beginning to drip down his fingers.

'Where are you from?' she asked.

'Broken Hill.'

'But before that.'

His chin rose. 'Afghanistan.'

As she opened her mouth, Rosalind was conscious of his eyes on her. They were clear and clean. Like his hand.

And gave a cry that Oliver must have heard over in the South Mine.

She reeled back, choking. What she was recoiling from were two strands of wool. She had swallowed one. She produced the other from her mouth – damp, long, scarlet-coloured – and held it out between her fingers.

How quickly he sprang up, like a sitting camel bounding to its feet. He was new in the job, he apologised. He couldn't imagine how this wool . . . how it could have got itself into the ice cream.

He snatched the offending strand from her, and insisted that she sample another spoonful from a different tub. And ran around to fetch it, this time yellow in colour and more generous than before.

She tightened her mouth.

He was standing beside her, holding up the spoon.

What had started in fun had become serious. Rosalind no longer had any desire to taste Mr Lakovsky's most delicious buttermilk ice cream. What she ought to do, she knew, was walk off. But she felt sorry for him. This strange man, the lost foreigner away from his family, ice cream in the heat, dripping down his fingers.

'All right,' she relented. 'But you can't object if I take a closer look.'

She examined his second offering. Which did on this occasion seem hairless.

After all, well, they were probably only shaken from some rug, and gingerly pushed out her tongue.

'That's the stuff,' in his English from Lakovsky.

It was icy cold, like a blast.

What was the flavour? She was curious to know.

'Pineapple,' his smile growing now.

'How much?'

'Threepence.'

She drew in her breath. There was the smell of hot canvas.

'All right, I'll buy one.'

Rosalind fished around in her purse while he filled a cone. 'I've got sixpence only,' giving him the coin, and in the same motion taking his ice cream.

He looked crestfallen – he didn't have change. Mrs Rasp had used up his last pennies with her sovereign.

It was suddenly all very irritating. 'Keep the sixpence,' she told him. He could bring it to her later, what he owed. She worked at Stack & Tyndall's. 'I will be there tomorrow.' And the day after, she said to herself.

It was easier than returning the cone.

'But who do I ask for?' he said.

Her hazel eyes looked at him. 'Rosalind Filwell.'

'Rosalind Filwell, I will see you tomorrow.' There was

nothing casual about his promise or about the way he spoke her name.

'I am Gül Mehmet.'

The following afternoon in the drapery store, Mrs Rasp tried on a straw bonnet on which Mrs Stack had reduced the price. She planted her feet apart to assess herself in the floor-length mahogany mirror. Her flat white face was an envelope, but with nothing inside except a thank-you letter from the League of the Helping Hand. She should stop trying to convince people she was not a whale, thought Rosalind.

With a toss of her head, as though a young woman again, Mrs Rasp addressed Rosalind in the glass. 'Do you imagine you'll be here, behind that counter, for the next twelve years? Looking at people like me in the mirror? Don't you have other ambitions?'

'I don't know.'

Mrs Rasp contemplated Rosalind's breasts, which always aggravated her, and the accumulated years tumbled back. 'There are good shops in Adelaide. You could always try,' she said in a distant voice. She rotated her plump body, and laid the bonnet on the counter. 'I'll take it.'

Mrs Rasp had left Stack & Tyndall's by the time Gül Mehmet appeared in the doorway. His glance ricocheted around the store – tablecloths suspended from the ceiling; hats on wooden stalks, like planets on an orrery; the petticoats, stockings and brassieres – and dropped to the floor.

41

After a moment of indecision, he advanced in long strides and placed a threepence on the counter, then withdrew his hand.

Mrs Stack sat out of sight in the millinery room, talking in a loud voice to Ern Pilkinghorne about the morning's headlines in the *Barrier Miner*. The Ottoman Empire was being mentioned. And something about a Holy War.

'Of course the Huns are behind it!' shouted Ern, who had seen action in the Eastern Transvaal with the Victorian Mounted Rifles.

Gül turned to listen, but the news from Europe was getting muffled in the bonnets and a large notice which read: 'If you're not one of our clients, we're both losers.'

His eyes found hers. He asked if she knew what was going on. Had the Allied armies reached Turkey?

Rosalind confessed that she hadn't been following events. She sympathised with Mrs Brodribb, who only the night before had said to her, 'It's too depressing, the news, so I listen to music.'

Gül talked about the war for a while. Four of his friends had enlisted with the Expeditionary Forces. They'd left by train last week. He referred to the Gurkhas' bravery in the fighting in Europe. He seemed to take great interest in the fighting.

But his manner had altered from the previous afternoon. He was agitated about something. He looked at Rosalind with a brownish hawk's eye that tore through her. 'Why so many go to war?' he asked, no longer in Lakovsky English.

She pointed outside. 'They want to go. They want to leave. There's nothing much doing here.'

In the street, a woman was shouting at a small boy.

He had not followed her hand. '*We* are here.' He said it with a laugh.

Her eyes sparkled back in irony. 'Yes, we are. But don't you reckon that says more about us?'

He looked at her reprovingly. 'You believe we enemies?'

'Enemies?' Then, not wishing to be evasive, 'How do you mean, enemies?' and raised the back of her hand to her mouth to suppress a cough.

'What you bin say to him?' He threw the question at her.

'Who?'

His eyes were darker. 'Meester Dowtah. You bin spoke to him!'

'Mr Dowter?' She looked back up, and her body rose and fell.

'He bin say ice cream dirty. He say I pay fine.' It was all coming out now, in his husky voice. He was angry as two sticks. 'He bin say – oh, why you tell him?'

Hearing voices, Mrs Stack appeared. 'Rosalind, is everything all right?' Sometimes in Stack & Tyndall's someone wanted more than a hat.

'Yes, yes.'

When she turned round, he had gone.

In fact, Rosalind had said nothing to Clarence Dowter about what had made her cry out. The one person she had told, and not in a serious way, was her best friend Mary Brodribb. That was in the Red Cross Society tea-room in Argent Street.

Now, without quite knowing why, she sought Mary out after work. Had Mary mentioned the story to anyone? She was struck cold to discover she had, only that morning – to Oliver, of all people.

Mary had repeated it to Oliver in Harvey's as he pondered which ring to select.

Because, Rosalind accepted with a small smile, this is what you did in a place that wasn't even on the edge of things, but in the centre of nowhere. A hole in the earth, and beside it a heap of earth, and no neighbours for hundreds of miles, and those neighbours that you were fortunate to have all of a sudden now in Egypt. So when someone walked into Harvey's – a person who had a jokey way of looking at you that made you feel you were funny and intelligent – to detain them in the jeweller's a moment longer, you ended up glancing over their shoulder at a brass bell clanging and a white cart clattering by. And then leaning forward, cheeks between two hands, you told them about a spoonful of buttermilk ice cream with something gross concealed in it, and even quoting Rosalind's words, 'It looked like a red worm!'

It was clear that Oliver had felt obliged to report the matter to his uncle.

And something else Rosalind learned from Mary. 'That engagement ring was for you, Ros!'

Rosalind wished that she had been able to respond with a better smile. After Mary confided in a voice from which she could not keep her envy that she knew where – and when – Ollie was intending to slip the gold-framed garnet on Rosalind's finger, Rosalind did not see Oliver on his knees in Umberumberka Creek, but the two black beaks of Gül's eyes tearing at her.

For the rest of that day, Rosalind could not shake off her concern that Gül had suffered all because of something she had told Mary in a giggle over a late biscuit. Clarence Dowter was such a stickler for the rules.

In any case, the way ahead was not so clear or exciting as Mary imagined. A decision would have to be made. And before that an apology.

He came into view at the corner of Sulphide Street, shaking his brass cowbell. From a long way off she could make out the green canopy shading the ice chest, and the cart like the four-poster. She saw her parents on it, on the street in the brutal light.

But when Rosalind waved at him, as if hoping to make reparation by her display of recognition, he gave her an offended stare and urged his horse on, kicking so hard against the cart that his left boot fell off.

He had to jump down and retrieve it.

Rosalind didn't see Gül again for two more days in which she was conscious of her revolving passions. Part of her hoped he hadn't noticed that she cared. But she caught herself scouting the streets and shopfronts for a pale bay horse, listening out for his bell. The Afghan had started to become interesting now that she had hurt him.

A mistake had been made. She had made it. But it annoyed Rosalind that Oliver had not said a word to her. Wasn't it her story to tell? Definitely, it hadn't been Oliver's to pass on to his uncle behind her back. So when the Sanitary Inspector approached her counter one morning and asked Rosalind to verify an allegation that concerned Gül Mehmet, she gave him a pale smile.

The denial plopped out of her mouth like curdled milk. 'No, it must be a misunderstanding.'

Clarence Dowter had stared at her. 'Are you sure about that?' Everything about him was downturned and suspicious. Her father laughed with his whole frame, but in the case of Oliver's uncle, only his lips moved on the rare occasions when he couldn't conceal his mirth. They were motionless now.

'Quite sure,' said Rosalind cheerfully. 'The ice cream I had was delicious. It was pineapple.'

'Pineapple?'

'Pineapple. That's right.'

The Sanitary Inspector put his homburg back on and did not thank her for her time.

The Red Cross Society tea-room was in the basement. Rosalind turned around to see if it was Mary descending the metal steps, but it was Mrs Kneeshaw, who gave her a friendly greeting and disappeared into the kitchen. That was when she noticed the woman in the corner. Thirtyish, long blonde hair, with a mole on the side of her nose, like the jewel on an Indian. She sat less than ten feet away, in the shadow of the spiral staircase, stirring her tea.

They caught each other's eye through the cast-iron banister, and the woman smiled a peculiar smile, then picked up her cup and saucer, and walked over. She wore a long print dress, plum-coloured, and sandals.

'Don't I know you?'

Her gaze did seem familiar.

Now where was it, each one wondered, that they might have met? In the drapery store? The grocery? The Methodist church?

The woman put down her cup, and raised her arm until it was horizontal across her face and the distracting mole. Two green eyes looked over it at Rosalind, as though above a veil. 'Remember now?' and held out her hand.

She seemed thinner than the shrouded woman in blue clustered about with four small children; more angular.

'Sally Khan,' and asked if she could sit down.

Rosalind introduced herself. She had been keeping the chair for a friend. 'But she's late,' she added superfluously.

Sally was intrigued to know what had taken Rosalind to the camel camp.

'I wanted to see if the Afghans would get me,' Rosalind said humorously.

'And did they?'

Rosalind heard herself laugh. 'I'm more worried about the Australians, to tell the truth.'

Sally cast her an eye of surprised curiosity. 'But you're Australian?'

'I suppose so.' If having two sets of grandparents from Ireland made you Australian.

'How old are you?'

'Twenty-one. Nearly twenty-two.'

'I remember twenty-two . . .' as though it cleared something.

Sally had been that age when she met her first husband in Port Pirie. Alastair. There was a sense of closeness around the wide mouth at his mention. 'He was one of those difficult men. He cared more about his horse than he did about me. With Badsha, I am number one in his life. What did I ever get from Alastair but sneers. It was probably my fault. I did some stupid things. But.'

She laid down her cup with a crack. She was sick to death of Australian men. They were so weak. There was something to be said for an ancient culture. It never made Badsha snaky if she went into town on her own.

Rosalind admired her good humour. Sally seemed to have a happy life, although she did miss her ginger snaps – and Mrs Kneeshaw's were the best! Which was why Sally liked to pop in to the tea-room when her kids were at school. Only now and then, mind you.

Then she was all apologetic for gabbing on so much.

There weren't many Australian women in the camp, and Badsha had no gift for talk. She came here when she wanted to thrash things out in her mind. She thanked Rosalind for being a sympathetic listener. If there was one thing she couldn't bear, it was being told to shut up. 'You don't get to my age to be having someone always yelling at you. Or to be crawling to them for every penny. Badsha gives me half of everything he earns. Like I said, with Badsha I am number one. You're not eating those?'

'Help yourself.'

Sally took the biscuit with a grateful smile. 'I'll have one more and shove off.'

Eventually, Mary arrived. She was sorry to be late. She had bumped into Oliver on his way to the South Mine. They had stopped to chat about his garnet ring, for which he had left a deposit, and about his calling in to Harvey's to pay the final instalment.

Rosalind was leaving Stack & Tyndall's at the end of a trying Friday afternoon when she heard Gül's bell again.

She continued on down Oxide Street and then stopped and checked a non-existent watch, and paralysed by her own recklessness, turned and trod in heavy steps along the pavement she had once tripped over, scraping her knee, when she was a girl.

There was a cardiac thump underfoot. Horses tethered beneath shop verandahs jerked back on taut reins. Rosalind was accustomed to muffled subterranean explosions, although since August these had become less frequent. New was the reverberation in her chest.

She saw the white cart trundling along Argent Street and walked towards it with a face that Gül immediately knew was for him.

The fracture in his glance came from what people like her had done to him, she told herself. He shook the reins, but she grabbed the harness and held it. She knew how to stop a cart.

His horse snorted like a flag unfurling. There was the smell of animal sweat.

She raised her eyes. 'I have something for you,' and dug into her pocket.

Curious, he looked down at what she had given him, coiled in his palm like a young tiger snake, before awkwardly stretching it out: a lace from one of William's boots.

Rosalind waited for Gül to thread it before she questioned him. And though he was not in the mood to talk, she did eventually get it out of Gül: what Oliver's officious uncle had said when he called at Lakovsky's ice house in Blende Street.

This was the story Gül told.

Dowter interrupted Gül in the little front room, damping casks, and asked him what he was doing, and Gül said, 'Damping casks.' Dowter then said, 'You will get into trouble.' Gül said, 'How will I get into trouble?

Mr Lakovsky makes the ice cream in that room over there that has been made by the rule – as you know.' Dowter then stepped into the refrigeration room, but on this occasion not to check that the motor was functioning, or that the temperature was at twenty-two degrees below freezing point, or that none of the cans had their lid off, or that his instructions to Lakovsky as to the concrete floor had been carried out. The Sanitary Inspector seemed to be looking for something else.

Whatever Dowter hoped to find, it was not in the cans that he emptied with tremendous fastidiousness onto the floor and examined in messy succession.

Dowter was on the point of leaving when he saw a rolled-up object at a lean against the wall. He walked over and unravelled it with a kick. He bent down, a deceptively cheerful expression on his face, and plucked out, with no apparent effort, a length of reddish wool.

Looking at Gül, Rosalind remembered the rug she had sat on in the camel camp, its strange patterns and motifs, lozenges and zigzags, woven in brown, crimson and indigo. With unusual clarity, she saw Gül laying out his mat in the refrigeration room, where no one would see him, to say his noon prayers. Later, some loose strands must have brushed off him when he was filling a can, and fallen in.

So my guess was right, she exclaimed within herself.

'And you haven't heard from him again?'

Gül shook his head, but he could not shake from his

mind a very angry Meester Dowtah threatening him with a large fine.

Rosalind pieced it together; it was easy to piece together. There was only one reason why Clarence Dowter had taken no further action. He did not possess a sample of the contaminated ice cream, as the Pure Food Act demanded. Rosalind had swallowed the only proof. And felt a tickle in her throat from the woollen ghost of it.

'He was angry because he realised he couldn't fine you.'

Rosalind was so absorbed by where her thoughts were leading that she scarcely registered Gül saying he had to go – he had glimpsed the flustered shape of Mrs Lakovsky, his boss's wife, pushing a large perambulator across the street. Rosalind watched him kick the side of the cart, and was pleased when his boot stayed on.

The incident brought them together. Whenever Gül's horse and cart appeared, Rosalind felt an internal tugging combined with a surge of relief.

How often did they meet in the next five weeks? There were blanks which no one would be able to fill in. But it wasn't hard to bump into each other in Broken Hill.

It became harder to tear herself away. Rosalind's fear of being discovered in conversation with a 'Turkey lolly' was mingled with an unfamiliar feeling, a loosening of something inside her in which excitement and possibility were present too. His skin might be brown, and yet Gül had a heart not so different from hers, and a good heart, it seemed to Rosalind.

She would not have been able to talk in a coherent way about their relationship, if that is what it was. It was something private, mysterious, and she felt it spreading. She began to spend the money that she had been saving for her wedding dress on ice creams.

People who observed Rosalind with Gül saw a young woman at the head of a queue of snottering children wiping their noses and bawling at her to get a move on. Sometimes she stood there with Lizzie, who from the start associated Gül with the sugary tastes that she liked so much. Over the past three years, it had become automatic at mealtimes for Rosalind to contract into a state of vigilance – to ensure that Lizzie didn't choke on her food. But ice cream was safe, the way it slipped down your throat. Good for invalids, too, apparently.

Lizzie became her alibi.

By Christmas, there wasn't a single one of Lakovsky's flavours that Rosalind hadn't sampled, to say nothing of the sodas, milkshakes and Bijou syrups that were Lizzie's favourites.

Once, Rosalind caught Roy Sleath looking in her direction, his nose jutting out like his father's truncheon, and said, 'I have to go.'

Otherwise, only Mary Brodribb appeared to sense anything. 'How's your new boyfriend?'

'What are you talking about?'

'I saw you with him outside Harvey's.'

'Oh, Gül Mehmet you mean . . .' and said something about Lakovsky, the boss, needing extra milk in a hurry.

Mary did not believe her. 'Positive you're not keeping something back, Ros?'

'I most certainly am not!'

Mary glanced at Rosalind. She heard a lot of things in Harvey's. 'You know what everyone says? It gives you the fits, not to say what you feel.' The truth always came out in the end. When a woman had something on her mind, to stop her saying it was as foolish as trying to cover a shaft head with a handkerchief.

But it was dangerous to tell Mary what was on her mind. Mary was jealous of her relationship with Oliver Goodmore, and Rosalind had a sharp hunch that Mary would be willing to trade in her friend for the fiancé, without really knowing or understanding that that's what she was doing.

Mary aside, no one came forward to say that Rosalind Filwell had developed an uncharacteristically sweet tooth all of a sudden, or that she and Gül seemed to be doing more talking than the act of buying an ice cream required. At the intersection of Wolfram and Kaolin Streets. Outside the Freiberg Arms Hotel, while he watered his horse. Coming out of Lakovsky's ice house holding a churn. And on another occasion, going into Gilbert Bros, the saddlers.

Lakovsky's decision at the end of November to order

his milk from Rosalind's father made it easier for their encounters to pass unnoticed. The stickiest beak in Broken Hill wouldn't have found reason to linger over the sight of Albert Filwell's daughter walking with a metal pail in each hand to the ice-cream maker's factory in Blende Street. And if the white cart with Lakovsky's name on it sometimes stopped in the street to give Rosalind a lift with the milk, this too was nothing remarkable.

After an initial wariness, Gül asked her questions, what she believed in, where she'd been, about her ashen-haired mother, who washed and darned for extra income. And about Lizzie, whose condition he appeared to understand. Rosalind's friends knew Lizzie as a peculiar girl with a big forehead that she compulsively rubbed, and who talked to herself as though permanently frightened by something inside her. In Gül's village near the Khyber Pass, he'd had an aunt like that, he said, with a lot of stones in her head.

Curiosity was strong in Rosalind. Gül seemed to have travelled the world. One afternoon, he produced from his waistcoat pocket a creased postcard of Hagia Sophia, and described with passion the vivid colours that the grainy black-and-white photograph failed to evoke. He put his hands on hers when she tried to return the postcard. 'No, keep it.' Their hands stayed together for a moment, one on top of the other.

The following afternoon, he quite badly ripped the back of his hand on a splinter while shifting the ice-cream chest to make space for one of her milk buckets. She produced her handkerchief and used it to wrap the torn skin. It gave her a small charge, dressing his cut, to have confirmed what she suspected all along. His blood was the same vermilion shade as the red that bloomed in her underwear, and which she was never able to anticipate in time.

She was envious of what he had seen. His visit to Istanbul, the sailing boats and minarets and tiles bluer than the sky. Is this what Miss Pollock dreamed about behind her sun-faded curtains on Oxide Street, and which accounted for her starved look? Broken Hill was resistant to comparisons. Milk, cakes, mining were what Rosalind could talk about. Gül represented life beyond the mullock. He was proof that Rakow Street was not the only street in the world.

The things he knew! He planted images in her mind. Suffocated by inevitability, she longed for what she was lacking. All she had was this flat landscape and this huge sky, black snakes, brown snakes, and the tan-coloured slag heap with its blue and green stains on the rocks indicative of the minerals that had been extracted. And Oliver Goodmore, of course.

She was reminded of Oliver every time the ground shook and the horses neighed. But she kept him out of their conversations.

What Rosalind learned from Gül was what he chose to reveal to a twenty-one-year-old girl who had been nice to him when no one else had. In time, others would take

56

part in a frantic scramble to piece together Gül's history after treating it with disdain.

Back in January, she had asked her father, 'Where do you think *they* come from?' and nodded across the road at the team of camel men who were noisily rescuing the Filwells' bungalow from the sand. Her father had been going on with thwarted pride about Rosalind's grand-mother, a Doughty, who had come from a cottage in Farranavara in County Cork, bringing out with her to Australia the four-poster rosewood bed that he and her mother now slept in, and in which each of the three Filwell children had been conceived as well as born. Yet he never exhibited a smidgen of interest in the background of anyone in Ghantown, their origins or names. Turks, Hindus, Afghans, Indians – they were much of a colour. His eyes darted over to the pot-bellied foreman, whom she afterwards realised was Molla Abdullah, and he said simply, 'He looks like he comes from a good paddock.'

She could have written it on Gül's postcard, all that she knew about him. In her strong, small hand, as Miss Pollock had taught.

Gül was an Afridi from the Tirah Valley who had landed in Australia seventeen years before, in the dark hold of a ship chartered by an Afghan who had promised him £3 a month to look after camels. Gül's idea was to send money back to his family and at the end of a three-year contract go home. But there was not enough work as a cameleer, and he had found himself destitute. With no money for the return passage, he had raked stones for ballast, done a bit of bore-lining, and cut up sleepers for the railway extension at Wilcannia, before he drifted down to Broken Hill where he coaxed an Irish miner to teach him how to use a hammer and drill, wangling himself a position as an underground trucker for seven shillings and eightpence a day. He saved enough, he told her, to travel to Turkey, where he stayed for a time, but on his return to Broken Hill he found that the miners had been laid off after all contracts with the German smelters were cancelled – the Germans being the principal buyers of lead and zinc from Broken Hill. He went back to cameleering, walking strings out to the sheep stations with post and provisions, and returning with wool bales. But the war did not spare the camel trade either, and in early November he had bought an ice-cream cart off an Italian. His initial encounter with Rosalind in Argent Street took place after he had been hired to ride his cart around Broken Hill to hawk Leo Lakovsky's ice creams. He admitted to her that it wasn't Lakovsky who had taught him his English, but a team of sandalwood cutters from Tarrawingee. He also said that he had not given up his intention of going back to settle in his native land.

Rosalind could not have said that she *knew* Gül. She never penetrated his mystery or understood him; they were different as two coloured threads crossing each other at right angles. He went into that box of people like Miss Pollock who had prised open her curiosity. But he had the effect of the cockatoos that screeched in the gums bordering the creek; he made the place less lonely by his presence.

For Gül, too, the chaos stopped when he saw her, his horror of what had been done to him faded, as did his fear and continual loneliness among infidels.

Afterwards, people said in stunned amazement: 'We didn't see it coming.' Yet it wasn't the mullock obscuring their vision, but some barrier within themselves. Gül's radicalism had not been a willy-willy that blasted in from nowhere.

Who persuaded whom? To some in town, Gül was the mastermind; to others, it was Molla Abdullah. Most likely, they evolved their plan together in the days after Gül was ejected from the Trades Hall. It wouldn't have required much instigation. Gül, by then, had endured a bellyful of derision. And Molla Abdullah was going berserk anyway, having been fined a second time by Clarence Dowter.

According to who you listened to, the two men hadn't known each other long. Or else they had known each other many years. Not in dispute was that Molla Abdullah, following a fire at his home in Williams Street, was living in temporary accommodation in a ripple-iron shack right next to the hessian humpy that Gül had moved into when he returned from his latest travels.

Gül was friendly and open, more thoughtful. His neighbour was an old cameleer with a limp. Some years before, Molla Abdullah had got between a raging camel in *musth* and his cow, and the bull camel had torn a chunk from his right leg. Ever since, Molla Abdullah had walked in a doubled-up manner, like someone battling indigestion or waiting for the next stone to land on his head.

Children go for you in a small town, where stone throwing too often is regarded as one of the joys of life. Different skin colour, strange clothes, not Anglo-Saxon – Molla Abdullah, a reserved, simple, childlike man, presented a target that was irresistible. Boys laughed when he shambled by and chased him down the street. He never retaliated, but he complained on more than one occasion to Sergeant Sleath, who each time promised to have a word with the rascals.

Molla Abdullah had other reasons to feel embittered. As well as acting as the imam at the camel camp, leading the group prayers on Fridays and performing burials in the absence of a permanent religious leader, he served as the butcher of his community, killing their meat in the correct Muslim manner. The fact that he was not a member of the Butchers' Employees Union in the most unionist town in the country had brought him into confrontation with those who needed no excuse to treat a Pathan from India's north-west frontier as an enemy alien.

Since his arrival in Broken Hill eighteen years before, Molla Abdullah had slaughtered and prepared his meat in the North Camel Camp, out of sight of the town. He had received no reprimand from the council up until the moment, a year before, when Oliver's uncle became the local Sanitary Inspector.

Perhaps it was because Clarence Dowter was not qualified that he was overzealous. He had tried twice to get his inspection certificate, and failed. 'Why should the council carry Mr Dowter in its arms?' was the inflexible opinion of Alderman Turbill. But after Turbill was dismissed and asked to hand over his keys, Mayor Brody had turned to Dowter, whom he had got to know when Dowter was in charge of the gang laying the Silverton–Broken Hill water pipe.

In 1913, Dowter was appointed Acting Chief Sanitary Inspector. He might not have a certificate, but he had a bit of push behind him. Plus he was a union man. He wouldn't be another of 'those silvertails who gave no fair deal in the Sanitary Department'.

Dowter set to work, and no one enjoyed immunity from him. On discovering the state of the floors in the council toilets, he installed a penny-in-the-lock slot, and chastised the men and women in the council whose sense of cleanliness, he said, did not redound to their credit.

Determined to prove himself in his war on scarlatina, diphtheria, pneumonia and typhoid, Dowter became a tyrant against all filth. To keep Broken Hill's premises in conformity with the requirements of the Pure Food Act, he fined a shopkeeper who sold butter which, in Dowter's opinion, was 'not fit for greasing boots'. He chased a man riding in a suspicious milk cart – 'The more he cried whoa!

the faster he'd go,' reported the *Barrier Miner* – and when the cart toppled over, after striking a stone, stayed only long enough to collect eight samples. He prosecuted one woman for selling a verminous stretcher; another for tipping her soapsuds into the lane.

As well, he hunted down anyone he suspected of contravening the Broken Hill Abattoirs, Markets, and Cattle Sale-yards Act.

During his first year in office, the uncertificated ex-pipe layer issued summonses to two butchers for transporting their meat in uncovered carts. He stopped one man in Slag Street who was actually riding on the meat, with flies following like seagulls. His dungarees were saturated in blood all the way to his ankles, and a leg of lamb was about to fall off. Dowter charged a third butcher for storing his minced meat on a floor covered with a 'quantity of slimy stuff'; plus the owners of two piggeries for failing to keep their premises clean. But the person he monitored with the fiercest attention was Molla Abdullah, the Ghantown butcher.

Already, Dowter had found reason to caution Ghantown's residents, after discovering that they had dug an unauthorised grave in the town cemetery, in the small plot reserved for Muslims: all graves had to be dug by council gravediggers, Dowter was stern in reminding them – although it was permissible for Afghans to prepare the body and place it in a coffin, provided they left the screws undone.

Dowter found it offensive that local Afghans and Indians would not eat meat killed by people other than their own. Soon after his appointment, he had received a letter from the Ghantown community appealing 'in the name of religious liberty' for Molla Abdullah to be able to kill their meat at their camp and not in the abattoirs, where sheep and cattle were slaughtered alongside pigs. ('One of the tenets of our faith is that the latter is a contamination.') The Abattoir Committee had turned down the request on Dowter's recommendation. 'There are people of fifty different religions who will want the same privileges.'

Molla Abdullah was not going to be made an exception.

Dowter prosecuted him for the first time that April, for slaughtering sheep at the North Camel Camp instead of at the municipal abattoirs. In court, the Ghantown butcher had read haltingly from a piece of paper: 'Me not guilty, not know break law, very sorry, not do again.'

Ordered to pay a fine of £1, or go to prison for seven days, Molla Abdullah had paid the fine. Dowter had not pressed for the heaviest penalty of £20.

A fortnight after he had walked into Stack & Tyndall's to question Rosalind about the purity of Gül Mehmet's ice cream, the Sanitary Inspector visited Ghantown again, and found four sheepskins strung out on the fence.

He cast his eyes about for Molla Abdullah and saw him crouched over a fire. Smoke gusted from a black pan where something was boiling.

At the sight of the Sanitary Inspector, Molla Abdullah

forced a smile which revealed two brown teeth, and slowly got to his feet.

He stood staring at the ground, waiting.

In an unemotional tone, Dowter recited the regulation that each butcher's carcass slaughtered at the abattoirs must be branded with a distinctive brand in indelible red.

'There is no brand on these skins.'

Molla Abdullah looked up. The sun glinted on his scalp. 'No unstan, no unstan.'

'You said that last time. But not understanding is no defence.'

Molla Abdullah repeated himself.

To the Sanitary Inspector, the man's store of English was annoyingly small. Dowter thrust his right boot forward and with the toe began to scratch a circle in the earth.

In the adjacent humpy, a woman pulled open the door and looked out and then turned and whispered to someone inside.

Inquisitive faces appeared at window frames to listen. Molla Abdullah's voice rose, imploring. Dowter said nothing. His foot went on circling. It might have been creating the world.

It was during their stand-off that Gül emerged from the humpy and walked over.

Dowter immediately recognised Gül from the ice-cream factory in Blende Street. When Gül offered to interpret, Dowter gave him a mistrustful and dismissive look. He hadn't forgotten the contaminating prayer rug. 'Don't think I haven't got my eye on you, too. But seeing as you're here, you can ask your mate if he killed his sheep in this yard.'

Gül turned to Molla Abdullah and the two men spoke animatedly. Yes, he had killed the sheep here. But the abattoirs had been on strike.

Dowter looked incuriously at Gül. The fact that the abattoirs may not have been *in use* did not mean that they were not *open* for use. It did not relieve a butcher of the necessity of complying with the Act. Nor did it justify a man killing surreptitiously and in an underhand way. 'What he's done is not legal. So he's going to be fined for doing it.'

Grabbing Gül's arm, Molla Abdullah wanted his position explained to Dowter. He swore by the beard of the Prophet and the bones of his seven ancestors that he sold only to his own people, and not under any circumstances to the general public.

'Is that right?' said Dowter meditatively. He reorganised more dust with the toe of his boot, as if he might find something buried there. 'Then maybe you can ask your mate here if he is a member of the Australasian Federated Butchers Employees' Union?'

This time, Molla Abdullah was fined £3 and ordered to pay the six-shilling costs of court. The police magistrate gave him until the end of December to pay, or face imprisonment for one month.

A desert was closing around the old man. He heard his

name in a denigrating tone being knocked about the courtroom, in a language he did not speak or write, and he wondered how his life could have ended up so soiled.

After leaving the courthouse in a rush, Molla Abdullah bashed his way up the street. A hard object struck him on the shoulder and he spun round, glaring. He grabbed the stone from the pavement and hurled it back at the goading group of boys and girls, causing one girl with sores on her face to yelp.

He lumbered on. His temples ached. Back in Ghantown, he wallowed for the next two weeks in an apathy from which no one could stir him, save for Gül Mehmet.

Late on Christmas Eve, Gül returned to the camel camp and entered Molla Abdullah's shed, looking agitated. He produced a small fistful of dried pituri leaves and they sat on the ground smoking them through a long-stemmed bamboo pipe, discussing grievances.

Gül was pugnacious after his eviction from the Trades Hall. He had maintained his composure until he stepped outside the building, but as he walked home with his two companions, he couldn't rid himself of the image of Rosalind Filwell, her look that went through and beyond him.

Yet she had done nothing to restrain Oliver Goodmore and his jeering mob.

His thoughts streamed out as he recalled Goodmore's face, and how Alf Fiddaman and Roy Sleath had shoved him towards the exit, calling him a mooching Turk. These white men and their families were honoured guests at the festivals in the camel camp. Why should Gül and his friends be denied entry to a dance in Broken Hill? Wasn't this Gül's town as much as it was Goodmore's? Didn't Gül Mehmet and Molla Abdullah have British passports too?

So they raked over old grouses. As the night wore on, their sense of injustice magnified along with their impotence to redress it.

Molla Abdullah still felt utterly dejected by the fortnight-old court case. He had no means of paying the £3 fine by the end of December. The fire that had destroyed his uninsured two-roomed house in Williams Street, while he was boiling a pan of fat, had burned his possessions, including all the money he had. He had lost everything. And in less than a week, Dowter's strict application of a set of regulations that contravened his religious principles and made no sense to him threatened to take away his freedom.

Both of them should have returned home a long time ago, said Gül with a thoughtful sigh.

Molla Abdullah tugged at his beard and shook his head from side to side in anguish. Even if he could have afforded the passage, none of his family in India were alive. He had nothing to live for – and thanks to Dowter's unions, he wasn't even allowed to dig his own grave!

Ever since he had arrived in Australia, nearly two decades before, Molla Abdullah had been cooking his humiliation and shame, rendering it down, and now, sitting in this smoke-filled shed with Gül, it exploded into indignation.

The Turkish Sultan was right. Europeans like Clarence Dowter were an offence to Islam – and Oliver Goodmore and his friends no better. They were cutters of the veins of life. They were unclean pigs.

Neither Gül nor Molla Abdullah needed reminding that Turkey was at war with Australia, and that the Sultan, only five weeks earlier, had appealed for a jihad against the Entente Powers, 'the mortal enemies of Islam', obliging all Muslims young and old, on foot or mounted, to support it. Had war broken out sooner when he was in Istanbul, Gül admitted, stretching out his long legs, he would have joined the Turkish army and fought.

Probably it was then that Gül made his bold proposal: they should answer the Sultan's call to arms, and seek a glorious death by attacking his enemies thousands of miles from home. Branded as Turks, what did they lose by behaving like Turks? Instead of living this persecuted existence in Broken Hill, wouldn't it be better to die with the guarantee of happiness in the next life – by killing as many Australians as they could? The Australians were doing all these terrible things to true believers, not only in Broken Hill, but also in Egypt and no doubt imminently in Turkey. Why not go for them here, in Broken Hill, in the desert?

Molla Abdullah's eyes sparkled like flames spitting up

from a heated pan, catching fire, running across the hessian. So did his house in Williams Street burn down.

But in the morning the heat and light had not diminished.

The decision made, Gül felt serene, weightless. The only person who had treated him well in the community which he now saw as his duty to destroy was Rosalind, and possibly her sister. But he no longer thought of them. He had crossed into an existence parallel to the one in which he woke up next day and went about his business, that enveloped him in a rapturous calm.

Gül and Molla Abdullah never again smoked pituri, but over the next six days they had conversations. They discussed what form their crusade should take. They made a reconnaissance of the railway line – coming back from this, Molla Abdullah's camels had collided with Albert Filwell's milk buggy. And they fixed on a time and a day: the morning of January the First, when Molla Abdullah was to be arrested if he didn't pay his fine.

Date and location agreed, they acted swiftly. The butcher took charge of tailoring the Turkish uniforms in which they had vowed to fight; the ice-cream seller, because he spoke English, organised weapons and ammunition.

Gül required the rifles for hunting rabbits, he told the publican in Slag Street who sold them to him. He said nothing to Frank Pincombe, at whose store he paid two shillings for eighty soft-nosed Snider cartridges, but

Pincombe was more than pleased to get rid of such old stock. Across the street, Gül bought two extra-strong cartridge belts, each three foot nine inches long and one and three-quarter inches wide; and two pairs of leggings, which he picked up on New Year's Eve.

In the same hour of that same evening as Rosalind prepared the lamb-and-lettuce sandwiches in her mother's kitchen in Rakow Street, the two men sat in Gül's humpy and dyed a cotton tablecloth with sheep's blood. Onto this crimson background, Gül stitched a yellow crescent moon and a star to resemble the Ottoman flag. They folded it away in the ice-cream chest, along with the cartridge belts, a Belgian navy revolver, a new butcher's sheath knife, and the two rifles: a Snider–Enfield for Molla Abdullah, which Gül had bought for £5; for himself, a Martini–Henry breech-loader with a long steel barrel.

As the sun fragmented behind the date palms, each wrote out a confession to tuck under their cummerbunds.

In his confession, written in a mixture of Urdu and Dari, Molla Abdullah explained that he bore no enmity against anyone except Clarence Dowter.

One day the Inspector accused me. On another I begged and prayed, but he would not listen to me. I was sitting brooding in anger. Just then the man Gül Mehmet came to me and we made our grievances known to each other. I rejoiced and gladly fell in with his plans and asked God that I might die an easy death for my faith. I have never worn a turban since the day some larrikins threw stones at me, and I did not like it. I wear the turban today.

Owing to his grudge against the Inspector, Molla Abdullah's intention was to kill Dowter first.

Gül wrote:

I must kill your people and give my life for my faith by order of the Sultan because your people are fighting his country.

He thought to add that he had informed no one else of his intentions – he did not wish to implicate Rosalind Filwell.

That night, the two men walked back and forth three times through the doorway of the mosque and read from the Koran and said their prayers, in accordance with Molla Abdullah's instructions. The idea of his death did not frighten Gül, when he considered the glory which awaited and the luxuries bestowed on those who died in the struggle.

With their heads pointing north, they snatched a few hours' sleep, then rose early to perform a ritual shaving and cleansing. They washed their bodies thoroughly with water from a billycan, massaging hands, forearms and feet with perfumed oils and musk. After scissoring off his beard and razoring his chin, Molla Abdullah put on a collarless shirt trimmed with silk. He wore rings on his fingers and toes, kohl around his eyes, and on his bald head a small blue skullcap decorated with mirror fragments and embroidered with a frieze in the style favoured by the desert tribes around Kandahar. Last, they put on their red jackets, leggings and white silk turbans.

Shortly before 5 a.m., the two-man army of Allah climbed onto Gül's ice-cream cart and rode out of Ghantown behind his bay horse, down Rakow Street, following the railway line towards Silverton, to declare war on Australia.

3

'Grab your seat for the joyride!'

'Don't push!'

Above Rosalind, the smoke from the Y-class locomotive hangs vertical and motionless in the air, like one of Oliver's pipe cleaners.

Almost the last to board is Miss Pollock, who creates a flurry on the platform, in an orange dress down to her knees, high white boots elaborately laced, and with scarlet and emerald ribbons twisted around her calves in tango style.

There's a three-note whistle. Jim Nankivell, the driver, leans out of the locomotive and waves. At 10 a.m., after various jolts, the longest and most crowded picnic train ever to depart Broken Hill pulls out of the station.

Beneath hats and parasols, hundreds of passengers settle

down in the forty cleaned-out mining wagons, happily talking and waving; hampers and rugs tucked under the benches, and the swings that will be slung up over branches.

Rosalind looks around at her open ore truck which once carried zinc and lead to Germany for bullets, and now carries Mrs Rasp, who is tinting her mouth with rhubarb lipstick.

Mrs Rasp has given up on Mrs Kneeshaw and is telling the Sanitary Inspector, between dabs, about her friend Alderman Turbill who shot himself in Adelaide two weeks ago – 'although he had no worries'. She licks her lips. These picnic outings make her talkative. She finds it a comfort to brood on her friends' failures and to feel exaggerated pangs of pity. 'He was found unconscious with a wound in his temple and holding a rusty gun in his right hand.'

Oliver is missing all this. Already, he has taken off his jacket and has gone to sit with Roy and Alf; they are bent over in a huddle, discussing the rugby. At least half the Rugby Union players of the state have joined the war, Oliver says severely. The local league will have to be re-organised for next season, and takes a long swig from Roy's water bag.

The talk around Rosalind, who guards Oliver's place with her hamper to stop Mrs Rasp spreading herself, is of the foot-running at Silverton.

Mrs Kneeshaw from her corner catches Rosalind's eye. 'I think I know about Oliver' – his name becomes rather ugly in Mrs Kneeshaw's mouth; she suspects Oliver

Goodmore of being one of those extremists who hurl stones and insults at departing recruits like Mrs Rasp's son Reginald – 'but will you be competing, too, today?'

It's something else that Rosalind has not decided. She moves the hamper a few inches to the right. The ore truck has been hosed, but it still smells metallic.

She feels breathless, more than the overheated air warrants.

'I might do the single ladies' race.' And afterwards, while her mother and Lizzie visit a garden in Penrose Park, Oliver will walk her up the creek.

Mrs Kneeshaw is sympathetic. 'The extreme heat made it difficult for my daughter to reach the tape last year. And today might be hotter, I have the feeling.'

'Or,' pursues Rosalind, her breasts itching under her blouse, 'I could do the ladies' hammer-and-nail competition.'

Mrs Lakovsky utters bird-like coos at her newest baby, who smells of sour milk, while trying to stop her three-year-old Ivan from crawling under the bench. Small black flies go on sewing in the air. And Mrs Rasp continues to mourn her dead alderman. She looks very white inside her large dress and new straw bonnet. She could blot out the sun.

'They say the gun was faulty and may have misfired after he looked down the barrel and poked the live cartridge with a nail.'

'Something he sure was capable of,' remarks Mr Dowter, not hiding his venom. Alderman Turbill had been the one hotly opposed to the council carrying the uncertificated Dowter in its arms.

Mrs Kneeshaw is still looking at Rosalind. Thinking, *She has a good figure and thick black hair; her face is rather plain.* 'Are you happy at Stack & Tyndall's?'

'Oh, yes, Mrs Kneeshaw, I think so.'

'The Red Cross Society has a vacancy for a nurse,' and smiles. She has white teeth, some longer than others. 'Miss Pollock is convinced you would make a first-rate nurse, Rosalind. I am inclined to agree.'

'Me . . . a nurse?' Rosalind could not have felt more inarticulate if she had been asked to summarise Cornelius Hayball's Sunday sermon. Nothing has happened to her, and so she does not know anything. Oliver has his machines and his toolbox. How can she hope to repair anyone?

She looks down at her palms. 'I'm not certain I would be so good at *that*.'

'Well, if you change your mind,' says Mrs Kneeshaw, and leans forward. She wants to reach out. She has watched Rosalind with Lizzie. With Oliver as well. 'You know, Rosalind, you must always feel able to speak with me – if there is something you want to say.'

Suddenly, there is something Rosalind would very much like to say, but Oliver is wedging himself back in beside her.

The mullock lies in sunlight behind them, leached of its shadow and power to intimidate. Oliver in his hat instead lours over her.

Out of habit, he starts packing tobacco into the bowl

of his pipe. But it's too hot to smoke – even Clarence Dowter's cigarette has been returned with a snap into its silver case.

Oliver sits back, Mrs Kneeshaw too.

Over the low rim of the truck, the morning is a tangle of fences and roofs. The train passes along the houses, past the gardens, smelling a little of manure, slowing down at the Rakow Street crossing.

In the yard, the cows and heifers are lapping at the water trough. Their shadows stretch in puddles of black.

'That's your room, isn't it?' says Oliver, pointing with his pipe stem at the window, wanting to draw her in.

Her eyes linger on the small hard round shape in his shirt pocket, on the hairs in his nostril, on the mouthpiece of his cherry-wood pipe. Once, toying with it, she had sucked and tasted the bitterest thing, a globule of gungy tar. *That* had made her scream.

'Yes.' She twists her lips; she has not stopped condemning him, the dirty fingernails of her future husband.

Oliver, on the other hand, is radiant. An hour ago, he was buying fruit for the picnic when Alf Fiddaman told him he had a house to let in Mercury Street. The couple who lived there were relocating to Hobart with their two small children.

'Would you come and see it with me, Rosalind?'

'If you would like.' The words, positive but neutrally spoken, hide her dismay.

'What about tomorrow?' He cannot look at her enough,

76

although his uncritical gaze does not suit his face, which the sun is painting red. He moves closer. 'Alf says it's perfect for a young family . . .' And their shadows join on the floor of the truck, to melt into a rearing, tussling creature.

She looks as though about to turn herself into something sweating.

'I think . . .' The words are too big to get out of her mouth. She senses Mrs Kneeshaw watching as she answers at the second attempt.

'Maybe tomorrow,' and adjusts her pink hat.

There is a veil between them, but he doesn't seem to notice.

The train creaks and bumps forward again.

She shuts her eyes to stop him seeing. The sound of the Bosphorus is inside her ear, and white triangular sails are tacking across her eyelids. She pictures herself on the edge of the Red Sea, dressing wounds.

When she opens her eyes again, Clarence Dowter is removing his jacket. He takes out a watch and notes the time, then stares glassily across at her as if he can read what she is all about in a notice under her chin. She remembers the carpet that she denied swallowing, and smiles.

'Emmy didn't want me to come, but I have yet to miss an Oddfellows' picnic.'

Her father's familiar injured laugh gives Rosalind an excuse to glance away. Up against the end of the truck, backs to the engine, her family are seated in a row.

Rosalind had not wished to sit with them. She had

boarded the train without resolving her argument with her mother about Oliver. But now she doesn't want it left untreated.

Arm in the fresh sling which she had fitted on him that morning, her father is chatting with a small, cheerful-looking man wearing a large bow tie.

Rosalind leans forward, and waves to catch her mother's attention; it concerns her that she might still be feeling unhappy. But her mother is engrossed in Lizzie, who is rubbing the fuzz off the peach that Oliver gave her.

Her sister was the sensitive one, her mother believed. Who would sit up in bed, shrieking.

But for Rosalind that was always William.

If Lizzie was all sky, she and William had been earth.

She remembers after her brother's accident when her father took her into the mine. Hurtling down. Water dripping from a dark rock face, and the terrible heat. The cage stopped. There were lots of lights. And at the end of a tunnel, an office with a man in shirtsleeves standing over a huge ledger, like the ticket office in the railway station, and men signing in. 'This is William Filwell's sister,' her father said. 'She wanted to see where he worked.'

For the first time, the darkness feels thicker where she is. Her brother is behind her and she cannot hear him. As if a bell jar has descended and silenced her.

She's had her tongue cut out too long, she tells herself. In the passive feminine way which, once silenced, becomes poisonous. And yet here she is, about to choose a man, a good enough man, but one who wants to participate in the cutting of her tongue.

The train builds up steam near the Picton sale yard, then slows abruptly as it approaches the cutting.

Clarence Dowter volunteers the reason – the stickybeak has heard it from the mouth of the driver himself: Jim, he says in his dry voice, has been instructed to take it easy here, since the previous week the express was held up after the wind blew a foot of sand over the rails.

Rosalind twists around and stares down over the side of the truck, but really to escape Mr Dowter and his small grey eyes.

She gazes at the humps of sand beside the tracks, at the intricate lace-like paths of the sandhill beetles foraging for food, and thinks of the wedding dress worn by her cousin Louise, now living in a tiny room in Beryl Street while her husband is fighting in Egypt.

Rosalind has exhausted on Gül's ice cream the money she had saved up for her dress. And suddenly feels tedious, she who has received a postcard from an Afghan; her parents and Oliver never knew about that.

The designs tremble and fade. She is left with Oliver's hard arm pressing into her thigh. She sees the veins snaking under the backs of his hands and remembers Gül's hand, and how she had wrapped it with her hand-kerchief – actually, her grandmother's handkerchief – that he has yet to return.

The palms of her hands are sweating. She feels it under

her skin. The ingrowing wick of her unlit, and perhaps unignitable, passion for Oliver. Lost in the shadow of his brim, he is not the answer to any mystery.

Her thoughts are running over each other up the bank, and sliding back. The train picks up speed. Soon it will burst out of this cutting into an ocean of baked red earth, of opalised shells and fish and long-extinct sea monsters, but already she is retreating into her own tableland of five-inch rainfall, denuded of mulga scrub for miles around, all removed for fuel; a bald and empty region like his sandy-haired head would become.

By the time the train draws parallel with the lime kiln, Rosalind has decided what she will say to Oliver Goodmore.

The cutting is the perfect spot from which to mount a surprise attack, and will be cited as proof of Gül's military experience. Because of the lime kiln, none of the passengers have a full view of the line. The Ottoman flag comes into sight separately to each wagon only as the train sweeps around the curve.

Lawrence Freer, the fireman, is standing out on the footplate when he notices a red cloth fluttering above a white cart. His first thought: *Someone's exploding defective ammunition.* But he dismisses it. No one would be venturing out with a powder magazine on New Year's Day.

The cart is parked near to the tracks, on the other side of the trench with the water pipe. The train steams closer. Freer reads the words italicised on the side, and relaxes.

'A bit late for the ice creams to be going out to Silverton,' he observes to the driver.

Jim Nankivell smiles. 'I suppose some poor old beggar's hoping to make a bit for himself.'

They chug past, and Nankivell sees what looks like an insignia on the red cloth. A breeze has sprung up, ruffling it.

At that moment, a pair of white shapes bob up from the trench – dark faces, the tips of rifles – and he hears two gunshots. One bullet hits the sand, spraying dust against the engine. The second bullet strikes the brakevan, embedding itself in the woodwork.

Ralph Axtell is sitting in the brakevan with the Mayor and the Secretary of the Manchester Order of Oddfellows.

'What's that?' enquires the Mayor.

'It's probably the Germans,' shouts Axtell, who has postponed his return to Melbourne until after the picnic.

The Germans! In Broken Hill! Everyone laughs. They think it's a stone pinging against the side.

The two turbaned men continue to fire at the train, ducking down into the trench to reload, or to take cover in case anyone shoots back. But no one is shooting back. No one has any idea what is happening.

'Hurrah!' contributes someone, responding to another shot.

Jabez Herring, Clarence Dowter's deputy in the Sanitary

Department, scans the horizon through his gold-rimmed spectacles, and sees nothing. 'They're only firing blanks,' he reassures his wife.

Then: two puffs of red dust.

Miss Pollock in her orange dress feels impelled to lean over the side and call out at the empty landscape in her teacher's voice, 'Stop fooling around, or someone will get hurt!'

A pair of girls in Mary Brodribb's truck yell 'Happy New Year!' at the spectacle of two dark men in such candid white turbans and red jackets.

Mary smiles, but her eyes are unhappy, seized by the thought that this may be a surprise which Oliver has organised for Rosalind, and the shots are being fired in celebration of their engagement.

Next to Rosalind, Oliver jerks up his head.

'What the hell?' rising to his feet. He sees a cow on the right-hand side and wonders if some idiot is trying to shoot it. Just then, he spots Tom Blows ripping along beside the pipe track, his round face protected by a leather visor. He thinks, *It's Tom's motorbike backfiring!* and takes off his hat, waving it in the air, at the same time delighted to notice, strapped between the handle-bars like a crib tin, the small case containing Tom's camera equipment. *Even if I haven't managed to fix the problem, he should be able to make it out to Silverton.* Tom will be photographing the running races at the picnic ground. In return for Oliver repairing his motorbike, he has offered to take a joint portrait of Oliver with Rosalind.

Clarence Dowter leaps up next. He registers two men lying on the embankment above the trench which contains what the Sanitary Inspector has come increasingly to regard as his life's work: the reticulation pipe that he laid ten years ago to carry 80,000 gallons of water per hour from the creek at Umberumberka to Broken Hill. He assumes something must be wrong with the water pipe – a leak perhaps – and these men are attending to it.

Lizzie is clinging to the side and waving the peach that she has started to eat. She is pointing it out – her beloved ice-cream cart. She wants the train to stop.

Rosalind, emerging from indifference, now stands up and squeezes in between Oliver and his uncle. Confusing matters, the *ka-bang ka-bang* of the motorbike. But she is puzzled by the white cart. It hasn't travelled far since she saw it last, five hours ago, outside her window in Rakow Street, and is turned about as though coming back to town. Has a wheel broken? Gül should be in Silverton by now. She feels a stab that he will miss out on so many customers.

It's then that Rosalind sees the yellow crescent like a banana, and a star.

She looks around. At the horse on its own under a tree. Less than thirty yards from the train, the Ghantown butcher lying on his belly. And crouching on the embankment another ten yards away – Gül.

Their turbans are frost white, like ice cream almost.

The train is carrying her towards them.

Suddenly, Oliver tenses. 'Get down, Rosalind!' and grabs her. But his hand on her arm does not comfort.

'I am not going to get down.'

Uncoercible, she raises her right palm to attract Gül's attention.

Behind her, Mrs Lakovsky is thrusting her children to the floor. 'Ivan!' she is shouting. 'Ivan!'

Earlier that morning, shortly after 9.00 a.m., Gül spreads out two horse blankets over the pipe in the trench. He sits there with Molla Abdullah, waiting more than an hour. When they hear the rails tremble, they jump to their feet. Gül shoots at the driver and misses. Molla Abdullah shoots at the fireman and misses.

Stooping to reload, Gül again asks Allah to accept his sacrifice. Then he levels his barrel at the line of passengers who have stood up.

In white shirts and hats, peering over the side, in the roasting sun – all those unbelievers, waiting to be picked off.

Gül fires, reloads, fires once more, startling a wood swallow from the mulga. He springs out of the trench to join Molla Abdullah on the embankment.

Legs apart, Molla Abdullah wriggles forward. He has only ever used a gun to shoot sick animals and is not accustomed to the kick. Still, what easy targets – these goggling women wearing ridiculous clothing. Like a row of rabbits in their soft cotton dresses, or a goat he has to kill for fresh meat when on a month-long hawking trip to Corona.

'*Rabbana inna aamanna, fa ighfir lanaa thunubanaa wa qina athaab el naar . . .*'

Molla Abdullah completes the '*Istighfar dua*' prayer asking for forgiveness, and fires.

In the second truck, Jabez Herring drops like a coat from a hanger. His spectacles fly off, clattering to the floor. Above him, one of his wife's brothers grabs Mrs Herring by the floppy sun hat which she has fastened under her chin, and tugs her down.

Molla Abdullah reloads. Another truck rattles slowly by.

He raises the rifle to his shoulder, and looks down the barrel at a man with an arm in a white sling – all at once recognising the rider of the milk buggy which had crashed into his camels. It wasn't Molla Abdullah's fault that the dairyman never reined in his horse. And this was the man whose house he had dug out of the sand!

The butcher is about to pull the trigger on Albert Filwell when his attention is diverted by Clarence Dowter squinting in his direction, as though he is beginning to interrogate him again. Molla Abdullah's eyes are black opals above his newly naked chin. If he could pick off the Sanitary Inspector, who has now removed his hat . . .

Abruptly, he shifts the barleycorn foresight from Rosalind's father until it hovers on Dowter's face.

At that instant, Gül notices Oliver Goodmore. He tries to quell his rage, asking Allah to give him patience, and takes aim.

Two loud reports, one after the other.

Pinioned between Oliver and his uncle, Rosalind feels a blow, followed by heat.

Lizzie lets go of her peach. It rolls under a bench, picking up grit and droppings. She jumps down to retrieve it, inspecting the moist flesh embedded with flecks of quartz and earth, and starts to shake.

Oliver, though, realises they are being fired at. He turns to Rosalind, but she has slumped forward.

He puts his arm out to support her, and as he does so blood streams down his wrist. He catches Rosalind by the shoulder and lowers her to the floor of the truck. Limp in his arms, she has never seemed so relaxed, so intimate.

She looks up at him in a perplexed way.

He stares back at her, his mouth wide open. Part of her forehead is missing.

'Rosalind . . .'

'But I . . .' Her voice sounds as if it comes not from within her, but from another place.

The train pulls up a few yards further on while driver and fireman debate what to do. Jim Nankivell can see people in the cutting ahead. Are there more attackers waiting along the line?

Molla Abdullah kneels and fires. He appears to be aiming at Jack Crossing, an assistant guard in the last wagon, who jumps down and runs off.

Gül has stopped shooting. He stands on the railway track, staring at the ever smaller train.

He knows that the bullets intended for Oliver Goodmore and Clarence Dowter have missed their target. The way he cried out when he saw who was hit made Molla Abdullah think it was Gül who had been shot.

Gül had noticed Rosalind too late. He can still see her waving at him.

In the fierce light, the confusion of the ore truck is laid bare. Children blink alarmed eyes at the panic taking place above them. Legs bumpy with varicose veins kick out from under skirts. The floor is a mess, suddenly, of dropped hats and parasols. Everyone is shouting.

Mrs Rasp has subsided on the bench in a cloud of white, from which red is oozing, spreading through the white picnic dress to her waist. Under her cream bonnet, she appears to have on a balaclava. The lower part of her face is knitted with blood from her masculine jaw, where a flying fragment of bone from Rosalind's skull has hit it. Blood drips from her mouth onto Rosalind's wicker hamper, and splashes to the floor.

Her moans mingle with those of Mrs Lakovsky, who has a big jagged hole in her left shoulder.

Amid the kicking and screaming and the scrummage to

get the hell down, only Clarence Dowter stands unscathed above the commotion. He remains at the side of the truck, staring out, with the serious, strained eyes of someone having their hair cut. Upright and remote, as if perceiving in a mirror for the first time the contours of his own skull, he seems afraid to unlock his gaze from the trench carrying his water pipe, and from which he appears to be under attack.

Behind the Sanitary Inspector's rigid back, Mrs Kneeshaw summons every ounce of her recent Red Cross training. She bends down beside Mrs Rasp, assessing her injury, and gently wipes her jaw with a handkerchief. Passing swiftly on, she twists her veil into a sling to support Mrs Lakovsky's shoulder.

But it's Rosalind Filwell who most needs help.

Her father is uselessly trying to shade her face. Her mother holds both of Rosalind's hands, stroking and squeezing them.

When the train rocks to a halt at Tramway Dam, Clarence Dowter turns around.

Some force has dragged Lizzie's eyes inwards. She is juddering and choking and rubbing her head vigorously, as if in the grip of a fit.

Clarence Dowter looks down at a semi-naked Mrs Kneeshaw. And a sight that remains with him until his death in Kogarah seven years later, of his nephew Oliver cradling Rosalind's unrepairable head.

Mrs Kneeshaw has finished tearing up her petticoat into bandages. She ignores Lizzie's shrieks and convulsions, and, nudging Oliver aside, starts to bind Rosalind's wound. The back and top of Rosalind's head is practically blown away, and her brain exposed.

Rosalind imagines that it's the Afghan who tenderly wraps the strip of white cotton around her temple.

She is conscious of a glaring light. The sun is a miner's torch bearing down on her.

'Goo . . .'

'I'm right here. I'm with you.' Oliver's shadow falls like lead across her blouse.

'I don't know why . . . I . . .'

She is bleeding from the mouth, but she wants to say something.

While Mrs Kneeshaw bandages Rosalind's forehead as best she can, Jack Crossing, the assistant guard, has hared down the track to the reservoir at Tramway Dam, where he finds a hand-cranked telephone in the pump shed. He turns the handle and waits for an answer.

Two more shots ring out from opposite the cemetery.

The receiver is picked up by the stationmaster in Broken Hill.

Crossing gasps that the Manchester Unity picnic train is under attack from soldiers flying the Turkish flag and that several passengers are killed or injured, and armed assistance is needed.

The message is relayed to Sergeant Sleath at the police station.

At 10.45 a.m., the Reverend Cornelius Hayball is driving Mrs Stack down Argent Street in his Ford runabout, having picked her up outside her store. They are on their way to Silverton when the policeman flags down the car.

'I need you to take these four men to the Freiberg Arms Hotel.'

The men climb in. Sergeant Sleath dives into a second car. The two vehicles, loaded with a total of ten armed policemen, accelerate off in convoy towards West Broken Hill, leaving Mrs Stack on the pavement.

With fresh rumours reaching shocked ears every minute, a spontaneous posse of about fifty men is raised from a crowd that has gathered in front of the police station. It comprises members of the Barrier Boys' Brigade Rifle Club, but soon embraces any able-bodied volunteer who owns a gun and would like to have a lash.

The local military commander is contacted. Major Sholto Sinclair-Stanbrook of the newly formed 82nd Infantry Battalion is leaving for the Jockey Club to watch the horse races, when his adjutant runs out to say that he is required on the telephone.

Appointed to his command because he 'looked the part', Major Sinclair-Stanbrook consents to Sergeant Sleath's request to deploy his men. Since it is New Year's Day and most of the battalion are off duty, the order is issued for any soldier who hears about it to muster in ten minutes at the Barrier Boys' Brigade Hall in Oxide Street.

All thoughts of the hurdle race suspended, Major

Sinclair-Stanbrook voices the confusion that many feel: Are they dealing with lunatics, or with highly trained troops? If the latter, where have the enemy sprung from? The mining town is 300 miles at least from the coast. And if the Germans or their Turkish allies have in fact reached as far inland as Broken Hill, in what numbers are they here?

Oliver never sees the shot that kills Tom Blows as he roars, exhaust pipe popping, towards the ice-cream cart. His motorbike slithers along the ground, spewing photographic equipment, and comes to a halt beside the trench.

The train has disappeared through the cutting when the two men stand up and walk over to where Blows lies jackknifed in the sand. Molla Abdullah has shot him between the shoulders.

Molla Abdullah kicks for signs of life. Gül stoops to pick up a lens that has spilled from the burst camera case. He peers through it – he looks like a camel who has strayed, with his inflamed rims – and tosses it aside. Molla Abdullah says that armed men will soon be chasing them, they had better leave this place. Gül nods in an absent way. This is wrong. He keeps seeing the white palm of her hand, waving.

Gül goes over to the ice-cream cart and tugs down the flag; and then they abandon their position above the water pipe, their horse and cart, and trudge back on foot towards Broken Hill.

They thread their way across a flat expanse of stony, treeless desert dotted with wind-twisted, blackened vegetation and the skulls of gourds and paddy melon, resembling two shepherds from the Holy Land in their khaki coats and turbans. Molla Abdullah has his rifle slung across his back, Gül carries his in his hand, and the red flag. It trails on the ground behind him, blurring into the red earth.

Quite soon they come to the isolated houses on the western fringe of town.

Old Phil Deebles, a retired fettler, is first to see them. Unaware of what has occurred, he calls out in a jocular voice over the wicket fence that he has all but finished painting. 'You won't get much shooting round here,' waving his brush.

Gül looks at him and walks on.

Terence Riley, a seventy-year-old tinsmith with a spade-sized black beard, is standing in his doorway when they pass. 'You'd better not do any shooting here,' he growls. 'There are children around.'

Without warning, both men raise their rifles. The tinsmith slams the door, but they fire through it, shooting him in the abdomen. Clutching his stomach, he staggers out of the back of his house and clambers down the granite slope to the Freiberg Arms Hotel.

They trudge on, skirting the West Camel Camp north of Kaolin Street, where several Indian and Afghan camel drivers live. Badsha Khan is milking a goat in front of his shack. Gül fires at him and shouts, 'Don't follow me, or I'll shoot you,' and fires again.

Near the Freiberg Arms Hotel, Sergeant Sleath notices two figures ambling along the ridge, and drives up, intending to ask if they have seen the enemy. The car is bouncing towards them when the men kneel and shoot. Constable Torpy steps out to return fire and is hit in the groin, twice. He lies sprawled in the shade of the Ford's swung-open door, cursing.

Gül and Molla Abdullah climb to the top of the hill, and look for shelter behind an outcrop of white quartz boulders. Moments later, something pokes up from between the rocks. It's their flag, knotted to the end of a dead branch, a bright red diagonal against the blue sky.

By the time the relief train arrives at the reservoir with fifteen armed men on board, Rosalind is dying.

Mrs Kneeshaw has had to take tremendous care in bandaging her head, as there's nothing left of the exterior of the skull to hold the brains in position. She uses Rosalind's hat to swat away the flies that keep congregating.

'. . . I can't . . . I thought . . . no . . .' Rosalind could have been sleeptalking.

Her eyes flutter. She can hear her sister screaming.

Lizzie's voice thins out – a long way above now. Because Rosalind is plunging, somersaulting into the earth. As when she went down with her father in a cage to see where her brother had died, and she sank in a clatter, the wind fanning her face, into a vast chamber of gleaming pinpoints, of lead sulphides twinkling in the darkness, or stars.

Oliver is leaning over, looking down. He is close to her face. She can smell his breath, a faint perfume of peaches.

'Gool . . .'

'Ros . . .'

'. . . So sorry.'

A vagueness enters her eye and then her shattered head falls sideways.

Gül and Molla Abdullah have chosen a good position to defend. The police are exposed and disorganised, dotted out in the open on the barren slopes below.

Sergeant Sleath's first attempt to dislodge the two men from their hilltop is met with defiant shouts of '*Allahu Akbar!*' and a brisk burst of gunfire. One shot chips a piece off the boulder behind which Sergeant Sleath skips to take cover. Another loose shot kills Ern Polkinghorne, chopping wood in his yard; deaf, the impervious veteran of Pongola Bosch has heard nothing of the battle taking place opposite.

In town, dazed shock has given way to fear and then to fury. Tom Blows's body has been retrieved from the cutting, his face still wrapped in his visor and with his sun-reddened ears poking above the strap. Also, the corpse of Jabez Herring; his coppery hair is matted with blood and a piece of gut protrudes from his back.

Argent Street is full of men charging about with rifles.

'The bloody bastards!'

'We're not safe while they're alive!' another shouts.

The correspondent of the *Barrier Miner* notes that in their desperate determination to leave no work for the hangman, the mob have developed little mood for compromise.

By 11.30 a.m., reinforcements are streaming towards the Freiberg Arms Hotel to assist Sergeant Sleath. They arrive by car, on foot, in a slopcart, in any vehicle they can obtain. All eager to repel an enemy that no one expected.

The white rocks are on a rise less than 300 yards from the hotel. In a wide circle around the summit crouch fourteen policemen; forty-three volunteers from the Rifle Club; thirty-seven passengers from the picnic train – some still dressed in white linen suits – including Roy Sleath and Alf Fiddaman, who have each run home and fetched their father's rifle; plus fifty-three members of the 82nd Infantry Battalion under the command of Major Sinclair-Stanbrook.

The battle lasts two hours and fifty minutes. Still, it seems to take an awfully long time. How two men, both not very effective shots, are able to keep at bay a heavily armed party ultimately numbering several hundred is not a question that anyone feels much motivated to pursue. It is, though, generally agreed that each and every member of the attacking force behaves splendidly.

Major Sinclair-Stanbrook is confident that he can position the Turks by the black smoke from their guns. He knows the battles of the Peninsular War by heart. Buçaco, Vimeiro. This was Salamanca. He is Wellesley. After assessing the situation, he stands up – broad shoulders, aquiline nose, a scar on his cheek from a clash with a nail – and in a firm, imposing voice calls on them to surrender. 'Come out with your hands up. We've got you surrounded.'

Two bullets enter the earth at his feet. Ducking, he hears a hoarse shout: 'Australians – burn in hell!'

A pair of miners have brought along sticks of dynamite to chuck as hand grenades, but more shots drive them back.

For a moment, silence. The sun burns directly overhead as if gummed to the sky. Heat waves dance off the slopes. There is the firework smell of gunpowder.

Then voices are heard from behind the rocks, chanting. The two men have no water. Their croaked prayers resound over the battlefield.

'. . . *La illah illaa huwa wahdahu la sharika lah, lahu el mulk wa lahu al hamd wa huwa ala kulli shai'n qadir . . .*'

Major Sinclair-Stanbrook, peeping with caution above a wool bale, spots through his field glasses a dark object flitting between the white rocks. He orders his men to fire at it.

The barrage does not let up for five minutes.

Shots echo back and forth. Chips of granite fly. The

red cloth crumples to the ground, the branch snapped by a bullet.

Molla Abdullah hurls himself after it, shouting, '. . . *La ilaha illa Allah* . . .' He staggers down a little from the rocks on the other side, and stands still, clasping his rifle, staring with abject eyes at his flag.

Major Sinclair-Stanbrook is momentarily nonplussed, but Sergeant Sleath bellows 'Fire! Fire!'

They all shoot at the same time.

Molla Abdullah flings up his arms and collapses, not moving.

Sergeant Sleath has run out of ammunition. He scrambles back behind the Freiberg Arms Hotel to obtain a fresh supply.

When Gül sees Molla Abdullah fall, he says another prayer.

'Allahumma inni astaghfiruka li thanbi wa as'aluka rahmatuka ya Allah!'

The skin below his eyes has a sunken look. He is still not afraid. Only for Rosalind, who might have died an infidel.

He pushes a cartridge from his bandolier and reloads. Twenty-two cartridges left. He wipes his brow with the end of his turban, lifts his rifle.

Gül keeps firing for about an hour and then his shots become less frequent, less threatening. He is evidently badly wounded.

Just before 1 p.m., he is observed rising to his feet. Short of breath, exhausted, he holds his arms out with difficulty. They are not carrying any gun. But in one hand he clutches what appears to be a white handkerchief.

Someone shoots at him and misses. He flattens himself against one of the rocks, glances around, and withdraws behind it.

'Reckon he's trying to surrender?' Sergeant Sleath asks.

'No,' says Major Sinclair-Stanbrook. The muscles show on his jaw.

When no more shots are heard, Major Sinclair-Stanbrook directs twelve men to advance in an open line. They wheel in from the left, climbing the hill in a series of nervous rushes, twenty steps at a time, rifles ready to butt.

Several bullets are fired in quick succession as they reach the top, before Sergeant Sleath calls out, 'Stop!'

A mixed mob of police, military and civilians then surges up the slope – to find the two turbaned men lying motionless on the ground a few yards apart. They trot forward like wild cattle to examine the bodies.

Molla Abdullah, still holding onto his rifle, has been shot between the eyebrows. Gül has sixteen bullets in his body – in his chest, neck, right forearm, and left thigh. The fingers of his left hand are lacerated, and his right hand is wounded, wrapped around by a dirty handkerchief with blood on it.

Sergeant Sleath notices a movement. Gül has opened his eyes and is trying to speak. A water bottle is put to his lips. He is barely alive, but he smiles as though he might have recognised the person who has appeared out of the heat to nurse him, and even has expected her.

Weeks later, in the Saxon town of Freiberg, the manager of the Berzelius smelting works opened the *Leipziger Volkszeitung* and read the following:

> *We are pleased to report the success of our arms at Broken Hill, a seaport town on the west coast of Australia. A party of troops fired on Australian troops being transported to the front by rail. The enemy lost 40 killed and 70 injured. The total loss of Turks was two dead. The capture of Broken Hill leads the way to Canberra, the strongly fortified capital of Australia.*

Not long afterwards, a force of 20,000 Anzacs lands on the Gallipoli peninsula in Turkey. The Third Australian Brigade consists largely of miners from Broken Hill. One of the bullets from the ore he dug up goes into the head of Reginald Rasp.

In Broken Hill, on the other side of the world, the confused happenings of that Friday morning take the rest of the summer to unpick. A narrative of sorts emerges in the *Barrier Miner*, which publishes interviews with survivors. Each survivor tells a slightly different story. Not only that, but they seem to reweave it with every recital, so that strand by strand the previous pattern of events unravels to be reworked into a fresh version, and the ritual repeated, pushing the experience past living memory and out of language.

*   *   *

Rosalind's undertaker delivered the coffin with her body in it to the Filwells' bungalow in Rakow Street, where members of the Manchester Order of Oddfellows, in regalia, had gathered with members of the Master Dairymen and Milk Vendors' Association, together with teachers from Rosalind's school and the staff of Stack & Tyndall's. A sizeable crowd followed her hearse to the cemetery, to the sound of the Salvation Army band playing 'Nearer My God to Thee'. At Rosalind's graveside, the mourners lined up behind her sister and parents, and joined the Reverend Cornelius Hayball in singing at the top of their voices 'Sweet By and By' and 'Safe in the Arms of Jesus'.

Hayball gave a brief address, a tall, thin man with spectacles that sat uneasily on his nose. 'No one can know when the golden thread of life might snap for us. No one can understand why this tragedy has happened.' He paused, quite out of breath. Privately, he felt overwhelmed by what he had seen at the hospital on that outrageously hot afternoon. Naked bodies on tables. Rosalind and Gül lying side by side, their knees and hands almost touching. And the perspiring figure of Dr Large on the telephone, trying to get through to Leo Lakovsky's refrigeration room in Blende Street, to order extra ice before the bodies started to decompose, so that witnesses might identify them and the coroner perform autopsies. Hayball could only tell the congregation that God understood and knew all.

Sergeant Sleath had contacted Rosalind's undertaker to

bury the 'Turks' as well, but he refused. The policeman next commissioned a municipal gravedigger to prepare two graves in the Muslim section of the Broken Hill cemetery. He began digging these on Saturday evening in a corner up against the fence, but being given no further instructions, beyond that the work should commence at once, he dug the graves at right angles to the fence, with no particular attention to where they pointed.

That night, a crowd roamed the western hills after torching the German Club in Delamore Street, and noticed a man digging. They protested: if these graves were for the Turks, they would tear up their bodies from the earth. The digger at once threw down his spade. He did not know who the graves were for, but if they were for 'those damned Turks', cowardly slaughterers of defenceless women and children, he was not going to finish the job.

The two half-completed graves in the cemetery, pointing not north to south, but north-west to south-east, remained empty until the next dust storm.

Over the years, the sand has filled them in. Still today, no one knows where the bodies of Gül Mehmet and Molla Abdullah lie buried. As if this strange and tragic event had occurred and then been blown away by the desert winds, until there's nothing much left or remembered.

The White Hole of Bombay

Now that I'm no longer living in India, whenever there's a hot day I think of a huge swimming pool in Bombay and Sylvia Billington.

We lay stretched out on canvas chairs – Sylvia, her husband Hugh and I – within splashing distance of the pool, on a strip of lawn facing the Arabian Sea. It was VJ Day, and sounds and perspectives blurred in the mid-morning heat. There was the hum of traffic from Breach Candy Road and a faint sweet-sour smell of garbage. If I half-closed my eyes, the world receded to an oblong of intense blue sky that seemed a projection of the pool.

At the time – the late sixties – I had only been in India for a few weeks, and as a temporary member of the Breach Candy Swimming Pool Club was new to its hierarchies. Ten yards away, staff from the Russian Consulate had their corner with a net that they strung up 'when not stringing up dissidents', to use Hugh's words. They didn't talk to anyone much, but thumped a leather volleyball back and forth. I could see a barefoot gardener in khaki shorts squatting as he pulled out weeds. Closer to, a woman paler even than I was squabbled with her teenage son in a needlepoint English accent very similar to Sylvia's. At the glass-topped table where Sylvia had insisted I join them, a waiter in a white jacket unloaded his thousandth tray of the week eyed by several sandwich-hungry crows.

Bogogoingg!

Sylvia squinted up, tensing. Above us, to our left, a muscular young man in tiny crimson swimming trunks bounced from the diving board.

Whoosh. He struck the water.

Seconds later, a blond head broke the surface. He smoothed back his hair in the way a man does who wishes he had a mirror and swam to the steps to do it again.

After another glance at the diver, Sylvia put on her reading glasses and picked up her *Illustrated Weekly*.

The Breach Swimming Pool Club was along the road to the Gymkhana Club. It never opened in the evenings, but on humid days its cold pool drew Bombay's expatriate community to jump in and afterwards enjoy a *nimbu-pani*, a refreshing blend of lime, sugar and water served in tall glasses. Aside from a couple of film stars, no Indians were members. In the circles in which the Billingtons moved, the place was known, good-naturedly, as the 'White Hole of Bombay'.

The Billingtons were among the oldest members in every sense of the word. They were 'part of the furniture' as much as the long planter's chairs that always needed repairing, or the glossy white plates from which we ate our buffalo-steak sandwiches. And rather like the swimming club itself – in pretty good trim but fractionally curling at the edges for being outdoors – they had about them a settled mediocrity. Other members exhibited a pragmatic energy knowing that they would be leaving in eighteen months. The Billingtons in all probability were going to die here.

Even before meeting them, I had formed the image of a couple in late middle age, thrifty, childless, who lived in a modest apartment on Malabar Hill. No one seemed to have visited their home, but the tone in which 'modest' was spoken hinted there were reasons why the Billingtons did their socialising at the club.

This was only our second poolside encounter. Our first had taken place the previous Saturday. I was walking past a chair towards the end of the afternoon when I grew conscious of tight blue eyes investigating me over the top of a magazine.

'You're not, by any chance, —— ' She said my name.

'That's right.'

The woman took off her glasses and stood up. 'Sylvia Billington.'

I looked into a face battered by the tropics. Her skin was lined beneath her make-up, as if stretched too much and then let go, and her straw-coloured hair, which she later assured me was once 'as long as my elbow and red', had retreated in thin curls close to her scalp. She wore a jade swimming costume that advertised the swell of her breasts.

My initial impression was of a wrinkled, garish, rather sad woman who obtained her leverage by knowing who everyone was – and making sure that they knew her. Much of what she told me I had already gleaned: how she had started coming here after the Second World War, after her husband returned from Burma. How her husband – 'Oh, where is he? You two would get on' – used to work for the British Biscuit Company and now was with Makertich & Co., importing textile machinery.

Sylvia Billington didn't think of herself as a transient ex-pat like the rest of us around the pool, but as a local with roots spreading far back. She had been born in India, the daughter of a Protestant Irish cotton merchant. India was where she had met and married Hugh before the war swept him further east.

On this first occasion, she alluded to her husband's 'heroics' and was fishing for me to ask questions. She was even getting quite annoyed that I wasn't playing along, when one of the Russians yelled out and I turned to see a leather ball bouncing in our direction.

It was intercepted by a figure I hadn't really noticed before: a human bulldog, obviously British, in white shorts and a maroon-and-blue bush shirt. He sprang forward and with a surprisingly adroit motion fielded the volleyball, returning it in a hard, accurate throw.

The action had wrecked his cigarette. He paused to heel out the embers before advancing towards us.

'Hugh, come here,' said Sylvia, waving him over.

Hugh Billington struck me then, and in subsequent conversations, as a man of decent instincts, principled, unbegrudging – and disarmingly dull.

'Have I intruded?' He brushed a fly from his fleshy nose.

'I was about to tell him about your time in Burma,' Sylvia said.

The saltiest morsel concerning the Billingtons was how Hugh's 'very good war' was stippled by Sylvia's disappointment that he had not made greater capital of it, as if in some deliberate way he had beggared himself. But her pride in her husband was touching.

'I have to sing his praises,' Sylvia said to me. 'Being brought up in a certain way, Hugh doesn't talk much about anything, do you, darling? But you remember everything.'

I thought I glimpsed in her look the intensity of Sylvia's nostalgia to recapture, beneath the pot belly and strands of white hair, the brave man who had disappeared into the jungle for three long years and made it out.

I also saw a firm resistance on Hugh's part to being recaptured.

He stood there in the afternoon light, shrinking slightly.

'I suppose I do,' he said, already puffing at another of his Indian cigarettes, 'but I don't want to know some of it.'

Then: 'We should be on our way.'

'What are you doing later?' Sylvia turned to me suddenly, and before I could answer asked if I would be their guest at the Lancaster nearby where they were having dinner.

In the hotel's inexpensive restaurant that night both Billingtons became quite tipsy. I had always enjoyed listening to older people and I must have seemed interested in their story. Besides, I liked them in their different ways. Sylvia, who had changed into an ankle-length dress and switched her lipstick from pink to mulberry, did most of the talking. I tried to bring Hugh into the conversation, asking him about his work, but he was evasive. These days, twenty-three years after Japan's surrender, he was, in his expression, 'a very small biscuit' whom local bigwigs offered up as a friendly, familiar face to British businessmen looking for opportunities in the textile industry. 'A lot of them are scared to invest because, will they get paid? The Indians have a track record of paying eventually, but "eventually" didn't suit my first company.' His indifference to his effect was laudable.

He was more forthright talking about the Russians ('no better than the Japs'). Or cricket (keeping wicket for his regiment). Or – after several beers – the sorry state into which Burma, where he had distinguished himself with General Wingate's Chindits, had disintegrated. The problem was: these days Hugh's bosses at Makertich & Co. were less subtle in their more recent demands for him to exploit what they supposed – absurdly – to be his lucrative Burmese contacts.

'Burma's a place not many people know much about, but a lot of people are interested in for the wrong reasons,' he told me, during one of Sylvia's trips to the bathroom. 'Its history is rather more hopeful than its future. I wouldn't rush back. If you like people who hate each other, it's paradise. But give 'em democracy and they use it to fight a civil war. Plus, it's not an easy place to get into. If they don't want you to come, they don't answer.'

Hugh implied that they had not answered.

Our second meeting was the one that took place a week later, on the morning of VJ Day. I had come to the pool to be on my own, but as I crossed the lawn I heard Sylvia say something in an unpleasant tone. Heads turned, and I caught sight of Hugh's harried face. I saw that that he wouldn't mind if I came to his rescue.

So instead of walking on to the chair that I'd earmarked, I stopped at the Billingtons' table and interrupted their argument.

'Look who's here,' said Hugh.

'Hello, you . . .' The effect was a little theatrical since Sylvia had watched me approach.

Whatever ploy I used to dissolve their tension, I can't recall, but soon there was laughter. Once the heads had turned back, I felt I could smile: *There, what was all that about?*

I was aware of the noon heat and the unresolved domestic humidity in the air and Sylvia telling me how outrageously Hugh had been treated. She was so forward, so un-English, that it crossed my mind she had been drinking.

'Hugh won a Victoria Cross for what he did there,' she said. 'A fat lot of good that is. It means when he applies for a visa they don't even reply!'

'A Victoria Cross?' I was unable to mask my admiration. I'd imagined a DSO, something like that.

'See!' Her irritation was vindicated. 'But if Hugh had his way, he'd forget the whole thing. He won't even attend the annual church service any more.'

'You sure you won't have one of these, dear?' said Hugh.

'No, I'm going for a swim. But he might,' and she beseeched me to pull up a chair and join her husband in a toasted sandwich.

Sylvia grabbed her bathing cap, which was covered with imitation petals, and turned it inside out before stretching it over her head. 'Tell him, Hugh. Don't tell me. It's not all stuff you can't speak about.'

She stood and manoeuvred her toes into a pair of flip-flops.

'My husband can tell you what he did on the night of 15 June 1944.'

So over a glass of beer and a buffalo-steak sandwich, which we both agreed was, as always, overcooked, Hugh opened up, without too much prodding from me. I wondered if it was VJ Day that had stirred him. Or whether it was to satisfy his wife. Some sort of concession for which the uneven calculus of marriage had ordained me the receptacle, like a loose volleyball punched in my direction which I had no alternative but to catch. Or maybe he was bored and sick of the heat and being stuck in Bombay.

'My wife wants me to jump up and down and make a fuss. Truth is, I don't want to go back to Burma. Not even for her.' He flicked his eyes to the pool where the orb of her cap stood out like a bull's eye. Then, in the same planed tone with which he had made his crack about the Russians, 'I wouldn't want to leave Sylvia on her own. She's not very good on her own.'

Maybe the most impressive thing about Hugh Billington was his indifference to his own heroism. After he had told me how he won his Victoria Cross, he lay back. 'I'm going to take a nap.'

I had hoped to steal away before Sylvia returned, but I was still sitting there when a shadow fell across my chest and I jerked up, preparing to bat away a hungry crow.

'Well? Did he reveal all?'

'I think so.'

Sylvia glanced at her husband's prostrate figure, eyes closed, a dribble of gravy at the corner of his mouth. He was a big man who could move when he wanted to. Even so, it was hard to think of those legs and arms crawling back through the mud and darkness to rescue eleven of his men; this was after he had been tortured and interrogated by the Japanese. He had escaped, disguised as a Kachin villager, resolving never to leave Burma without his comrades.

'Hugh?'

He nodded, not stirring nor opening his eyes.

'I'm glad. It's important for people to know.' She turned to me: 'He's so modest it makes one scream. Of course, he's spared me the details, but it was beyond horror.' Imitating what I took to be his voice, she tilted towards me in case he overheard her whisper. 'Think of the worst, most inhumane way you can treat people. Double it. The worst, the worst.'

Hugh made a sound for her to be quiet.

I said in a hushed voice, 'What Hugh did was extraordinary.' I knew lots of war stories, but nothing so brave, or selfless; and not because I had heard it direct.

Sylvia peeled off her bathing cap and shook her hair. 'You wouldn't think so looking at him, would you? I get upset when he leaves it to me to blow his trumpet.' She reached for a towel and patted her glistening cleavage. 'I don't go around asking people to listen to him, you know.' She stared at me in a way to suggest that Hugh, by speaking, had conferred a rare honour on me, and that we were very few, we appreciators of the courage of her husband, this far-from-successful machinery importer who had begun quietly to snore.

'No, he's a real treasure is Hugh,' creaking into her chair.

Sylvia let the towel fall to the grass and loosened her straps. Then she dipped her fingers into a shallow blue tin and started smearing Nivea into her calves and shins.

Like so many of us, Sylvia didn't see herself in the present, but ten years before. She was facing me, to make sure I was attentive, and maybe to intimate that she had been a good-looking woman when she was my age. But I was thirty, she in her mid-fifties. I didn't find her sexually attractive or even poignant – not then, not in that moment.

'You're catching the sun.'

Before I could say anything, Sylvia had leaned forward and was rubbing Nivea into my shoulders. I could tell that my back was red from the tender way her fingers smoothed in the cream; from her breath that she had had a nip of gin.

She lowered her voice: 'In some ways, it was a difficult war for me too,' and looked up.

I waited with dread for her to continue when her face stiffened. She had seen the diver looming above.

One couldn't not look at this great blond idiot. Wherever you happened to be around that pool, if you were talking to someone you saw, out of the corner of your eye, his emphasising crimson Speedo.

As he walked to the end of the board he straightened his body and gazed down on us.

'Someone please shoot that man,' Sylvia said, but went on watching him.

His chest was like a slab of factory chocolate. He stepped up and somersaulted into the air, entering the water in a perfect dive.

He reminded me in his vanity of a boy I'd been at school with, a restless troublemaker in the classroom, but out on the sports field fluent and focused.

'Do you know him? He must be your age.'

'His name is Jonathan,' I said. 'He's over from Michigan to work in an advertising agency.'

'I know that,' Sylvia replied, in her pointed middle-class voice. She screwed the lid back on. 'Something to drink?' I presumed that she had forgotten what she had been about to say, and our conversation petered out.

I beckoned a waiter and gave him our order, putting it on my tab.

Beside me, Sylvia seemed listless. She was grateful that I recognised her husband's bravery. And, also, she was oddly unsettled by the discovery that Hugh had spoken to me.

Sylvia picked up her magazine. But instead of reading it, she was looking at the diver. Thinking of her adventurous youth maybe. Boom. Splash. And it's over.

As he kept bouncing off, I became aware of the movement of his body as a series of outlines in a Futurist painting. There was a lot of tidiness, at least, on display. 'He's like a Hockney,' I said. 'He did a splash,' and I mentioned an exhibition I'd seen in London, although immediately I did so, I felt embarrassed: Sylvia wouldn't have any idea about painting.

It was then that she laid down her magazine and removed her glasses and turned to her husband.

'Darling, may I smoke one of your . . . Oh . . . darling's nodded off.'

She sneaked an arm under his chair and grabbed the packet, tapping one out.

'I used to know a painter once.'

While Hugh had been 'doing his heroics' in Burma, Sylvia had had an affair in Delhi with an Indian artist and posed nude for him.

I don't know how many people she had told the story to. Not many, I suspect. But some of the spirit had gone out of her and I wondered if she was hoping to retrieve it by confessing a hazardous experience of her own.

'His name was Bhero Sethi. He wasn't well known. We loved each other very much.'

She found an ashtray and struck a match. Her cheek-bones became evident as she sucked in.

'He had this Indian nickname for me, the only nickname I've ever had. He called me – oh, it's gone. Infuriating at this age how a word goes. Just wait. It'll come to me.' But it didn't.

I was curious that she should be telling me this story so close to her sleeping husband, and I kept glancing at Hugh.

How could she be certain that he wasn't awake? But Sylvia took it in her stride, although she quite often looked towards him in a peremptory way. Checking that he was asleep, then swivelling back to reveal more about Bhero.

'I loved his energy. That's what you miss as you get older. I won't explain the why of it. I hadn't heard from Hugh in a year. Bhero could see that I wanted intimacy. He'd say, "Where do your smiles go when you're not laughing?"'

Smoke streamed from her nostrils. I had a sense of the lines on her face melting. She looked younger.

'First time we met, know what he said? "Do you have a portrait in the attic?" Oh, he could never hide his attraction, could Bhero. Nor could I. Once, I had on a pleated skirt and he compared my waist to a Christmas cracker. Imagine!' She rested a hand on my wrist.

Again she inhaled, hollowing her cheeks. In memory she saw him. 'Not fat, not thin – what Mother called "neat". Slightly bloodshot eyes. Greying. A bit of black hair on his chest, a mole on his hip. He'd had meningitis as a child and wore leg-irons when young which left him with one very slightly withered leg, but he made sure he didn't limp when I was around.'

She had been seeing him for six months before he asked her to pose. 'He couldn't get a model who wasn't a prostitute, so I said OK. I had a body then. I had no problem taking my clothes off. Never did. Funnily enough, it was when my glasses came off I felt naked. You hide behind them if you're a shy child, which I was. But I was determined not to be what Mother wanted me to be.'

'What did she want you to be?'

'Oh, nice. Nice girls keep their clothes on. When I met Hugh, I thought, *Eighteen – get rid of my cherry now.*'

Her voice was light, but there was a seriousness in her gaze. Next thing I knew, her description was guiding me up uncarpeted steps into an artist's studio in west Delhi. She conjured a little verandah. A dividing curtain of yellow shot silk. I looked over at Hugh.

'I loved the smell of gesso in the curtain. Just loved it.'

He had done a few preliminary sketches, with pencil and crayon – and in different poses. 'Some standing, some lying, some sitting in the middle of the room, on this chair, his bed, whatever he said. Do this or that . . . Oh, what did he call me?' A worm of hot ash dropped to the grass when her hand tried to summon it.

'Names, names, they come back at three in the morning.'

Her small blue eyes had ignited and widened. She was catching one after the other the images that her past was eager to toss at her. And one image she held fast to with a passionate ache. Carrying it around with her like a tall glass of gin filled right to the top, not wanting to spill a drop. Of herself – propped up on her elbow on a ramshackle divan.

The sketches were for a single voluptuous oil painting. 'Bhero had this ambition for it to be his "magnum opus" – the work by which everyone was bound to remember him. He struggled with it for over a year. This one painting! He kept telling me it was his chance to "break through". I suppose all artists say the same.'

Sylvia smiled, animated, before her seriousness returned. She needed an accomplice to escort her, without stumbling, beneath that gesso-scented curtain, into the small back room where she had posed for him.

'I felt very special,' she said moistly. 'He wanted me to pose like that woman, you know, with her back to you, in London.'

'The *Rokeby Venus*?' I nodded.

She half-smiled, but without a smidgen of humour. 'Only, I was to lie facing the artist . . .'

Two yards away, Hugh fidgeted in his sleep.

She leaned further forward, her chin almost to her knees. 'Like I said, we loved each other very much – well above a passion.' Her voice was growing softer and softer. I moved my head closer. We were breathing the same air in front of her face. 'It wasn't anything to do with sex. Oh, it was in a way, but also not part of it at all. When you pose for people, you're sharing with them. Bhero never talked while he worked, but afterwards he'd say, "When I'm painting you, I feel like I'm touching you. I know what the texture of your skin is like. I know the texture of your hair in the way your husband does. I feel the bone under your forehead, I'm running my fingers over it . . ."' Her hand mimicked the motion. 'He taught me that turning someone into art is one of the most intimate things you can do.'

'How did it end?'

'Horribly.' Her arm descended slowly. 'Hugh came back and it was only with great difficulty that I returned to him. But he had been in the war . . .'

'Did you see Bhero again?'

She shook her head. Her face had taken on a painful, obscure look. She stared down at her gleaming shins, then at her husband – before hoisting her eyes up to me. 'But I saw his painting.'

Some years after the war, the Billingtons had been guests at a military club in Delhi. After dinner, they went into the officers' bar.

'It's totally Indian now; at the same time, more British than the British – wood panelling, regimental colours and the rest of it. Hugh was offered a whisky, I had one too. Conversation normal. The CO was pretending to speak to Hugh – the smallest of small talk – but I could see from his eyes that his mind was on me, doubtless hoping for some luck if my husband was away on a long business trip. Then he said, "I've got much better stuff. Black Label! I keep it my bachelor quarters over the yard."'

'I was slightly reluctant to go with this whiskyish man to his "bachelor quarters" – we knew perfectly well he had a wife in Poona – but couldn't see a way out of it.'

From the bleakness in her voice, I sensed that everything Sylvia had told me was a prelude to her journey across that courtyard.

'We went through a room and into a locked room tacked onto it. He said, opening the door, "This is my den where I prepare military campaigns." Eyes glowing, he added in a mildly lascivious way for my benefit, "What secrets it could tell!"'

'We walked in. Everywhere the usual swords and daggers on the walls and an inlaid Afghan rifle. There was a sofa with a blanket tossed over it. And in pride of place, on the wall at the end, this quite large painting in an ornate frame. I looked up and to my horror – there I was. Horizontal. Me with my red hair.'

She held my gaze, to see if I would understand.

'I kept walking, but in fact I froze. My heart pounding, my face on fire, this chill spreading through me . . .

'Our host pointed at the painting with the bottle he'd opened, eager to know our opinion. "Well, what do you think? I bought it in Nangloi – off a decrepit sort of a fellow with a limp," and he laughed. "He didn't want to sell it, but he had to."'

'I saw Hugh looking at the painting and with every cell in my body braced myself for his response.

'He looked at it and remarked in that jocular way he has, "I'm not the one to ask about modern art."'

I imagined Sylvia's relief – and said something to this effect. But her smile was very slight.

'By then, I was fifteen years older,' she said eventually. 'That can be quite a long time sometimes.'

I looked at her, puzzled.

Her voice had gone ragged and she had tears in her eyes.

Sylvia's expectation that I would understand lasted no more than a few seconds. She spoke in a fierce whisper. The heat of her breath was on my face. She no longer seemed tipsy. It could have been her in the jungle. 'It's hard to explain . . . but it went through me like a dose of salts to feel that nothing in my pose connected us. Not a hint.' Her mouth was trembling.

I reached out, touched her arm. I was able, now, to picture the scene: her terror that Hugh would recognise her in the naked figure, and then, almost instantly, her greater sorrow that he hadn't. And behind the fear and sadness, her concern for Bhero Sethi and the circumstances that had forced him to part with his magnum opus.

'I'm sorry,' she said, covering my hand with hers, squeezing it. 'I don't know why I'm upset. I get this decent, good man, my treasure . . .' She picked up her towel and wiped her eyes, doing it quickly so that she could put her hand back.

I shot a look at the slumbering hero. 'You're positive he didn't see you in the model?'

'I didn't think so at the time – you have to realise how out of context it was. Then as the years passed, I decided he had recognised me and was being protective. Now?

To be honest, I have no idea. I've lived so long with the uncertainty, I've come to accept it.'

Bogogogogoinnnngggg!

We both tightened. To our left, the diving board reverberated with a terrific judder, like a ruler twanged in the flap of a school desk. Afterwards, I couldn't help feeling that he had bounced higher to regain our attention. Sandwiched between distinct sounds, the silence was intensified by being prolonged. I remember my hand incongruously beneath her hand, and Sylvia looking sharply up. But not at the diver.

'Neelam!' she exclaimed. 'That was it.'

Whooooshhh.

He smashed through the surface of the water at a loose, untidy angle, jetting spray onto the lawn, onto us.

Behind her, Hugh started. He rose into a sitting position and looked around, blinking.

'It's nothing, dear,' said Sylvia, and moved away.

'Blasted Americans.'

'Don't panic. All is well.' She towelled the drops from her forehead, her swollen blue eyes. 'Our nice young friend has ordered you a *nimbu-pani*.'

Hugh relaxed. He turned in my direction. 'Has she forgiven me?'

But he had seen her face.

'Syl?'

'It's nothing, Hugh,' she said in her cross voice. 'He was telling a silly story that made me cry.'

The Princess of the Pampas

I

Isabel was watching the fields for Clem when she thought she heard hail. She switched her focus to the barn roof. A bird. Scrabbling for balance on the steep tin. It slipped down the far side, clawed back in urgent stabs to the summit, and stood tipsy in the wind.

She dropped the glasses and fetched the first volume of *Birds of La Plata,* flicking through the pages for a rotogravure to match the slate-grey feathers. She knew all their names, the birds which settled on the barn. It vexed her not to be able to identify this one. A crested screamer, she guessed.

Chauna chavaria. No illustration accompanied the text. Disappointed, she read W. H. Hudson's description, comparing its marvellous voice to a bassoon.

The bird plunged its bill under a tired wing, and from nowhere a crazy hunger seized her on its behalf. She desired nothing more than to run to the side of the barn and break a scone for it. Only the thought of her husband restrained her. Where *was* Clem?

The bird flew off, soaring in laborious beats over a narrow strip of maize until she lost it in one of the rain trails sweeping across the window.

She stood there, scanning the fields for the pickup.

The hill was bare, the crab apples bare, the fields had lost their sunflowers, lines of stiff stalks pulled to the level horizon and the gale continued to blow, clattering the windmill behind the house with such force that when the telephone rang an hour before she initially hadn't heard it.

At least it wasn't a dust storm. Two winters ago they'd woken to find the farm choking under a blanket of ash. Nine hundred and seventy-three sheep Clem reckoned the volcano in Chile had cost him: one for every mile to Mount Fitzwilliam.

At the horizon the brown muddy fields met a grey sky. She could always tell if anyone moved through Clem's empire. Horseback, pickup, on foot, she would track them with her field glasses. This afternoon nothing moved. A promising blur beside the barn turned out to be a solitary cherry tree. There was no one for miles.

She pulled her eyes from the lens, and feeling a sudden pang she sat down.

'Never look back at the past,' she told herself. 'It's a hawk that goes for the eyes.'

At the sound of an engine she leapt from her seat.

* * *

Clem had left at six in the morning for San Julián, to sell the wool.

Isabel ran to meet him. She waved him down below the house. He turned off the engine so he could hear her words.

Eager under her umbrella, she asked, 'How much?'

Last night, after they'd listened to the radio, he said he hoped for twenty-five pesos a kilo.

He looked ahead, to where the rain pecked the bonnet. 'Twelve.'

She lowered her eyes to his arm. 'A man rang. The lorry's on its way.'

'But it's meant to be coming on Wednesday.' His voice began to bruise. 'That's what we agreed.'

The butcher was arriving from Puerto Deseado to slaughter the bullocks. Twice a year, for a few hours, the barn became an abattoir.

She walked round the bonnet and opened the door and collapsed her umbrella and climbed in. She thought, *Twelve*. It's never been as low as that.

'Did he say anything else?' asked Clem.

'Only that they'd left and they'd be here tonight. Failing that, first thing tomorrow.'

'I might not be here tomorrow,' he grumbled. Since laying off his men, Clem relied on hired help from the coast. It wasn't always reliable.

He braked outside the kitchen door, engine running, waiting for her to get out.

'If they come tonight, I'd better bring the bullocks in.'

'You'll have a scone, won't you, Clem—'

He was already reversing the pickup.

It took Clem three more hours to bring in the bullocks. He appeared late and poured himself a whisky. The rain had extinguished his pipe, which he emptied into the grate and started to refill, then abandoned beside the sink. His features were blurred, as if it rained an inch before his face and as if the storm, which had lasted five days, had fallen not on his fields, but between the two of them.

The rain had reddened his ears and she could smell the bitterness of wet tobacco.

She'd been rehearsing her thoughts. 'Is it the Australians?' All last year there'd been a wool mountain in Australia. 'Are they still undercutting us? It's never been twelve before.'

He sat at the kitchen table and took off one boot, then another, leaving them under the table. 'I don't know what it is,' was all he said. Once, he'd talked enough to make himself hoarse.

'Did you accept the price?'

His nod was barely perceptible.

After dinner, her five-bean stew with rice, he continued to sit in silence. He had on a white jersey of ribbed wool with the mauve and black stripes of his school colours, and a pair of cream flannel trousers, turned up. It was the way he had dressed the first time they'd met, the way he always dressed.

On his feet he wore two olive-green velvet slippers.

'Don't say they're still worried about volcanic dust?' she persisted.

He refilled his glass. Drink had rounded his face and his lips relaxed together in an expression of discontent. She removed his plate, but he didn't look up and she could hear his feet fretting against the chair.

'What were you doing today?' he asked at last.

Isabel delayed her response. 'I saw a new bird.'

She avoided his recriminating glance. Brightly, she hurried on. 'I thought it might be a crested screamer, but the wings were too green.'

His chair juddered back. 'We'll miss the play,' he said.

He gathered his glass and went through to the front room and switched on the radio. Five minutes later she joined him.

'. . . *with Ian Carmichael as Lord Peter Wimsey* . . .'

Because of the storm, the reception tonight was not good. It was never very good. She sat opposite Clem, who sat under his father's circular portrait, and they listened to the actor's voice booming and fading from London. Clem listened as if he understood those silences. They had sat like this for almost a week. The play made no sense to her. Sometimes minutes went by when they didn't hear anything.

'What's happening, Clem?'

126

'Shhsh.'

She watched the inelegant tilt of his glass. He'd been trim-figured once, under that cricket jersey. Only his legs, protruding stiffly into their slippers, guarded their lean shape. She wanted to liken them to stalks, but they didn't suggest sunflowers.

Another silence, longer.

She met the eyes of her father-in-law, painted on a herring-barrel lid. That was always the story. She wanted to interrogate the old face: 'Was this how you spent your time? *Was it?*' At least, before they sent him abroad to school, Clem's parents had a child to look after.

Clem and she had only themselves, the BBC World Service, these books.

The voice of Lord Peter Wimsey returned to the room. She closed her eyes. She pretended to listen, but she was scaling a mountain made of wool.

Clem, after the play ended, pushed himself from his chair and switched the radio off. She collected his glass, came to where he stood beside the piano. She put a hand on his shoulder, but her fingers rested there untouched.

'Another?'

'I'll get it.'

He trudged out and she thought for the thousandth time, *Poor Clem, brought down by his upbringing.* He had no bright colours, no brilliant plumage. He was an ordinary person, but he had not pretended to be remarkable.

She heard Clem sneezing in the kitchen. He would

bring them both down unless she found a means to make him soar. She looked hard at a shelf behind the piano. Tonight, she could think of only one way to revive his spirits. Time after time it had proved infallible. She wandered to the shelf and plucked out a book with a faded lavender spine.

Never in their eight years of marriage, not at his lowest ebb, did he ignore the call of his favourite character.

When Clem returned to the room Isabel sat under the reading lamp. The story which lay open on her lap had been written a century before, but she knew its words by heart. She looked up, brilliant, steeled to give him this treat, cheer him up.

'Shall I be Princess Tatiana?'

He shook his head. 'That lorry's probably lost. I ought to put a light on the barn.'

2

They had met in mid-air, that's what he liked to say. He was flying to England for his mother's funeral, the first time he had been back since leaving school.

She was a stewardess. She had flown both flights. In neither crossing had she registered Clem Caskey. In her version, which she learned to keep to herself, they met in the lobby of a Buenos Aires hotel.

It was her first time on the Argentina run and she had

four days' leave. She thought she'd visit an estancia, go riding, maybe watch a tango show. Janis, another stewardess, warmly recommended a travel agent in Calle Junin.

She stepped out of the lift, a narrow-faced woman in her mid-thirties with large green eyes set wide apart and loose fair hair. She was pretty, but no more than that. Her eyes hadn't shrunk to bits by then. That morning she wore a knee-length maroon silk dress.

In the lobby, some journalists discussed the breakfast while she battled with the map. Clem stood before her.

'Excuse me,' she asked. 'This is a such silly question. But what street are we in?'

Respectful, he took her map, unfolded it, showed her. He showed her Calle Junin as well. Then he told her they'd met already.

'My headset didn't work.'

'Oh, yes, I remember.' She drew back, speaking automatically. She was suspicious of people who talked in soft voices. 'I remember you.'

'You were also on the London flight,' he said. 'You're thinner.'

He was right, she'd been ill. But it disconcerted her to think that someone might have noticed the difference, someone she couldn't recall.

She thanked him with a professional smile and was about to disengage herself when he invited her for coffee.

All her training obliged her to say no. The person before her was quite large with an untidy pink face and the forlorn appearance of an intelligent, graceless man who hadn't taken care of himself. He might have desired to cut a dash in his cricket whites, but something seemed undone in his character through which escaped the narrow, honest, awkward truth of it.

Everything about him was indicative of awkwardness: the tight white collar, the wintry eyes, the hands bunched into fists.

Then he dropped her map.

She started to bend down, but he lunged forward and in one seamless movement recovered it from the floor as if he was catching a ball at slip.

'Here.' He held out the map, boyish. There hadn't been a skip in his attention.

When she had forgotten all about Clem Caskey she would be able to recall his redemptive gesture: its energy, its ease and the colour of the backs of his hands.

'You look like you've been out in the sun,' she said.

In an empty café on 9 de Julio, Isabel outlined the itinerary suggested with such enthusiasm by Janis. The sun falling through the water jug caught the glint of her dress, making reddish ripples on the white tablecloth.

'No, don't do that,' said Clem. He gazed at her from a bottomless shyness. 'Come to La Lucia.'

His farm was nearly a thousand miles south. He was leaving that afternoon. 'You can ride. See the birds. We have wonderful birds. Do you like birds?'

He was horribly persuasive. What else would she do? Follow Janis, as always, then buy an expensive cardigan she didn't need with money she didn't have.

'It takes fourteen hours,' he was saying.

She looked straight at him. 'I want to make something perfectly clear. We're not going to have an affair.' She was being professional and decent – yet out it came, sounding brittle.

He tried to look comfortable in a cane chair, but didn't know where to put his arm.

'I mean,' she went on, and something was deserting her, 'I don't want to be presumptuous and there's no really nice way to say this. I just feel I should be direct. You've been very kind . . .'

Her cheeks were blazing when with his big man's odd precision he laid two fingers on her arm, putting aside her fear.

'Don't worry. We'll sleep in separate bedrooms.'

They went down on the overnight bus.

From Janis's description of an estancia, she'd expected something grander. Clem Caskey's house was single-storey, modest and built in red brick on a hill below a windmill that reminded her in its metallic greyness of a Birmingham sky.

He lived on his own and had turned off the refrigerator while he'd been in England. He could offer no cool drinks.

'Warm gin and tonic?'

The tonic tasted flat.

'Tell me if it's flat.' He prepared a grimace.

'It's absolutely fine.'

The kitchen smelled odd. No one had emptied the grate, and from the rafter a lump of decaying sheep fat hung in the shape of a white shiny skull.

Beer in one hand, he piloted her into the front room. A huge window overlooked the pampas. There was an upright black piano and, on two walls, shelves and shelves of books to the ceiling. She carried her glass to a shelf and ran a finger along the spines.

'What a lot of books you have!'

'All his.' Clem pointed.

She glanced at the herring-barrel lid, but the shelves interested her more: volumes of short stories mainly, dating from the 1920s, with gold on their spines. Turgenev, Maupassant, Somerset Maugham, Tchehov.

'Is that really how you spell him?'

'It's how you spelled him then.'

'What are you reading at the moment?'

A book rested open on the piano, its place marked by a woman's nail file. Careful not to lose the page, she sought the title. '*The Princess of the Steppes and other stories,*' she read aloud, and pronounced the author's name. 'No. Not heard of him.'

Clem stood. 'He was a friend of Tchehov. He's not well known, but I like him.' There was a defensive quality to his voice, to the way he held himself. 'No matter how many times I read him, I always find something new. You can't say that about many writers.'

Scrupulously, Isabel replaced the book as she had found it and joined Clem at the window. Below, she saw a small orchard of crab apple and cherry, and a wooden barn with a corrugated roof. The day was hot, the sky on the horizon a rich blue. She followed the sunflowers to the sky.

'All yours?'

'As far as your eye can see,' in a jokey voice, but it was true, and her eyes ranged over the view, the first time they had confronted a landscape owned by one person.

'What's that bird?' It perched on the barn roof, grey with a black tail and primrose chest.

Clem narrowed his eyes. 'I'm not sure. A cocoi heron?'

He produced from a shelf two green, leather-bound books, offering Isabel one. *Birds of La Plata, Volume I,* by W. H. Hudson, with twenty-two coloured illustrations by H. Gronvold. Published 1920.

For Isabel's sake, Clem spelled out the heron's name. He found it first. 'Cocoi! Here we go!'

She stood by his side. Together they read the description.

He asked, tentative, 'Is that it?'

'No.' She had read ahead. Impatiently, she turned his pages. Further on, there was a photogravure of another species. 'Look! Isn't *that* it?'

'The whistling heron,' read Clem. Their shoulders touched. '*Ardea sibilatrix.* You may be right.'

He extracted from an ancient leather case a pair of field glasses and gave them to her. She focused while he sifted the short entry.

'There should be a chestnut patch behind the eye,' he said.

'There is.' The discovery excited her.

'What about a yellowish tinge on its chest?'

'Yes!'

The colours matched those in Gronvold's illustration. '"*Its melodious notes prophesy changes in the weather,*"' quoted Clem. 'It's very scarce, it says here.' He sounded slightly surprised by his own enthusiasm.

When Isabel handed him the glasses, he went on, 'We do get wonderful birds. They always rest here on their way south.'

She was looking at him looking at the whistling heron when suddenly he turned his head. 'How's your drink? Another warm gin and tonic?'

Tired after the long bus journey, she took a siesta under a peach tree. She said hello, goodbye five hundred times a day. Here there was nothing to do, and it thrilled her.

Later, Clem saddled a bay for her and they rode. Away from the tumult of airports, her spirits revived. The fields stretched enormous before her. She sensed the freedom of the geese swishing overhead, heard each clear sound. The cry of a lapwing; the rasp of a tongue on a cow's flank; the clash of two bullocks locking horns, like the cutlery of silent diners.

She was riding ahead, thinking that in coming to La Lucia with a stranger she had done, for her, something quite extraordinary, when her horse stopped to urinate. She swivelled in her saddle, conscious of Clem's approach. She had slept under a straw hat and the strong sun had patterned her face. She looked at him between the lattice marks, listening to the urine steaming into the red earth.

Isabel didn't have the energy or the will to be embarrassed. She rose in her stirrups and stored her lungs with air.

It was after dinner when he introduced her properly to the Princess of the Steppes. She stood at the huge window, wearing an unprovocative dress, waiting for him to bring coffee. There was enough light in the sky to see the heron's lanky silhouette.

'"*Princess Tatiana intrigued Stolypin from the moment he saw her feeding the birds . . .*"'

She looked around. 'Say that again,' she said, struck by the conviction in his voice.

He repeated the line, placing the tray on the piano. 'You reminded me of Tatiana. You're just like her.'

'And who's she?'

'She's everything I desire.' No sooner had he uttered the phrase than he laughed at his own ridiculousness. 'What I mean to say –' his arm in a graceful sweep took in the shelves – 'of all the hundreds of people in these books, she's the one I'd really like to know.'

'It sounds like you know her already.'

'I've never heard her voice.' His face was boyish again, animated. 'But if she had a voice, it would be like yours.'

'What's she like, this Tatiana?' she asked, fired by her gin and tonic.

Clem, removing his mother's nail file, underlined a passage with the corrugated tip. 'See for yourself.'

Isabel read aloud:

There are people who feel in colour, that's what Stolypin believed. If he were to put a colour to Tatiana, it would be the pale blue of a lake in Oslo. He had visited the city as a student. There was one night's ice on the lake, and when he put down his foot, the ice broke with a pinging sound that he recognised in her voice. There was a crispness, a youthfulness about her . . .

'You think this is like me?' She could see Clem's body poised, as if watching the heron.

'That's the first thing I noticed about you, your voice.'

She read on, in silence. 'This is really good.'

'Growing up, we always used to read to each other after dinner.'

'You mean aloud? That's very old-fashioned.'

'There's not an enormous amount to do in the evenings. I should have warned—'

'But I want to know what happens!'

'Then you'll have to begin at the beginning.'

She sat in the window and started at the first line, reading slowly and clearly, pausing only to sip at her glass. Twice she raised her eyes from the text. Clem sat on the piano stool. His face, observing her enunciate the words, had life in it, and she felt calm and intimate, the room idealised by the gin, her voice, the story. She smiled at him. She became aware, for the first time in a long while, that she was feeling nothing professional on her face.

Tatiana lay waiting for him in her room. When she heard the door open, she propped herself on her elbows and looked at Stolypin with such intense longing –

Isabel stopped, glanced sharply up. He must have known this was coming. But his eyes were closed. When he opened them, she blushed, looked down at the page, continued.

She read to the end, hearing in her voice the cold sunniness of the stewardess.

Next morning, Clem showed Isabel round the farm in an old Ford truck. It was painted Bolivian Army green and the passenger door didn't work and she had to squeeze over the driver's seat.

At each gate she waited for Clem to climb out, open the gate, drive the pickup through, close the gate. The process bothered her patience. Clem, she noticed, didn't seem to mind.

They drove to a shed where he spoke to two men who

stood in shadow doing nothing in particular. One, spanner in hand, listened to a soccer match on a radio. The other, seeing Isabel, raised his hat, but it was to scratch his head.

Two more gates brought them to the boundary stream. Clem parked and they watched the parrots in quick flutters screech in and out of a cliff honeycombed with burrows.

Set back from the stream under a spread of acacias, the roofs of a dozen beehives poked from the rushes. They belonged to a neighbour, Clem told her. 'My sunflowers welcome the bees.'

'Does your neighbour give you honey?'

'No.'

'Why not? His bees make honey from your flowers.'

He thought about it. 'You live here, but you don't know your neighbours two away.'

On the way back, as if a decision had been reached by the stream, he opened up to her. His father had started the farm, he explained. Its history seemed a race that he had to finish before they reached the house. Before, he had spoken one sentence at a time. Now he talked at a gallop.

Alec Caskey from the Falklands was granted his land as a bastion against an Indian threat that never materialised. He had built it up as a sheep station. The price of wool had slipped ever since.

'No one's buying wool because everyone has central heating and wears acrylic.' From Bahia Blanca to Puerto

Deseado, the farmers were steadily going bust. This was why, after his father's death, Clem had diversified – 'although no one warned me about Patagonian parrots'. After losing one crop of sunflowers, he had planted a band of maize. That seemed to stunt their attacks. 'They're not very good at precision landing.'

He survived on sunflowers, sheep, a few cattle. The flight to London for his mother's funeral was an expense he couldn't afford. His father, he said, had bankrupted himself through spending so much on Clem's private education.

'Like Alyokhin's father,' he said.

'Who?'

'A character in Tchehov.'

Alec Caskey had died five years before, but his presence clung to the farm he had hewn out of nothing and passed on to his son like an illness. After Clem and she were married, Isabel would come across half-sucked lozenges wrapped in tissue in the pockets of his suits, which Clem sometimes wore. They still smelled of a man's saliva.

At the time, Isabel thought Clem had simply inherited a love of the land that was not yet requited. She would learn that it more resembled the energy of an illegitimate determined to outrun his stigma.

Clem's economic situation was indicated by the Ford pickup: Isabel's unopenable door rattled at the slightest rut.

'You're sure it can't be opened?'

'It's always been like that.'

He got out to open another gate. As he walked back to the pickup, two sharp bangs startled him.

He raced forward. 'Isabel! Are you all right?'

Isabel opened her door, stepped down, stretched. Apologetic, she said, 'We were trained on doors like this.'

'I don't believe it! But it's been like that for nineteen years!'

'You haven't used this for nineteen years? What happened to your passengers?'

'They always climbed over my seat.'

His gratitude was extraordinary. He was still smiling when the pickup halted at the last fence. 'Passenger side opens the gates.'

She read to him that night, and again the next. His favourite stories were Russian. 'They're so at ease with their landscape!' She saw by the way he listened that he was drawn to what she became when she read. It was the concentration of a man listening to someone read his own poetry aloud.

As the moment approached for her to leave, Isabel felt her heart go out to him, this man who was not an obvious part of the landscape he struggled with.

On Monday afternoon, he drove her to the bus station in San Julián, four hours away.

On the outskirts of town, a crop sprayer wobbled overhead. 'It's been lovely,' she said, breaking a long silence.

'Yes.'

'I'll wave down at you.'

'Next week where will you be?'

'London, Toronto, Cape Town.'

'You go everywhere.'

'I fly the world, but I don't know it.' Grim-faced, she contemplated her schedule.

He said something. The words stumbled out in a quiet, awkward rush, and seconds passed before their meaning penetrated. She was too stunned to keep the thought upright in her head.

She would have to think about it, she said.

A fortnight later he telephoned. 'The birds are missing you.'

She found herself smiling. 'And the whistling heron?'

'He's there every morning. He's pining for you – and he never got to know you.'

'Give him my love.'

'How was Toronto?'

'I slept.' In Clem's pickup, she had told the truth. She flew around the world, yet she didn't see anything. She was meeting all these people, but she didn't meet anybody.

'And you, Isabel, how are you?' he asked.

'Apart from some bruised fingers, I'm well.'

She had returned to work unravelled, with a reckless energy. Two nights before, on the flight to Moscow, a passenger had poked his head round the pantry curtain, pulled Isabel's face to his, kissed her. When she didn't respond he had lingered, winking.

'With those legs you shouldn't sit down.'

In that moment, in that man's drunken leer, she saw the numberless bodies she had strapped, the mouths she had served with how many trays, the snot-encrusted noses of the children she had wiped. She put down on the floor the mineral water she was about to carry to 22G and her right hand formed itself into a fist and with all the energy that she had denied herself, with every regret at the passing of her impertinent hopes, she ploughed it into the man's face.

Since then the pinging in her hand reminded Isabel at the slightest movement of Stolypin, sinking with loud cracks into the ice. Clear, cold, true, beautiful.

'Have you thought about it?' asked Clem.

'Give me another week.'

A week later, her lungs still fresh with the air of his pampas, her eyes still filled with his yellow empire of flowers, Isabel accepted Clem Caskey's proposal of marriage.

3

She was unable to sleep. She had offered herself as Princess Tatiana and Clem had rejected her. She listened out, awaiting his return from the barn.

The windmill squeaked, and the light she had left on for him in the hallway stretched flat and pale under her door. They slept in separate rooms, but how she longed sometimes for Clem to open her door, come in with the rest of the light. She imagined that same light, unused, building up over the nights and weeks until the weight was too much to endure and he burst into her room, silent and fluent, with his body composed of the same athletic grace as when he had retrieved her map.

He never came.

At five in the morning, Isabel was woken by the sound of a lorry. Next door she heard Clem rise, feeling for his slippers in the dark. Her imagination followed him into the bathroom, through the kitchen, down the hill. In the hiatus of the abattoir and scraping hooves, of slaughter-house offal and the shouts of itinerant butchers, he would tread in a daze until dawn.

At seven she got up. The rain having eased, she decided to spend the morning riding. The need to be away from the house, the farm buildings, all of a sudden overwhelmed her. She never was able to harden herself to the killing, and Clem's behaviour last night disturbed her.

His boots stood under the kitchen table where he had left them. He must have taken hers in the dark. Clem's, although bigger, would do for her ride. She would watch the ewes lambing.

Isabel guided the bay up the hill, a pair of Dettoled

gloves in her saddlebag. Her horse trod in nervous steps through the damp char grass and once or twice a hoof slithered in the mud. Last time she rode this way, Clem was burning the grass and the stumps were black and the smoke got into her eyes and stayed there.

She came to an earth bank and kicked, intending to pause at the summit where the clouds were biteably close. At that moment, concealed in the grass, a chimango thrust itself from an armadillo carcass and beat into the air.

The horse shied in fright at the hawk, and when Isabel lost balance broke into a gallop. She tried to fall, but Clem's boots remained stuck in her stirrups.

By two o'clock, the men had finished loading the warm meat into the refrigerator van. Exhausted, they sat around on bloody bales, prolonging the ritual of maté, until the foreman barked, 'Time to go.'

Clem, surprised to find that Isabel had not prepared lunch, concocted a sandwich for himself. After eating most of it, he lay on his bed. Half an hour later he was standing at his window, buttoning on a clean shirt, when he saw her horse grazing on the hill.

He ran to the pickup, accelerated up the bank, wheels spinning and careering in the wet soil.

At first, he thought she was dead. Her body lay stretched out on the grass, not moving, the trousers splattered with mud.

'Isabel!'

She raised her head. There was a calmness about her. She tried to smile. 'My ankle. Can't move.'

He gathered her up. Only when he lowered her into the pickup bed did he hear the clicking. Her hands gripped his arm, her green eyes looked into his, and he could tell the pain was excruciating.

He drove her, covered in blankets, through the dusk to San Julián.

They had been travelling for an hour when he pulled in to check how she was.

'Absolutely fine,' she said, her nod as feeble as her voice. Her eyes moved away, lingering on the colours in the sky.

At the hospital, a nurse fitted a metal bib in preparation for the X-ray machine. It was hot in the waiting room, and Isabel fainted.

Two men lifted her onto a trolley. The nurse brought a pair of crutches, and a smooth-looking young doctor came to reassure Clem. 'You can go home.'

Clem said, 'I'll come by tomorrow afternoon.'

'By then, we should have her in plaster,' said the doctor, as if he was a dance teacher and was going to take her in his arms, one two three, one two three, one two three.

At four the next day, Clem returned. The doctor took him aside. He had lost some of his springiness.

'How is she?' asked Clem. Seeing Isabel at the end of the ward, propped up on pillows, one leg raised in plaster, he waved his unlit pipe.

'She's obviously taken a bump. She was in and out of consciousness, and she's now a bit forgetful.'

'What do you mean?'

'The fall has disturbed her. She's not herself, quite.'

Clem approached the bed. Isabel's face twisted in his direction, awake.

'I saw you talking to the doctor,' she said. 'Isn't he nice? He's been so good.'

He sat beside her. 'Yes, he does seem nice.'

She gave him a look, curious but bright, and he was relieved.

He asked, reaching out to touch the plaster with his pipe stem, 'How's the pain? I called this morning to check up.'

'Are you a doctor too?'

'Am I—?' The words stopped, waylaid in his throat. 'No, darling,' and with the mechanical response of someone who has driven an empty road for hours, he said, 'I'm your husband.'

'My husband?' She seemed rather indignant.

He noticed the stoop of her gaze. He was sweating slightly, and bits of straw stuck to his forearm.

In a voice very formal, she said, 'You look like you've been out in the sun.' Her eyes rose up his arm to meet his stricken smile. 'How long have we been married?'

It was the nausea of feeling himself alone. A most terrible wrong had been committed. 'I delivered her to you with a broken ankle,' he told the doctor.

At some point in the night, Isabel's mind had turned blank on itself. Her own name, who she was, what she'd done: she could not remember anything from her life previous to the accident.

'The lesion may have been there before the fall,' the doctor cautioned. He was acknowledging something serious, while making an effort to sound upbeat. In every probability, her memory would return. Full recovery occurred usually within a short space, he said. Either gradually, or unblocked suddenly by an isolated memory. Patience, that's all that was required.

For three days, the hospital kept Isabel under observation, without medication. Urged on by the doctor, Clem compiled a list of details which might stir a memory. She greeted each with the same devastating expression. Lord Peter Wimsey. The whistling heron. La Lucia. They had no meaning for her, produced no bombardment of associated images.

Only one detail elicited any sense of familiarity. Asked about volcanic dust, she said, 'Is it to do with the Australians?'

'Darling . . .' Defeated, Clem tried to hold her eyes, and it was as if he was feeling for two lost slippers in the dark.

On the fourth day, the doctor started her on a dose of valium and sodium amytal. His diagnosis: severe retrograde amnesia.

'It's still a grey area, with a lot of debate.' The best

course was for Clem to talk to her, remind her of who she was. 'Sometimes we only know what we're told.'

Late on the fifth day, Clem reappeared with a holdall.

Isabel, when she heard his footsteps in the corridor, told the nurse, 'That's him!'

Alert and inquisitive, she observed him unpack, arranging in turn each object on the bed.

'I've brought some things for you to look at,' he said.

She accepted the framed photograph. Engrossed, she scrutinised the wedding in the chapel of St George's, Quilmes.

'She's smart,' she said, indicating Janis in an Hermès scarf. 'Who's she?'

'Your bridesmaid.' Agitated, he retrieved the photograph. 'What about this map?' He showed her the hotel where they had met on Calle Lavalle. She did not recall a single circumstance of the episode.

'Does this ring any bells?'

She inspected herself in the silver stewardess badge.

'No.' She pushed it away, distressed at his distress. Fear and tension scored her face. She glanced at him with the withheld breath of an animal under threat, and suddenly he was back in the darkness of the barn, watched by living creatures he couldn't see.

Then she said something in such a quiet way that he had to ask her to repeat it. 'Did we have a nice time?'

He sat back, staring into the bowl of his pipe. 'Yes, I think so.'

She searched his face. Her lower lip trembled. 'I can't remember. I can't remember,' and she sounded as if she was snowing.

From the holdall, he selected another object, a book which he rested on the bed. 'What about—'

Isabel, unable any longer to contain her frustration, kicked out under the blanket. 'What is the point of showing me these things, what's the point?'

The book slipped from the blanket, but Clem with an acrobatic gesture lunged forward and scooped it from the air. When he stood up, he noticed a change in his wife. She held her head at an angle, bird-like, her eyes fastened on the backs of his hands.

'Don't you remember?' said Clem. He gripped even tighter the faded lavender cover. 'You were my princess.' It was a sigh from the marrow.

'Princess Tatiana?' She gazed at him in a concentrated way. And then in an altered, interested voice, she said, '"*Princess Tatiana intrigued Stolypin from the moment he saw her feeding the birds.*"'

4

Ten days later, Clem Caskey drove his wife home.

'What a view!' she said. She rested on her cane, breathing in the hill, the windmill, the fields. When he offered his arm, she squeezed it trustingly, and with a coltish rub pressed her head into his shoulder. Like that, they entered the house.

He had prepared for her return with painstaking care. He had stripped the front room of shelves, of books, of his father's portrait. In her bedroom, too, he had removed all traces of her past. Of anything that might trigger premature memories of Isabel Caskey.

'Stolypin, look!' Taking his hand, she gestured through the window at the barn. 'That's where I fed the birds.'

Garaged word for word in a corner of her memory was the story of his favourite character, which she understood to be her story. It was the only part of her life she remembered, to which she had access. She knew it by heart.

And Clem, responding to her warmth, couldn't help himself. He knew that he could choose at any moment to break the spell, but why do it? Hadn't the doctor advised him, in the hope of one spontaneous recovery leading to another, 'Just play with her, go with it. With luck she'll remember everything else'?

No. He would respect the natural law of things. He would say nothing.

She touched his face. 'You're very withdrawn.'

At her touch, he felt a mad charge of omnipotence. 'I'm just happy to have you back.'

'I'm happy to be back.' It was a sensuous smile.

Nothing in her change of manner could have prepared Clem for the joy he felt that night when, with clattering heart, he opened the door to her bedroom and saw the light fall on her eager face. She lay propped on her elbow in an attitude of the most intense expectation, as if she had waited a hundred years for him.

Over the following weeks, the familiarity which had built up in a vague but confident sort of way in the hospital developed into a childlike sense of awe at her surroundings. This was true especially of her feelings towards her husband. Or – as she called him – Stolypin.

Whenever she addressed him by that name, he felt the same charge of energy. He didn't care if Stolypin wasn't his real name, that Tatiana wasn't hers. Who was there to challenge Isabel's new sense of herself? As far as her eye could see, she was his Princess.

Under his guidance, she learned very well. Soon all concern vanished about her defective memory – although, because of her cast, she continued to walk with difficulty. The injury to her ankle restricted her to Tatiana's universe of kitchen, bedroom and the orchard that she looked out on from the window.

She moved through that world with splendid ease. Surfaces gleamed for the first time. She scoured the floor tiles, rafters, pans. She stewed jam from the young crab apples and cherries, labelled the jars, lined them up as little gifts for her Stolypin. In the kitchen the warm, sweet smell of baking cakes replaced the odour of sheep fat.

Sometimes he heard her in the front room naming the birds in a sing-song voice. 'That's a J, could it be?' At first, she was able to recall them by their first letter alone, not by the whole word, and her evident frustration worried him to the extent that one day he arrived home with a gift which thrilled her more than anything: a pair of bird books entitled *Birds of La Plata*. They were the only two books in the house, but it both relieved and gratified him to see the satisfaction they produced in her. From that day on, she spent at least an hour each morning reclined on the window seat, one or other volume resting against her leg.

Nowhere did she move with greater ease than in bed. In the bedroom, she was not hindered by her ankle. Each night when he opened the door, her eyes looked up at him, open and shining.

So with each day did Clem come into his own. He completed projects long abandoned. He reorganised the vegetable garden; he mended the cracks in the swimming pool, so that Tatiana would be able to exercise once her cast came off; he extracted from his Basque neighbour a box containing twenty-two glass jars of acacia honey.

Neighbours who met him in the street in San Julián noticed that he had gained authority. He walked straighter, with a leaner body, and seemed in every respect to be taking care of himself. The few whose business took them on the cinder road past La Lucia noticed how amazingly healthy, all of a sudden, his crops looked.

Even the price of wool responded.

Two months went by like this.

* * *

One morning, Princess Tatiana was watching the tin roof through her field glasses when she heard a rattling noise. She lowered her glasses. When she saw what had caused the noise, she focused adoringly.

Stolypin stood at the barn door, struggling to pull open a padlock. Finally, he succeeded in wrenching it loose. He opened the door and disappeared inside.

Moments later, she observed him emerge from the barn, heading in brisk steps towards the pickup. Over his shoulder, he carried a woman's red dress.

Only a short while before, at breakfast, Stolypin had announced he was going into town and was there anything she required.

'Yes,' she said. 'I need a new dress.'

On the point of leaving the house, he had come back to find her.

'I forgot to ask. What size are you?'

Puzzled at his question, she stared down at herself. 'I don't recall.'

His behaviour struck her as peculiar long after he had driven away. Until this morning, she had never spared a thought for the inside of the barn, only for the birds resting on its roof. She couldn't help noticing that the man she loved, in his haste to be off, had left the door unpadlocked. Mildly curious, she wondered what he stored inside.

She was now able to walk short distances without discomfort. She estimated the distance across the orchard. With the aid of her stick, she ought to be able to manage.

Half an hour later, her knees brushed in the dark against a bale. She collapsed on the straw, panting heavily. The tendons pulled at the top of her foot, and she couldn't work out why her weight on the stick had woken in her right hand such a throbbing pain.

Glad to rest, she looked about, her eyes adapting to the gloomy interior. The barn smelled of urine and animal sweat and dust from the hay. She sneezed, frightening something on the roof.

Down at her feet, two pale track marks curved across the bare planks. She followed their direction, surprised to see various cardboard boxes stacked against the wall, and, beside the boxes, a black tin trunk. Somehow the trunk, even more so than the boxes, looked out of place.

After recovering her breath, she hauled herself up.

The lid was unlocked.

Inside, the trunk was packed to the brim with a woman's clothes: skirts, shirts, scarves. And, laid flat on top, a book. She picked it out, stepped back a pace and rotated the cover.

The book's purplish colour pricked at her. She had the sensation of having seen this precise tinge before. But where? On a bird? A fruit? In a sunset?

It was too dim inside the barn to read the faded words on the spine. In less than a minute, she had reached the door. She stood in the mid-morning sun, leaning against the frame. She did not see the Kentish cherries on the trees, or the water sparkling in the pool, or the ruffled feathers on a pigeon's neck as it skimmed the surface with its beak. Her eyes were on the book in her hand.

With great care, she opened it.

The book was published in London in 1922 by Chatto & Windus, and translated from the Russian by Constance Garnett. She noted that it had first appeared in print in 1897.

She turned to the first page.

Freshwater Fishing

The lounge of the Copacabana in Kenora is a white man's bar, but Ned is like his dog. He's happy if anyone steps through that door. You always see a few old Indians sitting in the corner window, silent as stones. The Copacabana is not what you'd call a popular bar, and maybe that's the reason. I haven't been in town long enough to tell this to Ned, but you shouldn't let just anyone walk in. You have to find a bottom line.

Today's the longest day of the year in Kenora. Already, it's six in the evening, and the only white man in the lounge apart from Ned, who as I said is like his dog, right down to his small ears, is me.

Personally, I like to read my paper at the bar. From where I'm sitting you have a good view of the lake. I can see the pier where summer cottagers leave their boats, and I can see a couple of girls standing on it.

There's a splash. A white face breaks the surface. It's the taller of the two girls. She treads water, laughing.

Then an arm comes out of the lake and flings something onto the dock, bright blue – a bathing suit.

I watch her for a moment. The Indians watch, too, their eyes expressionless like the water. The shorter girl stands against the dirty waveless lake, deciding whether to dive in. I'm waiting for her to make up her mind when the lounge door opens and the Indians smile and I know with a true weight in my heart who it is.

It all changes in the Copacabana when Silkleigh walks in.

'Hello, Richie!'

I turn and squint. For a moment he's indistinguishable from the coats and shadows. And then I begin to make him out. He's standing in a black rubber diving suit with his hair wet, and he's holding a pair of yellow goggles and some flippers of the same colour, and an oxygen cylinder. I won't dare ask why he's dressed like that, because there isn't a whole lot to dive for in that lake. We're talking about bathing suits which have missed the dock, or lost watches.

Silkleigh's a tooty-fruity Limey who's come to Kenora, so he tells me, to write the story of his life, as if anyone would read a page of that. He only has to say his name for you to savour the full palate of his bullshit.

'Hello, Sickley.'

'How are you, old soul?' and he comes back at me as if I'm his best friend. You have to say that for the Brits: their manners don't skip a beat.

Actually, we've met only once, but even in a place like Kenora where it would be nice to have a conversation, a single meeting with Joseph Silkleigh in his flood pants and paisley cravat was enough to satisfy me for the remainder of the summer. That's when he told me about his years as a diver in North Africa. 'Deep seas, old soul. Deep seas,' and he tapped his nose. He looked about as capable of deep-sea diving as Plywood Pete over there.

Silkleigh plonks his diving gear by the door, where it starts a sizeable puddle, and goes over to the Indians. He's the only white I've seen cross the floor to chat with these Ojibwa. He pinches Plywood Pete's purple, drink-ballooned cheeks, and says a few words as though he's speaking Pete's special language, but I don't believe he is. He's only been in Kenora four months. If you ask me, he's just old-souling them.

While he's listening out Plywood Pete, I'm thinking, *These colonising bastards, they walk into a room trailing water and a waft of England like sulphur.* Because let's face it, Silkleigh's not like Ned or me. He has a different relationship to space, like he owns it. And now he's chatting up the other Indians as if he's been here longer than they have, and you know what? They're like Ned's dog. All over him.

Anyways, they laugh at Silkleigh and then he squelches to the bar and without a blush asks Ned for a pint of the girl's beer, Molson Golden. 'And a packet of Humpty-Dumpty crisps.' By the time Ned comes back from the storeroom to tell him he's only got Old Dutch Ripple, I'm lost in my paper.

Actually, it's not my paper. I work for the *Manitoba Business*, which attempts to celebrate entrepreneurial spirit in Manitoba. This is the local rag I'm reading. It celebrates the obituaries of Ukrainian immigrants who've never left Kenora. How to remove scratches from furniture. Recipes for kiss-me-quick pudding. The same things, I recall, which used to go down well in the Midwest. You see, I'm not from Kenora either, which is, I guess, the only trait Silkleigh and I might ever hope to have in common.

So I'm reading this paper, drinking in the spirit of the locality like I tell you, and in particular a story headlined 'I felt the devil inside me', about a dry-waller from Gimli who destroyed his wife's beauty parlour in a rage after he discovered she was cheating on him, when there's a shout.

Silkleigh follows the trajectory of my stare. We're both looking out at the pier where the short girl is standing in her Speedo high-cut one-piecer, hugging herself. She has a farmer's tan: shoulders white, arms brown as if she's wearing long dark gloves. Her friend waves from the water, urging her to jump. And it's hard not to watch. They'll be girls from the city. They take the Greyhound and their boyfriends come up on motorbikes and collect them from the bus depot. Local girls don't swim off the pier. The water is full of diesel fuel and rainbows, but girls from Winnipeg are not water smart. They haven't figured it out.

For a moment, we watch the girl on the edge of the pier looking out at her friend with the long hair and long white body and not much else besides swimming in the slinky water. I see the old Indians trying to avert their eyes, and the young ones not bothering, and Silkleigh with an expression which makes me want to say to him, 'Your type?'

But the son of a dog pre-empts me.

'Richie, old soul,' says Silkleigh, all conspiratorial. 'That's the one ship I'll never sail in again. A relationship.'

That's how Silkleigh is, I suspect. When he sees someone intently reading a paper he wants to distract them. I say nothing. I'm hoping he'll go and dive back into the lake, but he dins on. He's like a child when his mother gets on the phone, he really is.

'Temperament has a lot to do with size, Richie. The smaller they are, the more you've got to watch out.'

He sips his girlie beer and waits to see if I've taken his bait, but I'm reading on. I've developed a hunger to finish the story about the dry-waller with the devil in him.

Noisily, he tears open his Old Dutch Ripple. And starts to read over my shoulder, munching his chips.

After a while he says, 'How do you know if you've got the devil inside you?'

'Oh, you know,' I say, and I also know my quiet time's up.

'Yes. I suppose you do.'

With the most extreme reluctance, I raise my eyes. By

the set of his chin I can tell he's thinking an enormous thought, which no one in the Copacabana shall prevent him from sharing.

'I know it's traditional to suppose that what happens to us is scrawled in the stars . . . No! I'm not allowed to feed you,' but turns out he's speaking to Ned's dog who's pawing Silkleigh's padded swivel stool with what you call a worshipful stare in his eye, much the same as I detected just now in Plywood Pete.

I'm in the middle of trying to establish Silkleigh's drift, when he says, 'Crisp, old soul?' and holds out a hand, in the same gesture dripping half the lake over the page I'm reading.

'They're called chips,' I tell him.

Silkleigh gazes past me once again at the small, thin girl on the pier. She curves her back and prepares to dive. Seeing her neat form strike the water like a match going out, he suddenly looks very tragic as if he's remembered something quite awful. Beneath the surface her white legs catch the sun, but Silkleigh's no longer smiling. In fact, he's all in a heap and lonely.

'You know, Richie, old soul, you and me are both men of letters.'

I am seriously content to leave our conversation at this, but he wrist-wipes some beer from his lips and swivels to me and says with an urgency which I have not observed before in our acquaintance, 'You're probably the only person in Kenora who has the smarts to understand this.'

'Understand what?'

He waves his hand in the air as though it's surrounded by flies, scattering more drops. 'You know, old soul. Of course you do. How people can separate or stay together for the most tenuous of reasons.'

I look around for Ned, but I hear him in the storeroom stacking bottles. I tilt my empty glass, waiting for him to reappear, but Ned's a sensible fellow. 'Not sure I know what you're talking about, Silkleigh.'

'Shall I tell you, Richie, the secret of the sexes?'

With two Molson Ex under my belt I am equipped to study him. Silkleigh, to be brutal, does not look at this precise moment like someone who can tell the difference between the sexes.

'No,' I say.

You have to hand it to him, he's uninsultable. 'Tell you all the same, old soul,' he says. 'Women hope men will change. Men hope women will stay the same,' and he leans so close I can smell the sour cream and onion. 'They never do.'

I'm investigating the top of Ned's bar through the bottom of my glass in a contemplative, microscopic way when Silkleigh says, 'And can I tell you something else, Richie? Something I've never told anyone.'

'Ned!' I call.

'Coming . . .' Ned answers, but that's a lie. He stays in his back room clinking the empties busy-busy while Silkleigh starts to tell me what he's never told anyone.

I'm not listening, to be honest. Being a nice guy, I'm nodding, but what I'm really trying to do is to glance at the dry bits left in my paper. Anyways, I gather it's about some squeeze Silkleigh was once married to and how she left him pretty soon after, which does not shock me in the way, evidently, he thinks it should.

'Terrible,' I manage. Ned may have told me that Silkleigh was married, I can't remember. Everyone gets married in Kenora at some point.

'You're bound to have met her father, old soul. Bound to.'

'Who is she?' I feel obliged to ask.

'She's basically a very selfish woman,' says Silkleigh, and then adds, 'She doesn't love me.'

Here I am able to relate. 'Name?'

He scrunches up his chip bag, claps his hands and tells me.

'You were married to her!' I say, much astonished, and Ned's dog starts barking.

'Don't be such a pain, Snorri,' says Silkleigh, and caresses the dog's head.

'Stella Fotheringham,' I repeat.

Now all I know about Stella is that she's supposed to be bright as hell and beautiful with it. The only other thing I know, she works up north with animals. Two weeks ago I was up at her father's lodge for an article I'm writing about Big Business on the lake. Stella wasn't there, but the office was hung with pictures of a lovely-looking woman standing in the snow beside no one, and certainly not beside Silkleigh.

'I had no idea Stella was married.'

'Wasn't,' says Silkleigh. 'Until she met *moi*.'

He peels the rubber down his wrist to reveal a swanky-looking watch. 'See this.' He holds it to his ear and when he listens his face positively ticks with joy. 'She gave it me. Wedding present. Water resistant to three hundred metres. "Like you, sweet," she said. But that's just the Silkleigh cover. I can tell you, old soul, I was a bit leaky after she left.'

'Why did she leave?'

'Now you're asking too much,' and he sits there all in black and dripping.

But I want to know. 'Silkleigh, that's not fair. You were about to tell me.' And seeing he's undecided, I make a vicious appeal. 'One man of letters to another.'

At this, he drops his wrist, and all of a sudden it's the face of hurt I'm looking at. 'She left . . .' says Silkleigh, and I'm not sure if he will continue, but he manages to find the words. 'Because I took her fishing.'

They'd met on a ship in some fjord. Stella, as it happens, is an Arctic mammalogist with a PhD from Tromso. 'She hated everything south of the sixtieth parallel, and that, in the end, included me,' says Silkleigh. 'But not in the beginning. Ah, the beginning . . .'

Eleven months of the year, she lived by herself in Nuuk,

tracking walruses and their cubs. The other month, she gave lectures on adventure tours for rich folk who wanted to see the north. She talked about reindeer, polar bear, walruses. Nobody talked to her. 'Too intelligent, old soul.' Except one night on deck as they sailed into Tromso . . . Silkleigh.

'We had the wilderness in common, and one thing led to another. I will not detail how she took her comfort, but when she danced the waltz that night she almost carried me in the air. I was arse over tea kettle about her, old soul,' he whispers. 'Arse. Over. Tea. Kettle. But there was just one problem.'

'Tell me.'

'I wasn't a walrus.'

I try to nod. 'You weren't a walrus?'

'Not that I knew this at the time. At the time I was tumbling gaily into the old free fall. "Want to come diving in the Gibraltar Straits?" I whispered as we danced. "Why not?" she said. We stepped off that boat and flew to Abyla, cold to hot. She thrilled at the idea of it, just as she thrilled at the idea of me. Contrast, old soul. Women love it. And all that cold, it melted in the Mediterranean sea. I showed her giant turtle and squid and cuckoo wrasse, and if I could get her south once more, it would happen all over again.'

I'm gathering from Silkleigh that Stella was as I have observed her to be in her photographs, small and compact. 'And beautiful?' I ask, to be sure.

'Does a fish swim!' says Silkleigh. 'But she didn't like to be reminded of her physical attraction and so I never did. "Beauty. Skin deep," I observed after one of her squalls. "Then it's lucky I'm so thick-skinned," she snapped back. And Stella was that, which is one of the things I discovered in Abyla. Most people filter unpleasant things out. She filtered everything in. She was like a Dutch slaver, old soul. Miserable. On our honeymoon I had a name for her because she looked so sad. Viejita, that's what I called her. Little Old One.'

I'm about to say that I don't recall her looking sad up at the lodge, but Silkleigh grabs my arm: 'Know what Stella's mother told Stella on her deathbed?'

'No.'

'"If that's how you kiss a man, no wonder you don't have one." And her mother was right. She saved every endearment for her bobsleigh team. Old soul, you can't imagine. The terrible cruelty of animal lovers . . .'

At this moment, I notice something move into my line of vision, and ever so slowly a hand curls around the door frame, and then a nose appears, followed by an eye, some whiskers and an ear.

'Ned!' But he vanishes, and all I hear through the renewed clinking of bottles and a dog barking is Silkleigh's unstoppable voice.

'Which meant,' Silkleigh went on, 'that she had no interest in my writing. Couldn't cope at all. Can you imagine, old soul? She wanted to go to the top of a revolving restaurant, or put out forest fires. Anything but read my work-in-progress.'

'So where does fishing fit in?'

'Ah, fishing,' says Silkleigh, as if he might have forgotten the reason why I sit here nodding. 'Well, this part will especially fascinate you, Richie, being a wordsmith. I bet you're the same as I am. Never happier than when sixty miles from a pavement. We writers, we're like the Indians I reckon. We need our space. When we're in the woods with our .22 and our sleeping bag, no sound but the cry of the loons and the low-pitched rumble of the ice talking to itself, that's when we're at home. That's when we're at our peak, isn't it? I can see it in your face. So, Richie, you of all people will understand why not long after we married, I took this houseboat in Minaki to write my book and left Stella behind at the lodge.

'I ought to say that since the honeymoon there'd been a teeny weeny bit of tension. We hadn't been fighting, but things were a mess. Which is why I was careful not to say too much when I left for Minaki. No home is broken by an unsaid word, old soul. That's what my housemaster told me.

'Well, there I am in the woods scratch scratch scratch. I suppose you'd call me one of the last of the old-fashioned autobiographers,' and he spreads his fingers and glances from his hand to mine. 'Tell you're a calligrapher, too, old soul.'

'No, I'm on a computer.'

He looks from the back of his hand to the palm, closes it. 'And when I finish my chapter I ring her. As it happens, this chapter's taken longer than I thought. It's the writing bug. Once it gets you, you don't notice the time. But how do you explain that to someone who runs a Walrus Alert Team in Nuuk? I can hear on the line she sounds a trifle subdued when I explain that I've got myself to prep school and only thirty years to go, ta-ra ta-ra. But I do understand. It's hard to be married to an artist, and I expect she's missing me. So I say, "Viejita, don't be like that. I'm going to give you a big treat." You would have thought she'd be delighted to hear this, but she goes on in this voice, and that's when the old Silkleigh sixth sense ought to have clicked in. You see, she was using words she'd never used before.'

'What kind of words?'

'Words like "touched". "I'd be touched if you took me out to dinner." Poor Viejita. She's never been touched in her life. So I say, knowing what an animal lover she is, "No, I'll do something much better. I'll take you fishing."'

'You know that island opposite the lodge? Smoke-coloured pines on a pink rock. Well, that's where I decided to take her. I wanted to make it a day she would remember, and to this end I stopped off in Kenora to buy her a present.'

'What do you buy a girl in Kenora?'

'I bought her a spanking new split-cane rod and a lure.'

'Just what she always wanted.'

'What I didn't tell her was I'd forked out every penny of my publisher's advance to give her this treat. But that's how you are when you love someone. The old doh-ray-me doesn't mean a thing. So I row her to the island and tell her how lucky we are. It's a beautiful day for fishing, overcast, with the ice melting in a tinkle and the sun invisible behind the beaver-stripped trees. I start to put up her rod and she sits on the rock, pulling on a jersey. I'm just sorry she's not saying much, that's all.'

'Didn't you lay it on the line, Silkleigh?'

'When you're having fun you never lay anything on the line. And the rod is lovely, a twelve-foot state-of-the-art cane. I hand it to her and I say, "You know, Viejita, how mayfly live twenty-four hours? When I look at that rock face, I feel like a mayfly." Well, she stares at the rock as if she has twenty-four things she'd prefer to do, and she suddenly becomes inexpressibly sad.

'"Don't say that, Silkleigh. Don't call me Viejita. It's everyone's inevitability."

'By now, I'm tying on the lure. I've bought her a Five of Diamonds. Actually, if I wanted to be critical, I could say Viejita was a bit like that lure, bouncing along all shiny on the surface, glistening with hooks, but lacking in the what-it-takes to land a fish. But in the right hands, the Five of Diamonds can be lethal. As I tie it on, I do a little demonstration so she can appreciate the science. Biophysics, I understand, is one of the subjects she studied in Tromso, so she'll be pretty interested. I show her how the lure doesn't revolve, flips back and forth, does a full turn one way, then a full turn the other. "So you can use it all day without twisting the line," I explain. Still she says nothing. Just sits on the rock and holds the rod and looks at the lake. I'm thinking all she needs to be Britannia is a helmet, and decide maybe the best thing is to educate her more about the lure, which is named after a metal-worker from Alberta who was gassed at Ypres. I tell her how the doctors told Len that he needed a year of exercise and fresh air and how he took his sleeping bag and tent and went off into the woods. "Rather like me," and I bowl her a Silkleigh special, a smile which normally works a treat. And how, I go on quickly, not being able to afford fishing tackle, he got hold of some kitchen spoons and cut their handles off and drilled holes in them, so they revolved in water instead of going back and forth.

'"You wait. You'll catch everything on the Five of Diamonds," I promise. "In fact, my darlingest, I should be hiding behind a tree doing this so the fish don't jump out."

'What I'm saying must strike a chord because she says, "How do you know, Silkleigh? You've never fished a freshwater lake."

'And that's when I see it. As I finish tying the lure, a big fish rises about thirty yards from the rock.

'Stella looks at the ripple, concentrating for the first time. "I wonder if that's a pike." It would have to be a pike or a muskie. She only likes things that are big.

170

'"Probably a trout," I say, and I start to tell her about the first trout I ever caught, out of a Christmas tree in Hungary. "I was so excited that I hoiked it from the river into the branches."

'The fish rises again, a little further out.

'She stares at the disturbance. "Or could it be a sturgeon?" Her voice suggests that even if it was a beluga and she happened to catch it, she couldn't really care. But I do have a feeling she's more interested than she wants to be.

'I show her how to cast and she casts in a dutiful fashion for about ten minutes, but there's no further sign of the fish. She returns the rod. "Here. You have a go," and as I take it the fish rises again and I can see it's a nice one.

'I can also see that the fish is heading out slowly into the lake. I try to cast beyond it, but the lure falls short in the grey water. I reel in the line and throw the rod harder.

'"More to the left," she says at the splash, and I'm excited. "I said you'd get a taste for it." The lure bounces out of the water, and a little further off I hear another rise.

'A wind blows in from the lake, fanning water onto the rock face, and beside me Stella shudders.

'"You watch. I'll get it this time." I'm so afraid the fish might swim out of reach that I back-flip the rod and with a special effort hurl it forward, and that's when the wind catches the lure, and the Five of Diamonds, instead of dropping into the lake, buries itself in Stella's arm.

'I put down the rod, run to her, peel up her jersey. One of the hooks curls dark under her skin.

'"I can cut it out," I say. "I could boil a knife."

'"No," she says firmly.

'I row her to the lodge and drive to the hospital in Kenora and by the time we arrive two hours have passed. The nurse takes her away and I wait outside in the car until the nurse comes to find me. "Boy," she says. "Your wife's mad at you."

'That night, I take Stella out to dinner. Since we're in Kenora, I've booked us a table in the revolving restaurant. I thought she'd appreciate that. We go up in the lift and find our table. But when we're seated, I have to admit the old sixth sense is relaying to me that maybe she doesn't have every oar in the water. Even though she insists her arm isn't hurting, I can see she's all churned up about something.

'I bowl her another Silkleigh special. "Share?" I say. Not that I expect her to. She's close like that. Put it this way, old soul, I have by now ascertained that Stella isn't someone to wear a matching curling jacket with "SILKLEIGH" on the sleeve.

'"Order anything you like," I tell her, ascribing it to hunger, but she just asks for a children's portion of pickerel cheeks. When the pickerel cheeks arrive she looks at them, and after a while she picks up the pepper pot. Then she looks at me and she says, "It's not working."

'"No, my darlingest, it's a grinder. Give it to me," and I'm reaching out for it when she says, "I want a divorce."

'I put down the pepper grinder and I can tell you, Richie, it takes a second to sink in, this bolt from the absolute blue. Then I meet her gaze.'

Silkleigh plucks at the skin under his chin as if it's not me who's looking at him but someone else, and he picks up his glass. 'Know something else, old soul? She had a look in her eye that I'd only seen before in wolves. I've come across them in packs on the ice. They look at you for a second out of curiosity, a very intelligent look, and then walk on. Well, this was the look on Stella's face.'

Silkleigh finishes his beer.

'It was the last time I saw her. As a wordsmith, I know what's going through your mind. That Five of Diamonds in her arm was a symbol, the final straw. That's what I thought, too. To begin with, I even tried to blame myself. I know, I know. But one does. In fact, there was actually a moment when things got so squiffy that Silkleigh here nearly had himself shrunk. Shrunk, old soul! Then I thought, that's ridiculous, and for a while I blamed the old stars in the sky. I spelled it out to myself. There was nothing you could have done, Silkleigh. N.O.T.H.I.N.G. It was inevitable. Unpreventable. And then not so long ago I started to ponder. If we'd caught that fish . . . If instead of her arm I'd hooked that fish and we'd had a beautiful day on the lake, would not Stella Fotheringham and I still be man and wife for as long as we both shall live? I tell you, old soul, when you bother to think about it, our happiness, our misery, hangs by a nylon thread. And then I thought, if I could just get her south again, under the sea . . .'

Silkleigh's words are lost in the noise of an engine revving. Outside the Copacabana, it's getting dark. A girl arranges her legs on the back of a motorbike and I see it's the small girl from the dock. Her hair hangs in a long wet rope down her back. She lifts a bare leg high over the exhaust pipe and her skirt falling over the tail light of the motorbike glows red.

'But I'd do it all over again. The writer in me, I suppose. Remember what our brother Nietzsche said about artists, old soul?'

I watch the girl disappear down Waboden Avenue and dwindle into a hot dot. 'Remind me.'

'We never learn.'

The Death of Marat

Who is Dilys Hoskins? A fifty-five-year-old woman with white hair and sharp blue eyes that look out from unintendedly fashionable horn-rims. The mother of two children both now in their twenties. Widowed for eight and a half years. Born on the east coast of Africa – in a country of high-duned beaches, deep lakes, fertile plains, intractable marshes and deserts. Someone to whom the following words might apply were you to speak with neighbours in her run-down apartment block: detached, resourceful, a hard barterer, ladylike.

In other words, a most improbable assassin.

She is at the end of her long month in London. Her daughter Rachel has just given birth to Dilys's first grandchild, a nine-pound boy with a piercing cry. Dilys has been staying in the converted basement of Rachel's terraced house in Putney, helping out. In five days' time, she will fly to Australia for her son Robin's graduation ceremony, from his school of architecture in Perth, before returning to her one-roomed flat in her African capital, into which she moved after the government confiscated Coral Tree Farm. She does not deny the surplus of fear that spills out when she considers the chaos that awaits her, or the poisonous sense of her own impotence. She is only one untrained person. What can she do to help? She is not a nurse, not a doctor; she is a farmer's wife who for the past eight and a half years has wanted a husband and a farm. But her mind is made up.

Her children have been emailing each other. They don't think that she should return. She has a strained relationship with both.

On a rainy evening in the last week of her visit, Dilys stands in her daughter's kitchen in Oxford Row, waiting for a pot of tea to brew, when she hears Rachel call in an urgent voice, 'Mum, you've got to come. He's on the telly.'

The word 'he' burns on her breath.

Dilys impatiently fills two mugs, then takes them into the living room where, seated on a large sofa beside her breastfeeding daughter, she watches, over her tea, the still-boyish features of her President denying the epidemic.

It is a novelty for Dilys to observe how outsiders report on her country. There is no one to contradict the President from within. Foreign journalists are forbidden. When Dilys is at home, her short-wave radio is jammed to blazes. Russia says nothing; China is just as feeble. But here on the BBC

– British Bum Cleaners, the President refers to them disparagingly – there are regular news items.

'Nay, there is no epidemic,' the President insists in his mission-school, old-fashioned English, jabbing his forefinger at an appreciative crowd. It is a rumour put about by the nefarious white minority, with the Europeans and Americans behind them. It is the Europeans and Americans who are responsible for the food shortages, the fuel queues, the billion per cent inflation; who even now are intercepting vital oil supplies on the high seas and scheming to recolonise the country with the assistance of greedy racist usurpers . . . He is dressed in his signature blue kaftan and a white baseball cap which looks ridiculous perched on top of his thick black shock of hair.

Rachel listens to the hectoring voice.

Her baby, unlatched momentarily from its breast, gives a small air-sucking convulsion, then reclamps its gums around the dark purple bullet of Rachel's nipple.

Neither woman says what's on her mind. The words have been used over and over:

You malignant bungler. Only one man is responsible for reducing the country to ruin; everywhere the stink of death, disease gnawing its way from village to village, farms deserted, motherless children grovelling for food through stacks of uncollected garbage; and night after night the pickaxe handles rising and falling, the bloodshed, the mutilations, the rapes, the abductions. One man, Mr Pointer.

What her daughter does say: 'I've had another message from Robin. He says you're mad. You've got a round-the-world ticket – all you have to do is keep flying till you get back to London and I'll pick you up again at Heathrow.'

Dilys swallows another watery sip of Darjeeling and says nothing.

Irked, Rachel cradles her baby. 'I know it's hard, Mum. It was our home, too.'

She lapses into silence. She has a blonde fringe and her father's small chin. Then, in a reasonable voice: 'Listen, I've spoken again to Tim about the basement. It's not what you're used to, but you'd have your own entrance.'

'Robin is getting quite serious about this Australian girl?' with great firmness.

'For God's sake, Mother!'

Rachel's emotions are running very close to the surface. She is, however, an old hand at manipulating her mother.

Dilys slams down the mug.

'I am going back, Rachel,' in a flaming tone. 'And nothing you, Robbie or your husband can say will stop me. It's where I belong.'

Her ferocity shakes them both. Arms folded, she sits at a perpendicular angle and watches her daughter cover the baby's ears, shielding it from the shouting.

'What is wrong with you?' Rachel hisses, and turns the child towards the television screen, giving it an un-interrupted view of an embroidered blue kaftan and a brushed-up halo of black hair. She prepares to leave the room. 'Where does this anger come from? You can be angry, but not that angry.'

Next morning, to avoid the stress of another argument, Dilys borrows Rachel's umbrella, leaves the already cramped house, and waits for a bus to take her to Piccadilly. It's a midsummer morning, but the rain has not stopped since she arrived in London.

At last, a bus sloshes to a halt. When a teenage boy – white and spotty, with wires trailing from under his woollen cap – attempts to barge past her onto it, she grabs his arm. 'Excuse me.'

She elbows her way ahead of the boy to buy her ticket, and is mildly astonished to be told that the price is the same as a week ago. She gives the driver the exact fare and a grateful, shaky smile, pockets her ticket, and moves along to the rear of the bus.

Settled into her seat, Dilys feels foolish for having exploded. She sits back and casts her eye around the other passengers. Their features are white, black, brown, yellow – and mostly British, presumably. As the bus crosses the Thames, she floats the opinion that what she is seeking is reassurance. She is looking for someone like her. Because isn't what she faces merely the lot of all fifty-five-year-old women of a 'certain generation' who have disappeared on themselves in the quicksand of domestic life?

She gazes out over the river at the dark mob of clouds

assembled in the London sky. But the tunnelling mole of her anger hasn't gone away.

When Dilys was a young mother, her friends called her Sleeping Beauty. A feisty and rather plump child, she had had the handicap of a late-blooming beauty. Suddenly to find herself at twenty-eight turning heads was almost more disorienting to her than the birth of her first child, which followed closely after. Along with the extra weight that had insulated her, she lost her pluckiness and confidence. With the arrival of cheekbones, she became benign, mild-mannered, accommodating. Now Dilys – she who flies off the handle at the tiniest provocation – has repossessed her childhood ferocity.

Other people might think that she has turned into someone new, but they are quite wrong. You can't remake yourself into who you are not. On the other hand, you can return to the person you once were. She is simply stretching the muscles, dormant for so long, of the unruly girl.

Four impervious rows ahead, the teenager watches the rain-spattered window, nodding his head back and forth.

Thirty-five minutes later, Dilys steps down opposite the Ritz and is walking past the Royal Academy, feeling cold and wet and oppressed, when she notices on a railing a framed poster for a Munch exhibition and is reminded of her daughter's face the night before. Dilys can't recall her last visit to an art gallery. Her fine, prematurely whitened hair twinkling with raindrops, she collapses her umbrella and goes in.

The painting hangs in the furthest room. Dilys doesn't see it at first. Her eyes glide dutifully from wall to wall and then her heart stops. A face looks out at her, into her – sparking a shock of recognition.

It's hard for Dilys to explain, the giddying affinity she feels for this young woman with tangled yellow hair. The small breasts and swollen belly remind her of the desperate black girls in her African capital. But the pale colour of the skin – squeezed fiercely from the tube and painted in rapid horizontal brushstrokes, like slashes – is her own. The colour of celery, white clock towers, pith helmets.

Only closer up does she see that the young woman is not alone: stretched out on a bed behind her, also naked, is a man with a moustache.

Dilys fumbles with her audio guide and learns from a dispassionate voice that the man is the French Revolutionary leader Marat; and the woman – who has gained access to Marat on the pretext of revealing a plot against him – Charlotte Corday. '*Munch completed the work in 1907, a year before his breakdown . . .*'

The subject of the painting surprises Dilys. The figures are so modern, like two lovers in a bedsit. And while she has heard of Marat, she knows nothing about Charlotte Corday – except that she famously stabbed Marat in his bath. She definitely wasn't in the painting by Jacques-Louis David. Who is she? How did she kill him?

She lifts her head and meets the stare of the assassin. The expression is vacant, corpse-like (even the dead man on the bed seems more alive), but it goes on snatching at Dilys.

Some time later, Dilys steps back from *The Death of Marat*. The painting has entered her marrow. The signalling emptiness of the young woman's face confronts Dilys with the bleaching of the canvas of her own existence. She feels boiling over all the things that she can't – or won't – discuss with Rachel and Robin. They are the one family link left, but their thrust to start again, to build new lives in Britain and Australia, has deafened her children. Dilys knows the pattern too well – she has taught it to them: In order to survive, you have to forget. You have to. But her oblivion, so painstakingly achieved, is unravelling.

As she walks back to the cloakroom, the outsized feeling takes hold of Dilys to challenge one of these people entering the Royal Academy: 'Are you aware that my President thinks you are supposed to be enjoying an unholy alliance with a few defenceless farmers who live in another continent?'

She'd expect shrugging shoulders. 'Sorry, the situation sounds ghastly,' as they shove past. And over the shoulder: 'Didn't you choose to stay? Isn't that what happens in

Africa?' Or, if they know some history: 'Isn't he simply taking back land seized by whites in the 1890s?'

In her obstinate mind she runs after them, shakes them, violated by their indifference. 'I'm sorry, but did you know that eight out of ten of these "settler vermin", my late husband included, bought their farms *since* independence – that is to say, *under the President's very own laws?*'

There is so much that she would like to get off her chest. She could stand here and talk all week and there'd be plenty left over. But how fast the blinds rattle down whenever she tries to explain – her parents had not come out until after the early days, when they were busy killing people; she does not carry a gun; did not call her dog after the President, or sing 'Climb the hill, baboon'. She is not one of those excruciating 'whenwes', who begin each backward-groping conversation, 'When we lived in—'. But even though she isn't one of those, Africa is the only place she knows. She is an African just as much as the President is. Britain owes her nothing. All she has in common with the original pioneers – and with some of the crowd in the Munch exhibition – is the whiteness of her skin.

One person who understands is a mad, dead Norwegian painter. In the catalogue, she reads that Munch said he was pregnant with his painting *The Death of Marat* for nine years.

Dilys is not due to leave for Australia until Friday evening. Tingling with the novelty of being truly herself, she will spend her remaining afternoons in London in the Putney library, digging out books on the French Revolution.

Charlotte Corday, the woman in the painting, arrived in Paris on a blazing July afternoon, battling her way through crowds dressed in tricoloured cockades and soft Liberty caps, and booked into the Auberge de Provence, a stuffy first-floor room overlooking the rue des Vieux Augustins. The porter put down her bulging leather bag and without saying anything drew open the heavy curtains. The nosy summer sunshine picked out a marble-topped desk and an unmade bed. She turned to the porter, a big-boned man, slightly deaf, with a box jaw that hung open, and asked him to fetch a chambermaid to make up the bed and then to bring her a pen, ink, some paper.

That afternoon, she set down the words she had rehearsed in her head on the journey from Caen. She wrote quickly, without pause. The peace of France depended on the fulfilment of the law. She was not breaking it by killing a man who had been so universally condemned. If she was guilty, then Hercules too was guilty when he killed Geryon or Cacus. But did Hercules ever meet a monster so odious?

She folded the sheet three times and pinned it to her baptismal certificate.

This was the conviction she had reached: Marat had to be killed and peace restored.

No one is so strong as the woman who stands alone.

She had asked nobody for help, breathed not a word of her plan to anyone. Those who knew her imagined that she was in England. Before departing Caen, she had written to her father, 'I am going to England because I do not believe one can live happily and quietly in France for a very long while to come.'

A whole nation can pay for the folly of one man. She was going to restore peace to the world by ridding it of a monster.

Who is this Dilys Hoskins who is so infatuated with Charlotte Corday and is now seated in the economy-class cabin on the overnight flight to Singapore? A woman in her imperfections and vanities not markedly different from any other passenger. Not a hero as a consequence of her determination to stay put, but a menopausal widow with nowhere else that she wants to go – except home. A woman who has no answer to the question: At what point are you entitled to feel part of the land where you were born; at what point do you earn your stake in its living earth?

She glances at the young couple in her row, engrossed in their film. Do you know what is going on, how bad? If you do not know, how can you help? But if you knew how bad it was, would you be able to help?

The newspaper in her lap tells her that the epidemic is spreading, aggravated by the rains. There is a photograph of an empty hospital, the wards deserted. Two children sit on the steps waiting for their parents to show up. The President has not been seen in public for several days.

'*The tragedy*,' says a representative from an aid agency, '*is that this disease is deadly, but curable.*'

Her hard-headed husband once said to her with reddened eyes in the days after they lost their farm, 'I would do it, given the chance.' His hand slashed the air.

'I know you would, darling,' and squeezed his hand as he had grabbed hers at the start of her labour with Rachel, and two years later with Robin.

That's how deep it was with Miles – he wouldn't vote again for the President to save his soul from hell. But if he ever got within a whisker . . .

Her meal tray cleared and the overhead lights switched off, Dilys tries to sleep. But her feet are swelling up, and a shadow flitting from side to side across the back of her mind is preventing her.

Charlotte Corday woke early on that hot Saturday morning in July, and put on a simple brown dress of piqué cotton, a white linen fichu that she tucked into her bodice, a black hat. All very quiet and sober.

It was 7.30 a.m. when Madame Grollier, the hotelier, unlocked the front door to let her out. The shops were not yet open. She reached the Palais Royal within twenty minutes and went for a walk around the public gardens. The plants were shrivelled and coated in dust. She made ten circuits, then left the gardens and walked up the Galeries de Bois to No. 177, where a burly man was pulling open the shutters. In the window, she spotted a display of cutlery. The man, Monsieur Barbu, the shop's owner, invited her in. She was looking for a kitchen knife, she told him; something to pare fruit with. He took out a velvet-lined tray and she chose a black-handled knife with a six-inch steel blade. The handle was carved from ebony and had two rings on it – and he demonstrated how it might be hung from a shelf or a cook's belt. She paid forty sous for the knife, which came in a green leather sheath, then slid it into her pocket, thanked him and walked out.

On her way back to the gardens, she bought a newspaper and sat on a bench to read it. The news from Orléans was that nine men were to be guillotined following an attempt to murder Marat's deputy. She put down the newspaper, the breath pushed out of her.

At that moment, a small boy running past fell over. He yelped in pain and looked up at her, chin wrinkling, his face pressed to the path. Their eyes met, and though from a different angle, each saw that the other wanted to cry, and perhaps because of this recognition both held back from actually doing so. She helped the boy to his feet and stroked his apple-red cheek, smiling, a small grave smile of sadness, and he stumbled off, rubbing the gravel from his knees, with an exaggerated limp.

'Black Robespierre' is what they had called him, some of the farmers she grew up with. The same ones who fled abroad after his election. 'You wait, Dilys,' as they packed their belongings. 'Beneath that preposterous kaftan, there'll always be a Mao collar.' She wanted not to argue, but believe. She was in her mid-twenties then, Rachel's age, and had faith in the President and the vision he articulated for their (yes, their) country in his shy, polite, wedding photographer's voice. These farmers were taking the Yellow Route out, she couldn't help thinking. She went to one of their yard sales and bought a Black & Decker drill with some bits missing and a Zenith short-wave transistor radio.

And how reasonable the President appeared at the outset. All that stuff about forgiveness, his passion for peace, of wanting to take everyone with him. 'You have given me the jewel of Africa,' he said to his outgoing white predecessor. He wanted the whites to stay, help rebuild. There would be no retribution, a little redistribution maybe, in time; but revenge, nay, not that. He appoints a white farmer his agricultural minister to safeguard the farmers' future. He listens attentively, in his blue kaftan. He has a new name: Mr Pointer, the people call him with affection – because he always points his finger when speaking. He's a messianic figure. Everyone wants to meet him.

Her husband takes Mr Pointer at his word. Her husband who loved lemon-cream biscuits and fine-shredded marmalade and the tangos of Carlos Gardel. Who saw the worst in others only after he had seen the best. One always admires the qualities in people that one lacks oneself. Miles's assertive manner was the same towards everyone. A man whose unbelievable bluntness went hand in hand with an extreme honesty. When they met, he was the owner of a thriving printer's shop on the capital's main street, but with a hankering for the land: land that Mr Pointer with outstretched arms was urging people such as Miles to take up.

'The secret of success in life,' Miles tells Dilys as if she were his apprentice and not his wife, and as she would later tell their children, 'is to be ready when your opportunity comes – and go for it.' He sells his printing business, and with their joint savings they buy a small tobacco farm twelve miles inland from the sea. They invest in a herd of dairy cows. They install a new hand pump in the chicken yard, to draw up water from the aquifer. They renovate the house, a modest whitewashed single-storey building at the top of a long lawn hedged with thorn bushes in which plum-coloured starlings like to nest, and a view beneath a thrilling sky over a horizon tufted with elephant grass. The sandy soil needed plenty of fertiliser, but the river gave water all year round. She would watch her children slide down the water-smoothed rocks, and go exploring with them on an escarpment that led down to an ancient stone terrace.

She needs to be useful. She starts up a school, employing two teachers; she creates a library for the village; she ensures that the workers have a nice place to live in. To use her President's words, she is doing her best 'to move forward together'. She has grown up playing with African children. It doesn't always make you a non-racist, but in her case the strong feelings that they all form part of one scrappy tribe have stayed. Although she is never so assertive or abrupt as her husband, she treats Africans as does Miles, as she would Europeans, and they like her for it. They notice that Sleeping Beauty is increasingly picking up her husband's ways, but at least they know that when she is being rude to them, she would behave no differently towards white people. Everyone waves at her when she drives around – unlike at the next property where the farmworkers glower.

Dilys was educated in the capital in the same school as her mother. In her French class, she studied Camus. She envied him when he wrote, '*This earth remains my first and last love.*' At Coral Tree Farm, she learns to understand Camus's sympathy for the land. During harvest time, she is never out of the tobacco shed. Each time she grades a leaf and rubs the ribbed arteries beneath the tips of her fingers, she feels an immediate connection with those who have cropped the plant and with the soil that has produced it; an involvement which passes beyond intimacy. The tobacco leaf, like the warm frothing milk that she squeezes from the cows, is tangible, something she can pinch and smell. It is life itself.

Unlike her liberal friends, Dilys is unsentimental about Africans; she has seen enough to know that Africa is a tough place – the Troubles have taught her that. But it's only when living on the farm that she experiences the authentic sense of Africa being *her* place. As though a book she is reading in another language has shifted imperceptibly into her language.

At what point did the truth come tumbling down on her that Black Robespierre had diddled – Miles's word – his people? At what point did the bluebottle settle on the lens to reveal that the President's promise of integration was just a fiction? Specifically, at what point did the quiet, shy, friendless wedding photographer become the raucous shock-haired demagogue in a baseball cap, urging his thugs to turn on settler vermin like the Hoskins family? In other words, at what point did Mr Pointer decide to punish her for the white taint of her skin?

The questions are like the furious horizontal strokes of Munch's brush.

The driver of the hackney cab in the Place des Victoires had no idea where Marat lived and had to climb down and amble along the rank asking his colleagues. 'Thirty rue des Cordeliers,' one of them yelled. 'Just off Faubourg Saint-Germain.' He heaved himself back up, and shortly before eleven o'clock dropped her off outside a tall grey shabby house with shops on either side.

Charlotte walked through an empty porch into a courtyard where two women chatted in the shadow of an arcade.

She asked: 'Citizen Marat?'

'Staircase on the right,' nodded one of them, her eyes lingering on this fastidiously dressed, rather beautiful young woman with enlarged blue humourless eyes.

She crossed the courtyard and ran up the steps, following the iron balustrade to the top of the staircase. The bell pull was a curtain rod with a makeshift canvas handle. She tugged it. Then stepped back, patting down her bodice where she had concealed the knife.

A muffled sound of females talking. The door opened and a woman stood there, biting her lip. The disarray in her face mimicked the chaos of the hallway behind. Tiles missing on the floor. Filthy wallpaper – patterned with broken Doric columns. And the rancid smell of over-fried fish.

'What do you want?'

She explained herself in a composed voice. She wanted to see Marat. It was urgent. She had vital news – about a planned insurrection in Caen.

'Out of the question,' the woman said brusquely. 'Marat is sick. He can't see anyone.'

'What if I come back tomorrow?'

Just then another woman appeared in the doorway: Marat's mistress, Simone. She seconded everything that her younger sister had said. No, Madame can't make an appointment. It's impossible to say when she'll be able to see him, when he'll be better.

'Then I shall go home and write to him,' she replied

calmly, resisting every particle in her body that screamed for her to fight her way beyond them.

Dilys breaks the long flight to Perth with a stopover in Singapore. At the insistence of her son, she is booked for two restorative nights into the Raffles Plaza. The steady hum of the air-conditioning drives out the noise of the city twelve floors below. But she cannot sleep. She wakes and does not know where she is, and for a moment her husband is alive and she is in Africa still.

She is sitting at her tinny little table, trying to lose herself in a novel, when Honour her housemaid bursts in.

'Mrs Hoskins, you must come . . .'

Dilys barely keeps up with Honour as they run to the end of the lawn. From behind the thorn bushes, the most horrible sounds.

The cow is stumbling and stopping every few steps, its intestines wrapped around its legs like South American bolas. The grass glistens red from the slashed udders. A head twists around at a strange angle, sensing her presence, and the look in the creature's eyes sends Dilys racing back to the house.

She grabs the keys, her breath coming in short thrusts. She has to kill it. And she doesn't know how. She needs Miles . . .

The agonised bellows continue to reach her as she struggles to unlock his gun cabinet. Hunting is men's business. But her husband has taken the children for safekeeping to a cousin's house in the capital and will not be back until the next day.

She pulls out the rifle and a handful of bullets. She has never killed an animal, other than a chicken when Honour was away. Miles had infuriated her by saying, 'Don't you worry, I'll do it. You'll never be able to do it,' and she had not let him – she had jolly well halal-killed the chicken exactly as Honour had taught her.

But a chicken was not a cow.

She stares at the bullets loose in her palm. The same panic has assaulted Dilys ever since Miles's cancer was diagnosed. The panic that tells her he isn't going to be around and she will have to do more and more and she doesn't know how.

Through the mesh window – another bellow. That unearthly lowing, it's intolerable. And she knows in a small, dry, cold and ruthless part of her, in a space beyond the emotions and the histrionics and the tears, that she has no choice. Only she can put the animal out of its suffering. There is only her.

The rifle is unexpectedly light. She walks with a pall-bearer's tread back down the lawn. It isn't that she's unaware of the path she must take. All her life, she has been an observant passenger. But she has never done the driving, and now she has to.

On the other side of the hedge, something is still staggering. A mouth wheezes open and a tongue curls up, stiff, blue, abnormally long. She fumbles and pulls the trigger.

In the dying light, she walks over to the office shed and raises Peter Trasenster on the battery-powered radio. The neighbouring white farmers do a security roll call every night. Until now the area has been peaceful; their road is the only road into the capital without a curfew. But a fortnight ago, Coral Tree Farm was gazetted in the government newspaper. Section 8. Compulsory Acquisition. Ninety days to vacate. Her sick husband is running around calling on lawyers to dispute it.

Trying not to sound melodramatic, she explains to Peter what has happened. He tells her to stay where she is, a local patrol will come by and check. She locks the rifle in the gun cabinet, crosses the lawn and bolts the doors.

Afterwards, no one believed it. Sleeping Beauty – this mild-mannered woman – shooting a cow. Her children were incredulous.

Back in her hotel room, Charlotte Corday manoeuvred the baptismal certificate out from under her breasts, along with the piece of paper attached to it, containing her manifesto. Next, she removed the knife and placed it on the desk behind the ink bottle. She stared at it for a moment, before reaching out and taking a fresh sheet of paper.

Her letter written, she folded it into an envelope, scribbled

Marat's name and address on the outside, and rang for the porter.

'Be sure to deliver this by seven o'clock this evening.'

Then she asked Madame Grollier to arrange for a hairdresser to be sent up.

It was something about the sisters, their strong, careless faces. She decided that Marat had a keen eye for women. She was too primly dressed this morning. This time, she would arouse the ex-monk's vanity.

The timid young coiffeur who knocked on her door at 3 p.m. found her waiting for him, already wearing a loose white bombazine gown, a low-cut bodice, and over her shoulders a rose gauze scarf. For the next hour he stood behind her, gathering the gold tresses from her round lovely face and braiding them into a single garlic string that fell down the middle of her back.

All this time, she sat there in the solipsism of her conviction, not saying anything. Detached. Her eyes on the marble-topped desk and the knife in its green leather sheath. Absolutely indifferent to what his hands were doing.

He sprayed her hair and throat with cologne and powder.

When she walked downstairs at six-thirty on this baking July evening, it took Madame Grollier a second or two to connect the white-gowned woman who descended in high-heeled shoes, wearing an emerald cockade hat and fanning her scented face with a gloved hand, and the person who had arrived three days earlier from the Normandy countryside with cake crumbs on her sleeve.

Dilys cannot hear them since bare feet make little noise; and then they are there.

A high-pitched voice draws her from her chair. She parts the curtain and when she sees who is out there, motions that she is coming. Before leaving the room, she pauses at Miles's desk to pick up something.

The angry voice speaks again as she lurches into the hall. 'Open this door or we'll fuck you up, *mamma.*'

She unbolts the door and stands in the feeble porch light. Assembled before her, a silent ominous mob stretching back to the tobacco shed. Leather jackets, green caps, red-and-yellow T-shirts printed with Mr Pointer's smiling face.

A few of the young men carry branches torn from the trees. Others clutch whips made from fan belts and bicycle spokes. Their faces gleam with the prospect of violence.

'What do you want?' addressing their leader. As if she doesn't know.

He raises a golf club. Solidified in its grooved metal head, the mood of menace and uncertainty that has lurked in the background these past months.

'We have come to take your land.'

She runs her eyes over the faces, recognising one.

'Elias?'

When he was a boy, she had bought Elias reading glasses so that he could study.

He looks away.

Disappointed, she turns back to the man holding the golf club. Fresh blood is spattered across his T-shirt.

'How old are you?' Her eyes angry. Thinking of the cow. She can sense the blue veins standing out on her neck.

The question makes him uncomfortable. He wipes his nose on his leather sleeve.

'Nineteen.'

'Then you were born after the Troubles. That was the year I bought this house . . .'

He shakes his arm. 'This land belongs to us. You white kaffirs came and grabbed it long ago from our people.'

'No, we didn't,' the rebellion rising in her voice. 'I have this certificate from your government' – she has stopped saying 'our'. 'It specifies that it is not needed for resettlement.'

She shows it to him. It will get her nowhere. But she wants him to see it, this annoying young man who has made her feel middle-aged and powerless.

'See there. "No Present Interest." Signed by the courts. *Your* courts,' harping on it.

He frowns at the legal language.

'Mr Pointer makes the law, not the courts.'

'This is still private property. If you don't leave, I shall call the police.'

He laughs. The arrogant, unedited laughter of someone with the sanction of the provincial governor's office. 'The police will do nothing. We can do what we like.' And rips it in half.

Dilys slams the door, bolts it, then seizing Honour's hand, runs through the house, out the back, to the office shed, thrusting her housegirl down beneath the desk. She's not worried about being raped herself, but the story among the local farmers is that these idiots have been told to rape women like Honour. To create babies who will vote for Mr Pointer.

Her hands vibrate as she radios the Trasensters. 'Oscar Romeo Four Five.' Across the lawn, she can see the lights being switched on one by one. She listens to the mob thumping on Rachel's harmonium and singing hysterical songs of liberation as they tramp through the rooms. 'We will find you, we will find you . . .'

'Oscar Romeo Four Five.'

At last, she raises Vanessa Trasenster. 'I need help.'

'Isn't Peter with you?'

'White bitch, where are you?'

A golf club smashes through the panes. Hands stretch through the shattered glass and grope for her hair. A black tentacle fastens around the cable and rips it from the wall. When all of a sudden the baying stops and they are running off, piling onto the tractor with their booty. Car doors slam in the darkness. There's the chatter of a radio. Then Peter Trasenster's voice. 'Dilys?'

In the morning, she walks through the rooms. The children's blackboard broken to bits. Miles's record collection. Her books. Even her son's watch in fragments. And an acrid tang of urine – coming from where, she can't tell.

Mr Pointer's response? 'This is a peaceful demonstration of people who are frustrated.'

Dilys is surprisingly undisturbed by the house invasion. She doesn't perceive it as a tea party at Government House – as one or two neighbours mutteringly suggest – but rather as part of her toughening-up process. What she can't get used to, what unhinges her, is the imminent loss of the farm and the deteriorating effect that this has on Miles. No one could be more finicky in the kitchen than her husband, but she notes with a weight in her heart that he has started to leave his knife by the sink, still covered in marmalade.

The hackney cab drew up outside 30 rue des Cordeliers. She asked the driver to wait, and walked in long strides through the porter's lodge – empty as before – and up the stairs.

Her gloved hand tugged on the bell.

The door was swung open by a fat, one-eyed woman, wearing a man's ill-fitting trousers. Visible in the dirty hallway behind was the pile of newspapers she had been folding – copies of *L'Ami du Peuple*, edited by Marat, and printed on the press which he and Simone had installed in their apartment.

Charlotte started to explain herself all over again.

But the fat woman interrupted. Marat was not seeing anyone. He was taking a bath.

Then would it be possible to find out if Marat has received her letter?

The fat woman glared at her. At the sight of that elegant hairdo and ravishing white bust, a vision of health and privilege, her face contracted. 'Oh, he receives many letters,' and turned to pick up another newspaper. 'Sometimes too many.'

Before anyone could say anything, two men ran up the staircase and barged past. One waved an invoice that required signing. Another had come to take a bundle of newspapers to the War Office. Chaos. Everyone distracted.

Angry, she stamped her foot and called out, 'I have come from far away with important information that I need to deliver personally to the People's Friend. There's a plot against him. I have names!'

Simone, the mistress, appeared, attracted by all the hubbub. 'Oh, it's you,' momentarily nonplussed by the summer dress and the hat with its knot of emerald ribbons.

'Did he get my letter?'

'Letter? I don't think so.'

'I have to see him.'

'Maybe in two or three days.'

But a male voice was shouting something from inside the apartment.

Simone excused herself.

She waited, leaning against the wall, watching the fat

one-eyed woman who very deliberately folded another copy of next day's edition of *L'Ami du Peuple*. Charlotte noted with horror that it called for the head of her friend Charles Barbaroux.

Suddenly, Simone was back. 'He will see you.'

Dilys wonders why on earth her son has insisted on her spending two overnights in Singapore, where she knows no one. Unable to sleep, she decides to set out early for a stroll through the city centre.

The humidity hits Dilys the instant she steps outside. She looks right and left before deciding to head off in the direction of Orchard Road. The shops taunt her, their windows filled with filmy sarongs and skirts translucent as flies' wings. Five minutes into her walk and sweat is meandering down her cheeks and neck. She feels disoriented, as if she has stood up in a hot bath. When she comes out into a park with spreading angsana and flame trees, and sees a bench, she flings herself down onto it. All she wants to do is strip.

Dizzy and flushed, she hauls off the burgundy alpaca cardigan that was a gift from her daughter. Her eyes blink with sunshine and sleep and the cardigan clings to her – she had exchanged it for a size smaller because she anticipated shedding the weight she put on in England. She allows it to fall on the bench while she lifts her elbows to let the air circulate. Then fishes inside her bag for a tissue and starts mopping her face.

She is looking about as if she expects the flame trees to lean forward and smother her, when the bench sinks a fraction beneath the weight of another woman.

Her dizziness passes. The park is still again when she falls into polite conversation.

The woman is waiting for her daughter to finish a swimming lesson. She speaks fluent English, but is not English. Tall, slim, mid-thirties, with her light brown hair pulled back, and dressed in thin clothes that show her youthful shape, she reminds Dilys of a backpacker who once stayed at the farm. There is something vivacious about her, indiscreet. A woman who likes a good gossip, Dilys senses.

'Are you from here?' Dilys asks, wiping her forehead.

'With a name like Van der Hart!' No, she's Dutch. She has been in Singapore two years. Her husband works for an investment bank; he is in hospital ('an operation for a floating kidney'); he should be home by the weekend. ('Fingers crossed – otherwise, I'll have to take him more books! Barend's always got a book in his hand. I sometimes think he's more interested in books than in me.')

Dilys half-listens, not really engaged. Not accustomed to this humidity. Even sitting down with her cardigan off, she does not feel herself.

Until Mrs Van der Hart looks at her. 'You're not from here either.'

'No,' stuffing into her bag the beige-stained Kleenex.

'Are you English?'

She could easily say yes. It's what her children do. Stifling a yawn, she replies, 'No,' and braces herself for the inevitable.

'Where are you from?'

Dilys smiles a little wanly. Even as her tongue moulds the word, she experiences the familiar embarrassment mingled with shame. But what answer can she give? She is not from anywhere else.

Certainly, she is not prepared for Mrs Van der Hart's response.

Instead of changing the subject or commiserating or getting up and leaving, Mrs Van der Hart says to her, 'Did you know your President is here?'

Dilys pales. She sits up, her back stiff as the cane that she always carried for snakes. Ever so slowly, she swings her head around. 'My President?'

'He is in the same hospital as my husband.'

'What, in Singapore?' she asks. 'Here?'

'He wanted my husband's room, but the hospital wouldn't allow it – he's in the next room, which is smaller,' Mrs Van der Hart says with satisfaction.

Her heart has stopped and her blood is flowing backwards. 'I had no idea he was ill.'

'Well, it can't be too serious, because yesterday he had a tailor in with him,' and before Dilys can ask how in God's name Mrs Van der Hart has come by this information: 'I get it all from Barend who gets it from the nurses. He's probably just having a service check. Dictators are high maintenance.'

Dilys drinks in the gossip passed on by those talkative nurses to Mr Van der Hart. The ban preventing the President from travelling to Europe. The Cuban urologist whom he always insisted on visiting in Kuala Lumpur. The recent transfer of this doctor, who has won his trust, to a senior position in a hospital in Singapore – 'where they do things differently. Your President decided to follow him here for treatment, but this being Singapore it means he has to leave all his bodyguards outside, except one, who sleeps on the sofa. Barend found himself standing next to him in the toilet, and realised that's who it was—'

But she is standing up and waving. 'There's my daughter. I have to go.'

Over the road – a crocodile line of damp-haired girls in white short-sleeved blouses and pinafores.

Dilys studies her long pale fingers that have interlocked as if the future is written in her hands and she can read it. The skin on them is cracked, like a farmer's.

Her head tilts back. 'Wait, what hospital did you say?'

'The Stamford – on Arab Street.'

Her palms prickle. 'Which floor?' trying to discipline her excitement.

Simone led the way along a dark passage, smelling of printer's ink, to a small narrow bathroom adjoining a bedroom. The air was thick and damper than a swamp.

205

He was lying in a clog-shaped copper bath, naked to the waist. A brown dressing gown was draped across his shoulders, and a wet towel wrapped his forehead. Her first impression: his head – crowned with bunched-up tufts of lank black hair – was grotesquely large for his body. Her second: how leathery and inflamed his skin looked. It was the same texture as the sheath.

Balanced across the bath was a pine plank with papers on it and copies of newspapers speckled with drops of bathwater.

Simone retrieved an empty jug from beside the bath and went out, not closing the door.

He was correcting proofs. He reached the end of the paragraph and looked up.

That face. Yellow-grey eyes. A crushed nose. Long sparse hairs for eyebrows. And scabby scales blotching the deformed body. Leprosy had left its rodent's teeth all over his bony shoulders, and there was a bitter reek of vinegar that she traced to the towel.

The man in the bath leaned back at an angle. His bloodshot eyes grazed over her throat, along her scarf, down her gown, exploring her with Calvinist intensity. No woman dressed like this, looking like this, had ever stepped into his bathroom.

He indicated with his pen a low stool below the window. She sat, her eyes sweeping the room, taking in more details: the map of their country pinned to the wall; a plate on the windowsill, heaped with sweetbreads.

'Your name again?' asked Marat.

'Charlotte Corday,' she told him, her gloved fingers fidgeting with her lace bodice.

Gravely, he assessed her perfect breasts. 'How old are you?' His voice was powerful, melodious; out of keeping with his undeveloped frame.

'Twenty-four.'

He tossed the proofs to the floor. 'Simone says you have come from Caen to see me.'

'That's right.'

The tone in her partner's voice speaking to this beautiful young woman brought Simone back into the bathroom with the jug that she had refilled with water.

She poured him a glass that he raised to his swollen lips. Pieces of almond and ice floated on the surface.

'All right?' his mistress wanted to know.

'You might give it more flavour next time,' grimacing, and handed it back.

She took the empty glass and the untouched plate from the sill. 'I'll heat this up.'

His eyes on the young woman, he nodded and seemed not to notice the door close.

Dilys shakes hands with Mrs Van der Hart as if pumping up water from a long way down. Then she walks back to the Raffles Plaza. The heat from the pavement rises up through her thick skirt, but she does not feel it.

She spends the rest of the morning at the swimming

pool on the eighth floor. In the old days, in the days when she was Sleeping Beauty, she would keep her hair above the surface, but she wants to dive under, soak herself. She comes up for air and swims out over the rooftop towards the empty sky and the city. When her fingertips touch the small blue tiles at the other end, she turns and swims in an even breaststroke, back towards the breakfast bar.

As Dilys finds frequently happens, the act of swimming – like dreaming – releases deeper thoughts. Her mind had stopped at the moment of revelation, and now it makes reckless see-saws to catch up.

– *This coincidence. His presence literally around the corner / my sudden obsession with Charlotte Corday. Isn't it fate speaking?*

– *No, it would be immoral, illegal. Besides, what difference would it make? Look at Iraq after they hanged Saddam Hussein. Look what happened to Charlotte Corday. She was guillotined and reviled and Marat became a martyr.*

– *But if Hitler had died in that suitcase-bomb, how many millions of lives would have been saved? Who would suspect a white, middle-class grandmother? You will never again have such an opportunity.*

Up and down she continues. After thirty laps, she climbs out. She knows that she looks a mess, and once she has towelled herself dry she goes down to the lobby to make a hair appointment – it needs a trim anyway. But the earliest they are able to take her is tomorrow at 9 a.m.

She considers cancelling it, then recalls a hairdresser once telling her that a new haircut can be as effective as plastic surgery. She had looked with puzzlement at the pregnant young woman who ran forward to greet her at Heathrow, until she recognised her daughter Rachel beneath the unfamiliar fringe. Dilys's flight doesn't leave until the evening. She confirms the appointment.

It's not yet noon. She feels renewed, less jangled.

Three hours later, Dilys returns to the hotel carrying two large brown carrier bags. The walk has sharpened her appetite and she orders a steak from the room-service menu. While waiting for it to arrive, she unpacks her new purchases and hangs them up. The smallest item is a laminated identity badge on a chain. She holds it out at arm's length, inspecting it. The lettering is not up to the standard of Miles's printing firm, but from a short distance it convinces. It looks official, she thinks.

Footsteps down the corridor and something squeaking and a rap on the door. A man pushes in a trolley with her meal on it. She has sat down to eat before he is even out of the room.

The steak is minuscule and Dilys plays an ancient game from childhood of carving it into smaller and smaller portions to make it last longer. She has picked the plate clean when abruptly she stands up.

She unzips her suitcase and rifles through it for the plastic bag in which she has wrapped the Munch catalogue. Was there a knife in the painting? I'm not sure there was.

Dilys digs out the catalogue and checks the illustration. No, not even a bath. Just two naked figures in a room with a bed. An anonymous room like this one – *like the room I'm flying back to*, she thinks.

She will never retrieve all the days she sat in a cane chair, not leaving her tiny cement-floored flat back in Africa. Severed, useless, shrunk. The time that was stolen, like the momentous loss of the farm, of her darling Miles – it is unreimbursable.

But does she have the courage to do it herself? In a battle, she can almost imagine killing a figure in the distance with a rifle. Or pushing a button to drop a bomb. But to stab someone . . .

Charlotte Corday didn't have a moment of doubt.

'Who taught you to pierce Marat to the heart at the first blow?'

'The indignation that filled my own. I was determined to sacrifice my own life in order to save that of my country.'

Dilys picks up the steak knife from the trolley and with the napkin wipes it clean, one side and then the other. Sitting on the edge of her comfortable bed on the twelfth floor of the Raffles Plaza, she remembers the breakfast knives that she kept finding in the kitchen, black with ants. And Honour leading her out into the chicken yard and reaching an arm into the coop.

Did Charlotte Corday sit in her hotel room and weigh up which part to stab? The heart or the throat? His throat would be above the bedclothes; she couldn't bear the horror of pulling back the sheets.

She tests the blade with her thumb, and an image of Miles slaughtering a springbok flashes before her. The neck tautened back, the swift slash of the sharpened blade, the bright spurts of blood on the tobacco-coloured earth.

'This is how you do it, Mrs Hoskins,' Honour had said, holding up the chicken like a lantern.

She drops the steak knife with a clatter, and goes to the bathroom. Coming back out, she changes into her nightdress. But she's not able to leave the knife alone. Once more, she walks over to the trolley and picks it up. Hadn't she managed to put that cow out of its misery – the bulging, all-seeing eyes meeting hers, knowing what she was about to do, and after she had done it, a whistling sound as awful in its way as the last sound that she would hear bubbling out of Miles's mouth.

Dilys looks around the room, her eyes settling on the bed. She decides to try out the knife on the pillows. But when she raises it, something in her resists doing damage to the hotel's Italian linen. It remains suspended at a ridiculous angle in the cooled air above her pillow.

And lowers her arm.

She weighs the knife one last time in her hand. Then she tucks it between the pages of the catalogue as if to mark a place, and lies down on the bed.

*   *   *

'So what is happening in Caen?'

She tells him.

'You have the names of those involved?' He takes up his pen, waiting.

She dictates. It's a roll call of her friends. Barbaroux, Buzot, Guadet, Louvet, Guadet, Pétion . . . Her voice is surprisingly even, without strain. Summoning them to her side.

He writes down the names, licking something from his tongue, followed by what sounds like a titter. In his excitement, the dressing gown slips further from his shoulders, exposing something ghastly.

She leans forward, suppressing a little cough, and her hand delves into her bodice.

'I will have them guillotined in a few days.' Less than two yards away, the pen hovers. 'Is that the lot?'

She leaps up, toppling the stool, withdraws the knife from its sheath, and in a single downward movement plunges it sideways into his chest. She skewers it in deeper, through veins and tendons. He has no time to respond, save with an exhalation of air as the steel tip punctures his lung. She pushes in harder, into his heart, until only the ebony handle protrudes.

The squelching sound when she pulls out the knife is not unlike a pumpkin hitting the earth. The blood jets up – over her wrist, her bare snowy neck – through the wound in the top of his chest that will be wide enough for Simone to fit her fingertips into.

He shouts out, but it is not his voice that is heard by the women who slam open the door. It is Charlotte's scream.

Dilys goes one more time into the bathroom to check that her lipstick is not too dark. She has had her hair done in the salon downstairs and is wearing a blouse of ivory silk open at the neck and a conservative foresty green skirt. She might be on her way to the Kennel Club Show.

Anyone who looked closer, though, would see the eraser marks. Children gone, husband dead – now it's just her. A woman left behind who has had to watch everyone leave. Her unresolvable fury is aimed as much at the President as towards her loneliness.

Her body tenses, as if it has heard one of Miles's favourite milongas strike up. She runs her tongue over her lips, and murmurs to her spectacled face in the mirror, 'Don't worry, darling.'

She inclines her head, and very carefully slips the chain over it, tucking the laminated badge down into her cleavage. The owner of the family-run print shop in the Funan Centre had given her a good price to have it made up, even throwing in the chain for free. It was another of Miles's beliefs. 'If you've got an identity badge round your neck, people won't stop you.'

Dilys returns to the room and gulps down the gin and tonic that she mixed herself from the mini-bar. She is no longer afraid. She picks up her bag from the bed and plucks the plastic room card from the wall socket, extinguishing the lights, and leaves.

The Stamford Hospital is but a short walk from her hotel. She gets through surprisingly easily. 'I'm visiting Mr Van der Hart,' she tells a harassed-looking receptionist. Before the young woman has time to formulate a reply, Dilys's face takes on the expression of blunt intransigence that so annoys her children. 'Ward C,' she says.

'Are you a relation?'

'I've brought him another book,' in a triumphant maternal voice.

The receptionist does not ask to look inside her bag. 'Then you know where to go,' and waves Dilys through.

The terrazzo floor is very soft. The sound in her chest as she walks towards the lift is like the tail of a dog beating on the carpet.

The Castle Morton Jerry

We called it the Castle Morton Jerry, though I never knew why. Ever since a child, I remembered that band of cold thick fog suspended above the river opposite our cove, sometimes all morning until the sun burned it off. When the jerry rolled in like that, you couldn't see anything. Walking home, you'd reach out your hand and you'd feel a hard object and you'd have to decode what it was, whether it was a gum tree or a fence post or the leathery, nearly round face of Old Stan jerking awake as he did on that day.

'Hey!'

'Sorry, mate,' when I saw that I'd blundered onto his deck. And when he'd seen who it was and relaxed, at least enough to stop hollering at me for poking him out of his sleep, I said, 'This jerry – I really do loathe it, you know.'

Old Stan must still have been half-asleep, because he stared at me almost as though he was seeing himself at my age, fourteen, and then he said in a careful voice, 'You shouldn't hate it, boy. That's the same thing as hating what you come out of.'

'Come out of this horrid fog? Sorry, Stan, I don't follow you.'

He looked at me in a thoughtful way. 'Granny Gordon never told you about the jerry?'

'Reckon only thing Granny Gordon told me was not to pick my nose.'

'She didn't hum you this song?' and his cracked voice warbled through the mist, thinning it a little:

So I hauled her into bed and I covered up her head,
Just to keep her from the foggy, foggy dew.

'Granny Gordon wasn't the humming type,' I said. 'And I don't recall her telling me no stories.'

'Well, maybe she had enough on her hands bringing you up to want to go spading about in the past. But if it wasn't for the jerry you wouldn't have a nose to pick, none of us would,' and that's when Old Stan told me about a ship called the *Castle Morton* and the story his grandfather Ralph told him who ran the ferry service at Two Mile Creek.

'You grew up knowing Huonville, but before it became "Hoonville" it was Victoria, and before that it had no name that I'm aware of. You've got to remember how remote Tasmania was then, before it was woodchip heaven. Believe you me, boy, this place was re-mote. It wasn't even called Tasmania, it was Van Diemen's Land. And this valley was one of the re-moter valleys in Van Diemen's Land. Why, there wouldn't have been more than three bluestone houses and eleven men in a hundred square miles of thick bush. Mr Gordon – your great-granddad – and his four convict workers; Mr Hacking and his four workers; and my granddad Ralph. All single men of notorious and immoral character, as the Governor in Hobart liked to put it. And in the whole district just one solitary female – Granny Lawrence, a noisy, irritable woman who was lame in one leg and had a fleshy mole on the side of her chin, and a scar on the tip of her crooked nose and over her right eyebrow, and whose rare grin opened on a row of missing teeth. Oh, and sheep. Sure your own gran never told you anything about this?'

'I already said.'

'Personally speaking, I never believed the stories about Mr Gordon's riding boots and Granny Lawrence's sore-ness at finding traces of a ewe's back leg in one of them. All I do know, the situation was pretty desperate for a lusty and profligate man. And don't imagine matters were easier in Hobart. It was common knowledge how Mr Gordon once rode on his horse for three days through the bush in order to dance at a ball – at the Bellevue, I believe – where he was much disappointed to discover that the settlers and officers all had to waltz with each other. You must realise that even in Hobart there were thirty men to every woman. Who knows what desperation would have done to Mr Gordon and the ten other fellas down here if it hadn't been for the Castle Morton Jerry.

'Well, like I tell you, things being so desperate on the island at that time, the Governor got in touch with Mrs Elizabeth Fry in London, and a committee was formed to send a transport ship to Hobart filled with 'desirable, free and single women'. This was the *Castle Morton*, built in Nova Scotia, 472 tons of copper-sheathed white oak and black birch. On board were two hundred young women, some of them the most beautiful and elegant ever to come out to Van Diemen's Land. Plus a chaplain, a naval surgeon and a matron to keep those women clean and orderly on the four-month voyage to "Hobart Town on the Derwent" – where they were to enjoy free board and a roof over their heads, and a lot else beside. Only trouble is, after four months at sea, the *Castle Morton* got disoriented in a southerly coming up the channel. Instead of sailing into the Derwent, where she was first sighted, she sailed, without realising it, into the mouth of the Huon nearby. Listening now?'

'Yeah, I'm listening.'

'You'll be listening real good, I reckon, when you hear what my granddad told me about that altogether memorable day. Ralph watched it all happen. He was settled on the sand spit here when mid-afternoon came through the cold front from hell. A storm blew up, and he observed a ship in distress. He didn't know there were two hundred eligible women on board, including some convicts from the London Female Penitentiary. All he saw was this sailing vessel off Bruny Island, dragging her anchors, and in danger of being wrecked. The southerly carried the ship past the entrance. Ralph could see she was in great danger. The rapidity of the tide made him fear that she might be forced on the west side of the sand spit, and he hoisted a bed sheet on a pole, but couldn't keep it up in the violent wind. So he ran to Mr Gordon's farm and requested two of his men to go with him and make a fire on Bluff Point and another on Norman Cove to guide the ship in.

· 'The smoke of one fire was seen on board. A stay sail was hoisted and the ship bore westward, clearing the sand spit with the help of the steering fires.

'Ralph alerted the crew to the dangers of another sandbar and directed them to sheltered water. He shouted "Starboard!" and they wore round. "Port!" and they did so. He told them, "Let go your anchor!" They did so. And then the gale died down as suddenly as it blew up.

'It was coming on dark when Ralph launched his whale boat and rowed out with the help of Mr Gordon's two men.

'The master who pulled Ralph on board was Mr Henniker. He was sufficiently wary to keep his passengers down below and out of sight until he had ascertained where he had anchored, plus the identity of his young saviour. Beside Mr Henniker on deck stood the chaplain who had fallen down a hatchway in the gale and dislocated his shoulder. Beside the chaplain stood the surgeon and matron. All four officials stood in a row and stared by the light of Mr Henniker's lantern at Ralph and the two disreputable-looking figures who had clambered with him on deck, systematic thieves and liars both of them, and both with faces blackened from the smoke of the bonfires they had lit and dressed in trousers and jackets stitched from the skankiest-smelling kangaroo skin.

'Ralph overcame his natural shyness to take control. He told the master that if he kept on the east shore on the mud flat he would be sheltered from any further gale.

'The master thanked him. Then he said, "I have 198 women on board bound for Hobart who have suffered much seasickness." And explained that he was most anxious to disembark them after so many months at sea and constant drenching by storms and heat. He looked again uneasily at Ralph's two companions and then at Ralph. "This is Hobart, right?"

'"Yes, yes," said Ralph, a quick-witted fella. "This is Hobart all right."

'"I was expecting," the master said, "I was expecting something bigger." He had seen through his telescope two clearings and a bark hut. None of his crew had been before to Van Diemen's Land. He had imagined a bend on the river surrounded by cleared banks covered in buildings.

'"No, you have arrived in Hobart," said Ralph, "most certainly. This is what we like to call the . . . the outskirts."

'"The outskirts," the matron said glumly.

'"We were expecting a Landing Committee," threw in the chaplain, wincing.

'"I will go this moment and fetch them," promised Ralph, and said that he would be back with the Landing Committee at first light.

'Well, as soon as Ralph rowed ashore he ran helter-skelter all the way to Mr Gordon's house. As it happened, Mr Gordon knew about this Girl Boat and its cargo of Reformers. It was because of the *Castle Morton* that Ralph found Mr Gordon saddling up, preparing for another long ride through the scrub to Hobart. Even so, Mr Gordon's spirits were considerably reduced at the idea of having to compete with three thousand single men at the wharf. And not only three thousand men. Also waiting in Hobart were the Ladies' Committee composed of all the respectable matrons of the colony and excited to inform the passengers of the *Castle Morton* that their committee had enabled each and every one of the one hundred and ninety-eight to be engaged in service and provided for respectfully. There were in addition at the dockside a small squad of police waiting to march the women under guard up Macquarie Street to the government hotel, the Bellevue, which had been appointed to house the newcomers. I tell you, lad, the arrival of this ship was a large and significant event, and it caused quite a stir. Once word got out that the *Castle Morton* had been spotted at the mouth of the Derwent more crowds turned out than for the execution of Matthew Brady. Mr Gordon didn't stand a chance. Nor did Mr Hacking, nor did young Ralph, nor any of the other eight assigned men in the valley. And that's when the jerry comes down the river to assist.

'In the night, the southerly eased off into a light offshore wind. Early next morning, a current of cold air tracked down from the mountains through the gulleys and marshes and fed into the river. It hit the warmer water in a tube of dense rolling mist, a big cloud of it that spilled out into the channel and locked the ship in a chill moist fog.

'On the *Castle Morton* they woke up to a virtual white-out. Couldn't see a thing. They knew it was a beautiful day, bright and sunny outside. But inside the jerry, the master couldn't see the matron shivering across the quarterdeck, leave aside the sourness of her expression. He certainly couldn't see that they weren't in Hobart on the Derwent.

'At eight o'clock that morning, Ralph rowed out Mr Gordon and Mr Hacking, both dressed in their neat Sunday best, to the ship. Noise travels over still water. They could hear the coughs below deck as the women put on the new sets of clothes that the matron had issued, the demure uniform to include, of all things, a veil.

'Mr Gordon introduced himself to the master. He had been at Harrow public school before he became a forger and spoke well, at least well enough to put the master at his ease.

'"I regret that this mist has kept away the Ladies'

Committee. They have sent me as their representative. You may tell me with complete confidence anything you would have told them."

'"Then I will tell you, Mr Gordon, that never have women been more commodiously accommodated as on this passage. You may be assured that much attention was paid to guard them against evil. From the moment they boarded in Woolwich, I urged upon them the most decorous and orderly conduct and a strict obedience to the regulations which the chaplain and matron thought needful to adopt. And this morning I impressed on them, I dare say for the thousandth time, how the Governor will take a truly paternal care of them on their arrival in Hobart Town."

'"As you say, they will now be in excellent hands," said Mr Gordon in his Harrow voice.

'The other officials were keen to follow the master's lead and trumpet their own contributions. The surgeon-superintendent was a long-nosed martinet called Guthrie. He said, "I was asked by Lord Goderich to land them as uncontaminated as they were sent on board. This I have done. No spiritous liquors were allowed, no visitors."

'The matron, who had mustered the women every morning to check their personal health and cleanliness, said, "I think they all have high hopes of marriage to wealthy settlers. Most have already been assigned as general servants. One or two are very bad, but a considerable portion of them are respectable and deserving characters."

'Then it was the turn of the chaplain: "I have told them the measure they have adopted in leaving their native land to go into a foreign country is a matter of vital consequence and under the Divine Blessing it may prove of the greatest benefit, but otherwise the very reverse. By their good conduct or the contrary they will form their own characters."

'"Well, let's get on with it," said Mr Gordon, enthusiastic to speed along the process of disembarkation. He urged the master in the strongest and most persuasive terms to remain with his crew on board, and promised to make it his topmost priority to arrange with the port authorities to have the *Castle Morton* fully provisioned with fresh water, mutton and oysters as soon as the mist dissolved.

'Relieved to be shot of his charges, the master ordered the women to be led up on deck and watched them step into Ralph's whale boat in groups of ten at a time. They sat with their faces obscured in their veils, their hands resting on their bags, and Mr Gordon and Mr Hacking were most careful to say nothing as Ralph ferried the first party ashore, where a cart and three men waited to escort the women to Hobart, that is to say 'Nettlepot', as Mr Gordon, who came from Cumbria, had baptised his three-roomed establishment.

'Once on shore, Mr Gordon and Mr Hacking were replaced in the whale boat by two willing rowers who laboured under the strictest instructions to remain in a state of cemetery silence until they had landed safely every single female. Only on the last journey did it prove impossible for the rowers to contain themselves. Ralph told me how the jerry had barely swallowed the *Castle Morton* behind them when his two crewmen began touching up the women and trafficking to obtain their services at the lowest penny. If the women couldn't see them, they knew where their hands were!

'The jerry lasted until late morning before the sun broke it down and it disappeared, and Master Henniker looked around and saw through his telescope that he was anchored in the middle of nowhere.

'I won't go into the disgraceful scenes that were enacted under Mr Gordon's roof. Let us simply say that the women who came ashore that morning swiftly became acquainted with our habits. But they turned out well, some of them particularly so. They'd have been wasted on respectable landowners, your great-grandmother most of all.

'Her name was Harriet Fay. She was the daughter of a Baptist minister from Richmond, a respectable servant and useful, delicate woman whose mistress regretted parting with her and who had been engaged by a gentleman as a governess to his brother's children in Hobart.

'As I say, I don't know what happened over the next days and weeks at Nettlepot or at Miles Cottage, which was Mr Hacking's place, or here at Two Mile Creek where Ralph had taken Mary Malvern, a pert and artful young pencil maker who'd been transported on suspicion of stealing fur and fourteen yards of bombazine. I do know that surprisingly many women chose to remain in the valley after the mistake was discovered, and these included Harriet Fay and Mary Malvern. Harriet's conduct especially was said to disappoint all expectation formed of her in London. When it was known that she was living with some men in the country in an improper way, a delegation was sent by boat, a sort of rescue mission to sail her back to Hobart, but she declined the advice of the committee, saying, "I'd rather be hanged than leave here." And after living myself in this same cove for eighty-two years I reckon I know how she felt.

'So don't go knocking the jerry, lad. Without it, you'd be piss in the wind. And now help me up. And when you've done that, you can look behind you. All the time I've been talking, it's been turning into a fine day.'

The Statue

The rue Lapin slinks like a pickpocket behind the back of the Théâtre Larache, joining the boulevard Denfert-Rochereau at the rue Saint-Anne. It is a narrow street, without distinction or interest apart from a medieval tower, now closed, from where the French navy claim the discovery of twenty-one planets.

Walk up the rue Lapin in summer and you might miss its other attraction: the statue of a man on horseback, cast in sea-storm bronze. The statue stands back from the road in a recess planted with four copper beeches. The head of its rider is lost in the trees. When the wind parts the leaves, he is revealed in a plumed hat. The hat is waxy with pigeon droppings, like one of the bottles used for candles in the bistro opposite.

Over 6,000 miles away, in the Bolivian mining town of Oruro and dominating a windswept square on its northern outskirts, stands an identical statue. The greyish-green rider not only looks the same, down to the bird shit on his chevrons. On closer examination, he is the same, cast in the Fabrique de Fer, No. 4 avenue Béco, from the same mould.

The plaque on the Norwegian granite base in Paris reads:

Le Maréchal Ney 1769–1815

It was erected to commemorate the hero of Borodino and Smolensk, who once threatened to bring Napoleon back to Paris in a cage.

The plaque on the statue in Oruro describes a man who died fifty-six years later, shot through the jaw while pounding his mistress's door in Lima. His plaque reads:

General Mariano Melgarejo
President of Bolivia, 1864–1871

Beneath in smaller letters, runs the inscription:

Riding out on his great march astride Holofernes

A March evening in Paris, 1910. A full house at the Gaîté-Lyrique. The audience stares. Lights explode across rapt faces. Red and blue gunfire igniting the dark horizons of bank clerks, apothecaries, charlatans, kings.

They watch Aladdin rub his lamp. With a Moorish leer, he wishes for all the charms of Paris. His words challenge the stage.

'All the charms of Paris . . .' The words echo in the underground cavern, empty but for a basket of flowers.

More lights explode. The petals stir, their movement mimicked in the audience by young King Manoel of

Portugal who cannot see flowers without smelling the japonica which his mother had poked into the face of her assassin, but who forgets everything as he sees a blonde head rising from the artificial leaves. For this woman, he thinks, gazing down on her breasts, each covered as if to restrain its prominence with a glittering starfish, he could imagine losing his throne. (Later, he does.)

She steps from her basket and trips. The audience inhales, in finer concert than a chorus line. She steadies herself. Her mouth swells into a smile. She turns to those in the dark at her feet, each imagining she looks at him. The orchestra strikes up.

'When I take my *bain de mer*,' sings Gaby Deslys, 'at what do all the men stare?'

One of the staring young men is a young Bolivian called Lizardo Real. He sits in the third row, tapping his foot against the seat in front, a habit which has caused its occupant to rotate twice. On each occasion, Lizardo has forced his eyes offstage to the woman next to him, whom later he will walk to the Restaurant Paillard (for the *choucroute impériale* which has become his favourite dish), and afterwards, to her room in quai de Béthune, fourth floor, front, where he will watch the large knot in which she has piled her peroxided hair untie itself with a magnificent shiver as he struggles to unbutton her boots.

The woman who steps from the black silk dress – his gift – is Marie. Her abnormally long eyelashes remind him of a girl from Oruro called Ana.

That night, holding her from behind, his moustache against her shoulder, his face in the cobwebbed tunnel of her hair, Lizardo hears the rise and fall of Marie in her sleep. She is far away, in Besançon again, a talkative little girl (who wishes she was as tall and pretty as her sister), helping her father, the glazier, to prise ducks from the frozen river. Lizardo feels someone else in his arms, awake. He feels Ana. He imagines the look in her eyes. He closes his eyes to avoid it. He cannot. She twists away from him, out of his arms. He dare not open his eyes. He feels her gaze pressing down, down, more unsparing than the Altiplano sun.

It is an April afternoon two years before. Lizardo Real, wearing his only suit, walks quickly up the stone steps into Oruro's town hall, a nondescript building on the Calle Pizarro. He is expected at a meeting of the municipal council, of which he is treasurer, by the town's Mayor, Guillermo Valencia.

Valencia has convened the meeting to discuss the erection of a public monument in the square opposite the railway station. He rakes his long beard with a hand, waiting for his council to join him. He rehearses his argument.

For over three centuries metal had been gouged from Oruro's hills, first silver, now tin. Its children breathed darkness from the moment they could walk. Every day its women leaned in the doorways having touched the shoulders of their men one last time in case they didn't return, watching them disappear into the river of heads, cheeks pouched with wads of coca, teeth green, hearts black as the shafts under the mountain known as Negro Pabellon.

That mountain had produced as much wealth as the Imperial City of Potosi, sufficient – according to the computations of the Fricke Company accountant – to build a silver bridge three carriages wide from South America to Europe. And what was there in Oruro to show for all this? Nothing, aside from two trees in the plaza, a peach and a twisted willow, which were covered every night with hessian sheets because of the wind, and a handful of foreigners from the mining company who fainted in the altitude if they tangoed so much as the length of the Hotel Terminus.

Otherwise, the town was one grey house after another, one street no different from the next, one street corner the same as every other corner, so relentlessly the same that it was common even for people who hadn't tasted a drop of Oruro's villainous maize beer to mistake their own doorsteps.

In another year, the men who nodded greeting in the town hall might have argued against Valencia's proposal. But in that year the railway between Oruro and Viacha had been completed.

The town was already connected by a narrow-gauge track to Antofagasta, 600 miles to the south. The new line opened Oruro to traffic from the capital, La Paz. Even the council's nervous vice-president, Juan Alonso, whose pale, thin face could have spent its thirty-four years in bandages, agreed that on leaving the terminus building, vistors from the capital should be greeted by something other than a grey monotony enlivened by two twisted trees.

'Gentlemen,' growled Valencia, when all were mustered. He looked purposefully at them. 'We have one item on the agenda. The monument in Plaza ——.'

Guillermo Valencia was fifty-five. He was small and squarely built, without a care for how he dressed, which might have been in a thunderstorm, his black corduroy suit flapped open by the same unseen gust that parted the ends of his long silvery beard into two ruffled scarves that could be thrown back over each shoulder, tempting the woman he loved, Chacita, the giggler, to tie their ends on certain occasions with scarlet bows.

In fifty-five years, Valencia had never been taken seriously by women. He was as helpless in their grasp as he would have liked men to be in his own. The truth was, men also found him a little absurd. Even if they didn't know about the red bows, they could have imagined them. But unlike the women of Oruro, they didn't dare laugh out loud. Irascible, single-minded, unforgiving, Valencia was a bad man to have as an enemy, which was why no one around that table listening to him could doubt the outcome. Valencia was able to make each of their lives extremely tiresome. His mind was set on this scheme. What did it matter anyway?

After a twenty-minute soliloquy he formally proposed the erection of his monument. The vote was passed unanimously. Valencia put a second proposal to the vote: the subject of the monument. He argued there was only one candidate – the man whose exertions had placed Oruro on a map that linked the town not just with La Paz, but with the most advanced nation in the world – and in so doing bound Oruro, briefly if splendidly, with the fate of France.

'You all know who I'm talking about.' He surveyed the eleven faces round the table. They nodded gravely. They knew who he was talking about. They knew their Mayor's inexplicable belief that he was in some curious way – which explained the length he grew his beard, the sudden flames of anger, the opaque gentlenesses – a blood relation to this man, a man whose 'exertions' they saw in a radically different light: the beam of dismal defeat. But what did they care? Napoleon, Bolívar, Melgarejo, Christ on his bicycle, it was only a statue. Valencia could let this meeting last all day if he chose, and they all had reasons for getting away. To see whether Lizardo's aunt, Hortensia, could produce something from her shawl to chase the pain from an abscessed gum. To win another trick off her husband in a room behind the billiard parlour. To sleep.

Valencia's eyes rested on the face of his protégé, Lizardo Real, who was dreaming of the stationmaster's daughter and the blue-and-white dress he was intending to buy her from the Fricke Company store.

'I'm talking about General Mariano Melgarejo.'

Lizardo, as the council's treasurer, but also as Valencia's

favourite, was deputed to make enquiries. His enquiries revealed that no foundry in Bolivia was up to the task.

'It seems that every statue in La Paz, Cochabamba and Sucre comes from Paris.'

Valencia approved. He knew the love, amounting almost to an obsession, which General Melgarejo had held for France. In Lizardo's reply, he traced the same hand of fate which made him share the name – perhaps a good deal more – of the man supposed to be Melgarejo's father.

Lizardo found the address of a foundry in Paris. He drafted a letter from Valencia, requesting an estimate for an equestrian statue in the best available bronze.

Within three months, a reply came from the *directeur générale* of the Fabrique de Fer. In his letter, Monsieur Clémenceau enumerated the advantages of phosphor bronze – used to great effect on the Orléans railway. For its strength, for its resistance to the abrasion caused by 'your Altiplano winds, your dramatic variations in temperature', for its close-grained patina, phosphor bronze could not be excelled.

There was one drawback: the cost. But Clémenceau warned that the modern custom of reducing costs was likely to increase them. 'A bad phosphor bronze is no better than a bad gunmetal.' He estimated the cost of casting General Melgarejo on his mount Holofernes at 165,000 francs.

In Oruro, the Mayor registered surprise at the amount, but nevertheless agreed to the terms. Clémenceau was informed that Valencia's trusted young treasurer, Lizardo Real, would be leaving imminently for Paris, armed with the necessary bonds and an aquatint portrait of Mariano Melgarejo on Holofernes.

Lizardo's departure for Paris was an emotional one. His mother wept for the first time since the Liberal Revolution of 1889 and gave him three bush chickens, as well as two blankets, one thick, one thin, to wrap over his knees on board the *Thuringia*.

His proud father kissed him on both cheeks and wished him well. 'Do nothing I would not do,' he said, the limp in his smile acknowledging the extent to which he had ever done anything.

His aunt, the sapient *chola* from Challapata, said she'd probably be dead when he returned, buried beneath the weight on her back. (What she kept in that shawl was a secret that not even her husband knew, but she had produced from it on occasions an ostrich egg, a Chimu christening pot, a small pig – even, to his delight, five bottles of Allsopp's India Ale.) But she'd pray for Lizardo. 'Far from your home town, far from health . . .'

Only Ana had stayed at home, unable to watch him leave.

One by one Lizardo was embraced by the members of the council. No one knew quite what to say except a jealous Good Luck. Few of them had left Oruro – and then only to Uyuni – but they had the word of Don

Maximiliano who sold bibles for the Gospel Society that Paris was a den of the vilest iniquity.

'Don't disgrace us,' said the Mayor, grasping Lizardo's shoulders and pretending to survey his brown eyes, but instead thinking how much he, Guillermo Valencia, would like to be stepping onto that horse.

'We'll expect you back by the next Diablada.'

The Diablada. That was why Lizardo was leaving now on horseback, his face in the shadow of a large straw hat (a present from Ana). That was the reason he would spend this night on a mud bench in a *posta* instead of reclined in a comfortable seat on the Antofagasta train.

The carnival of the devil dancers had ended at midnight. Long before Valencia's decision to send him to France, Lizardo had been chosen to play China Supay, the Devil's wife, whose role was to seduce the Archangel Michael.

Lizardo had trained rigorously for the part. Even Orureños needed stamina to leap for a week at that altitude, springing this way and that to the dirge of drums, the voices of hell.

For ten weeks, he prepared his costume: the wig with braids finer than a Paracas weave, the plaster-of-Paris mask fanged with mirror-splinter teeth, the horns representing the temptations of the flesh, which he had lowered lasciviously at Juan Alonso, encased in the feathers of the Archangel – and at the very moment of lowering them sneezed so loudly at the dust coming through his mask that he caused the council's nervous vice-president to jump a foot in the air (just as, aged ten, the short-sighted Alonso had leapt in the stomach of Negro Pabellon on coming face to face with a blind pit mule; he had mistaken its ears for the devil's horns . . .).

None of this would Lizardo have missed, but in not missing it, he missed the train which had passed through Oruro the previous morning. Fortunately, the train stopped a whole day at Uyuni, 150 miles away. He planned to join it there for the journey over the nitrate fields to the coast.

The morning was crisp. Earlier, it had been so cold that Lizardo was forced to beat his arms about his chest, frightening a bird which he mistook for a pink flamingo. Now the sun was melting the coolness in the air. As he rode onto the stony moorland, a cloudless sky above his head, the white peaks of the Challapata mountains before him, the long *ichu* grass, coarse with frost, brushing his horse's flanks, the only sound the squeak of the saddle, it came to Lizardo that he had rarely been so happy.

Lizardo Real was twenty-eight, the son of a shy wheel-wright who worked for the mining company. The source of his family's pride was his degree in law (third class) from the University of Cochabamba. It was a rare quali-fication for an Orureño. At an early age he had been elected to *corregidor.*

Others might have felt his salary too small to ensure

honesty in government. Not Lizardo. He took pride in the machinations of bureaucracy, in balancing the books, in administering funds for public works, as others might take pride in laying a mosaic pattern. His pride was not so much moral as mathematical. Mistaking it, Valencia elevated him to treasurer.

What few suspected, only his aunt who saw it in her bezoar stone but who knew no spell on earth existed to cure it, was the extent to which Lizardo was a dreamer. He only had to see a peat mound to believe it concealed a network of silver veins to outstrip Potosi; a vulture to think it was something infinitely more beautiful. That was the trouble with Lizardo: all his buzzards were condors. But no one knew. They delighted in the qualities which made him at the age of twenty-eight such a prepossessing figure in Oruro, with a degree from the same university that had given Bolivia three presidents, two generals and a poet whose work was read aloud in the squares of Salamanca.

From the moment when he was asked to play in the Diablada to the moment when Valencia entrusted him with the mission of the statue, Lizardo had dreamed of little other than China Supay and Mariano Melegarejo – to the exclusion even of Ana, whom he found one night after drafting a final letter to Monsieur Clémenceau, with her hands over her eyes, in such despair that his arm around her neck would not console her, nor a kiss on her flinching cheek, only the assurance that when he came back from Paris he would bring an amethyst embedded in a wedding ring of pure gold . . .

But he had not thought of Ana. He had thought only of China Supay, the Devil's wife, and Mariano Melgarejo. And now the masked dance was over, now that he had dazzled the whole town with his splendid head and his somersaults, now that he had spent four days, from Wednesday to Saturday, with hands on his hips, his shoulders wriggling to the same tune, played over and over again by a band as repetitive as the streets through which he danced, now that the Diablada was finished for another year, Lizardo was still not free to think of the stationmaster's daughter.

His mind was devoted instead to the man whose image he carried carefully folded in his saddlepack, who had himself ridden out on this same road forty years before, to the same squeak of leather: General Mariano Melgarejo.

Lizardo loosened his reins. He rummaged for the aquatint, tucked behind the three bush chickens, next to the envelope containing bonds worth 165,000 francs. He removed it from its cardboard folder and laid it flat across his horse's withers. The portrait showed a small-headed man with deep eyes blacker than ore dust, and a beard as thick as mesh.

Lizardo looked into the face, rising up and down with the horse's walk, like a piece of bread on the sea. And in this position, he dreamed of Mariano Melgarejo, the Hero of December whose statue he was going to fetch from France.

* * *

Melgarejo's favourite town was Cochabamba, though he had sacked it. At university there, Lizardo heard stories about him every day, in the library, in bars, on the benches of the Plaza Colón. So often repeated they became proverbially true. A hurricane of calamities, was the common reaction to his name; or else, it wasn't his army that was invincible: it was his ignorance.

But there were those who saw a different side to Melgarejo – the side that made him take the hand of a little lost girl, encountered in the street after an orgy, and lead her back to her parents' hovel; the side that made him shoot dead his favourite carriage horses as they careered, Whoa there! down a narrow ravine towards a mother and child, unstoppable except by bullet.

In Melgarejo's rise and fall, these others saw dramatised the possibilities which are given to men who believe they can stun the world. Guillermo Valencia was such an apologist. So was his protégé Lizardo.

To Lizardo, born as Melgarejo was on Easter Sunday, he was an inspiration for men to live out their dreams; and all men dream.

Melgarejo was born in a town that sounded like a bugle call, Tarata, 100 miles from Oruro, where the grass was so long you could lose your horse in it. He was born on Easter Sunday 1820. 'God decided,' he said, 'that I should be born in the same hour as his resurrection.' He was born a bastard, the son of a white man he never knew – Justo Valencia – and a *mestizo* whose name he took. A love child, he was also a child of passion, of drink, of women, of the army, of anything aromatic with the gunpowder of adventure. He could ride at a gallop through the coca fields before he could walk. When he could walk, he could do so with a horse across his shoulders. He supported General Ballivian, then turned against him, and was twice condemned to death before the coup of December 1864 which brought him into La Paz on the day of the Innocents.

He entered La Paz often in the course of forty-two insurrections against him, once astride a spur-scratched cannon as if his feet were in the stirrups of Holofernes.

Astride Holofernes, he compared himself with Washington, Bolívar and Napoleon as a man sent by Providence. 'Don't forget to send my warmest greetings to the Emperor,' he commanded his minister in Paris.

He was compared by others with Rosas of Argentina, Francisco Solano López of Paraguay, Monagas of Venezuela, Santa Anna of Mexico, and Nero of Rome.

He was proud, quarrelsome, puerile, vain, suspicious, vulgar and brutal, but he could caress you with his warm voice, Oh, yes, there was no doubt of that, you only had to see it in the face of his mistress, Juana Sanchez, when he stripped her naked before his ministers and generals, ordering them to kneel in homage while he stood, a glass of blazing rum in his hands, looking at her through its flames and watching her smile at him, only for him, while he whispered over their backs, 'I love you, Juanita.'

He trusted no one and nothing – not even his shirt which he shot every night in case its folds hid something from him. But he trusted Juana Sanchez. He loved her more than he loved Holofernes, and no one lived to deny he loved Holofernes, that gigantic black horse, its tail like a waterfall at night, a horse more intelligent than any of his generals. 'It's that horse who wins my battles,' he would say. 'I've a small head. Look! he has a big head. He thinks for both of us.'

But Holofernes was not only more intelligent and much braver than his generals. He also drank more. As Melgarejo proved when he laid a place for him at a banquet and commanded a bucket of *chicha* to be carried to the table. Holofernes plunged his nose into the maize beer, drank, lifted his head, inspected the assembled guests, among them two Chilean diplomats, and lowered his lips as they toasted his health . . .

Lizardo rode on. The sun which before had made the horizon beautiful now made it pitiless. He folded the aquatint into his jacket pocket and removed the jacket. He took two gulps from his water bottle, raising his eyes to the plain where nothing grew except for a freak amaryllis and the occasional crop of white buttercups known by his aunt as 'laughing celery', a flower that made you die insane with what looked like a vast smile on your lips.

He passed through a village where all the doors were shut. Beyond, he came upon a caravan of llamas loaded with coffee and coca. Three Indians stopped and cornered them, waiting for Lizardo to ride by. The llamas craned their necks at him, and tore loudly at the grass. Like the cutting of a throat, thought Lizardo. That's how he would choose to die, from a knife thrust, not the barrel of a gun, not even the barrel of Melgarejo's ivory-handled pistol.

Lizardo closed his eyes.

He thought of ex-President Belzu.

The year was 1865. It was March. Four months after Melgarejo seized power, Belzu had returned from exile in Paris. He had reoccupied his palace in La Paz, his balcony. The crowd filled the Plaza Murillo to cheer him. In the distance, Melgarejo the dispossessed entered La Paz. As he approached the centre, his troops seeped away. When they reached the cathedral, a handful remained. He saw the desertion in their eyes. He placed his pistol to his temple. 'Either you follow, or I blow my brains out.' They followed. They followed him down the Calle Junín. They followed him into the Plaza Murillo. They only stopped when he stopped. 'Pretend I'm your prisoner,' he ordered. 'Take me into the palace.'

So they led him through the crowd. They led him under Belzu, who waved his hand benignly, his wrist moist with French cologne after ten years in exile. They led him into the palace.

He strode to the first floor. He entered the large room where he used to command officers to dance together, where on his orders the Bishop of Sucre had made three circuits on his hands and knees, where he had seen Juana Sanchez naked through the blue rum flames. He saw the shape of Belzu on the balcony, over which he had marched two squadrons of his Invincible Army of December, to demonstrate their discipline. He saw Belzu turn to greet him, his face, habitually the colour of ashes, now glowing with victory. He opened his arms to embrace him, tickling Belzu's forgiving cheeks with his beard. Then he shot him.

He carried the body to the balcony. He laid it along the balustrade. He raised a hand for silence.

'Belzu is dead,' he informed the crowd. 'Who lives now?'

The crowd below, hushed for another second, pronounced. '*Viva Melgarejo!*'

The sun was at its hottest. It raged. In the hot air, the horizon vanished in a mirage. Volcanoes were floating islands. On their slopes the waterline of the old lake became waves. To the north, a cloud of brown dust spiralled from the plain. Lizardo thought he saw a condor.

His horse stumbled and righted itself. Between its ears stretched a dry river bed, the contorted road to Uyuni. On this road, along the banks of this very river, General Megarejo had set out on his greatest march of all. The march that guaranteed the unanimous vote of the Oruro council for his monument.

In the heat, Lizardo's mind slipped like the reins from his grasp. In that landscape, his imagination danced like China Supay. In the mirage, his horse became Holofernes. If he turned now, he would find an army of 4,000 at his back, following him to the ends of the earth.

They had been marching for several hours. It was long after midnight. The rain, falling thin and cold as they left Oruro, had thickened. The Andean night was freezing. No one spoke. They were numbed by what they were doing, by where they were going, by the dampness of their uniforms, by their general who rode at their head in a poncho the colour of blood.

Most of them had been asleep when the order came to assemble before the garrison. A drum rattled. There was the sound of hooves in the mud. Then he appeared before them on Holofernes. He raised his hand, his small head, his enormous beard.

Those who knew him well said he had never been so sober.

'Soldiers of the Invincible Army of December,' he began. 'Soldiers of Liberty.' Their allies the French were at war. Everyone knew the esteem in which he held that nation, in which he held her Emperor. Everyone knew the contempt he felt for frontiers.

'We must go to her aid.'

The rain pitted the square. Dimly, they absorbed his words. Somewhere in a room in the Hotel Terminus a girl screamed. Holofernes stamped the ground, retreating.

Still that voice, hard as a dagger, but soft too, like *carpincha* leather, weaved through the rain.

France was far, he heard them say. Yes, it was. 'That's why we must set off immediately.'

And how would they get there? He looked at them as if to suggest they were idiots, all of them, for not having thought of it already. His lips curled the answer through his long glistening beard.

'If need be, we'll swim.'

So, spurring Holofernes roughly in the direction of the sea, he led his men – men who had never before left the Altiplano, nor seen the waves break, nor known a language other than Spanish, nor drunk anything else but *chicha* – towards the combined armies of Prussia, Bavaria, Württemberg and Baden.

They marched into the night. They marched for an hour. They marched for two hours. They marched, chafing and squelching, for eight hours. It seemed like eighty. The monotony hypnotised them so much that they didn't even know they had left the plain. They picked their way through a narrow *quebrada*. Water followed them down the gulley, rising over their boots. They slipped. Their rifles clattered against the stones. In this way, step by precipitous step, the file of drenched men descended towards the sound of a river.

They reached it as the sun was rising. The river tumbled between two high sandstone cliffs, carrying away the banks, the trees quivering at its edge, the road to the sea.

Melgarejo looked at the dawn and the water, at the rain fading into a maize sky.

'What do we do now?' asked an aide-de-camp.

He looked over the black peaks, behind which, on the other side of an ocean, lay the country he was hoping to liberate, the embattled figure of his cousin in arms, Napoleon III . . . And in that awful moment, it came to him that so far from swimming the sea, he couldn't even reach it, that under the soaking red tent of his poncho, he was just a man with delusions common to all men on the Altiplano.

He raised his hand to order the turnaround.

'We're going to have to do something about our roads.'

Lizardo's horse had stopped. They had reached the river, a narrow street of water, twenty yards across. Lizardo stretched his legs in his stirrups and kicked. Hesitantly, his horse entered the shallows, then broke into a trot.

Refreshed by the coolness of the water, it cantered up the bank opposite and shook itself. Lizardo listened to the harness jingling. He looked at the path ahead, sloping through some dwarf juniper trees.

He looked back at the river he had crossed. Replacing his hat, he inhaled deeply. Where Melgarejo had failed so grandiosely, he, Lizardo Real, treasurer to the municipal council of Oruro and inveterate dreamer, would complete the journey.

*　　*　　*

247

In Marie's room in the quai de Béthune, Lizardo had lain with his eyes closed, but awake, all night. Above him, his phantoms kept vigil. Ana's admonishing eyes had given way to Valencia's, Valencia's betrayed, uncomprehending eyes to the impassive eyes of his aunt – so close together that only her nose stopped them joining – who understood him too well. He wanted to hide their gaze with an arm, but his arms were folded around Marie and he hadn't removed them for fear of disturbing her into one of those moments of silence which would make him think she was caught for ever between breaths.

But now he felt such a constriction in his throat that he had to drink water or he would stop breathing himself. Gently, he unwrapped his arms from the warm girl. She laughed, amused by something in her sleep. In the dark, it was a child's laugh. It laughed away Lizardo's demons. He smiled. He poured a glass of water from the jug on the side table. The pain in his throat made it difficult to swallow. His neck ached. He rose to his feet. The joints of his knees ached also. His head rippled with dizziness.

He felt his way to the window. It was open, but he opened it wider, his hands gripping the iron balcony outside as he inhaled the first of several deep breaths that made his heart knock furiously against his chest with more determination than the fist of his uncle, the gambler, who was always convinced after an evening of cards that he was being locked out of his house, unbolted in the next street, a peat fire glowing, a kettle on the flames, and the smell of burning birds' beaks in both rooms because his wife had thrown some chicken heads onto the grate.

Lizardo lifted his eyes to the skyline. The sun was coming up, above the toll bridge on the quai de Béthune, the roofs along the rue des Écoles and the snakeskin boulevards, their cobbles shining from the night's rain.

He turned his back on Paris. He looked into the room where Marie was sleeping; at the credenza sideboard, on which lay her black dress and petticoat, the blank wall where he could imagine a painting, the marble floor with more veins than the face of his aunt, the sorceress from Challapata who was whispered to know the language of animals and who spent her days making cicada oils and coral powder and buttercup broths with her husband, who had been lamed by the heat, by *chicha,* by the card table, by day after day in the tin mines under Negro Pabellon, hoping to cut into a silver lode . . .

A bead of sweat salted his eye. Lizardo rubbed his forehead. His face was masked with sweat. Something was the matter. Never had he felt like this. He felt terrible, as if his lungs were filled with dust from a rockfall. He lay on the bed. He would have to see a doctor. Dress, when the sun was up. Go back to his hotel. Ask the manager to summon a reliable physician.

Suddenly, Lizardo felt his spirits lift. Of course. He would have to cancel the meeting with Monsieur Clémenceau, a meeting he had been dreading every day for a week. And why had he been dreading it? Because if at that precise moment Guillermo Valencia had entered the room and ordered Lizardo then and there to give an account of his finances after one month in Paris, he would have to admit to his Mayor that he didn't know whether he had enough to pay the Fabrique de Fer for a statue of Mariano Megarejo, Hero of December.

One month, that's all, since Lizardo Real found the little hotel in the rue Henri-de-Bornier, a few streets from the Bois de Boulogne where he would spend at least two afternoons of his first week tearing bread for the tame white condors called swans, bewitched by trees which didn't need to be covered every night, the elegant neighbourhoods, the department stores.

One month since the hotel receptionist had asked, 'Bolivia, what country's that in, then?'

Already, on that first morning, his country felt far. In just the journey from the station, Lizardo had begun to learn the truth of Proust's remark that an hour is not an hour, it is a vase filled with scents and sounds.

On that first morning, he walked to the Pré Catalan where he ordered a *café crème*. Sipping it, he smiled a satisfied smile that after four weeks on the *Thuringia*, he was at last drinking milk from the udders of a French cow. He raised his cup to the street through the window and gave a silent toast to Ana, to his parents, to his aunt and uncle, to the council of Oruro and its irascible Mayor, without whom . . .

But he hadn't forgotten his mission. He was looking forward to a month in the French capital while the statue was cast. Perhaps six weeks. But no longer.

That afternoon, after tasting his first *choucroute impériale*, he visited the Banque de la Nation in the rue de Maroc. There he deposited all but 50,000 francs – the sum requested by Monsieur Clémenceau as a first instalment.

Next morning, having hardly slept at all, Lizardo took a cab to the avenue Béco. In his briefcase (purchased at Printemps department store with a month's salary), he carried Melgarejo's aquatint and an envelope containing the 50,000 francs.

An attendant led him through the foundry. A crane was unloading axle blanks. A man stood by the electric arc furnace with a wet towel in his mouth. The floor was gravelly with moulder's sand. He was led upstairs.

Monsieur Clémenceau sat at a large desk behind a small lead bust of Columbine. To impress Lizardo, and to refresh himself with his language, he was reading the Spanish priest Alvaro Barba's account of treating complex ores in *El Arte de los Metales*. He skipped several pages while waiting. When Lizardo entered, he closed the book. He rose on his short legs, tidily covered in zinc-coloured cloth.

'Ah . . .' he said, brightening.

Red-faced, with puffy cheeks, he had the old-fashioned manner of one who had been pushed into the century from behind. His office reflected his preferred taste. It was immense: a fireplace where a fallen beech could roast an ox, a bay window overlooking an internal courtyard known as the 'graveyard' (packed with the casts which for various reasons fell short of Clémenceau's standard, the standard of a Ponts-trained perfectionist), and three sturdy armchairs upholstered in coppery leather, all redolent of the days when the company had acted as principal statuarist to Napoleon III, before it was forced to corner the market in wide-flange beams, fence posts and ships' propellers – which was why Lizardo's arrival, bearing the commission from Oruro, excited his sympathies.

'. . . The gentleman from Bolivia,' he continued in passable Spanish. He showed Lizardo into a chair, informing him of his fascination for Bolivian Bronze Age chisels, and his prize possession, a pair of llama-headed Topu tweezers.

'Now, your general on horseback. Show me, show me, show me.'

The meeting ended an hour later with Clémenceau writing out Lizardo a receipt for the first instalment – 'the deposit' – and fixing a date one month ahead, by which designs for the twenty-six-foot statue would be complete.

'Then, if you're satisfied,' he said, filling two thin glasses from a bottle of grenadine, 'you pay the full amount – and we cast!'

One month. It was to be four weeks too many for Lizardo. Two weeks made him coltish. Four quite simply deranged him.

What broke him? Was it the first crack of the walnut which Dufay opened between her breasts at the Moulin Rouge? Was it his ride in the back of a Rocher-Schneider belonging to a rich young painter, at the wheel of which Lizardo may well have knocked down Gide's wife in the Place de la Concorde? Was it the sight of Gaby Deslys's blonde head emerging from the silk petals, or the sound of her voice singing 'La Parisienne' through the *théâtro-phone* beside his hotel bed?

Maybe there was never a single, identifiable moment, instead a gradual discovery that it was more satisfying to play the role of a rich South American in Paris – albeit one often mistaken for an Argentine – than to be a scrupulous administrator of funds on the Altiplano.

Maybe in his second week, one evening as he returned from the Restaurant Paillard or the Moulin Rouge or the Saint Louis theatre, having spent more of Melgarejo's money, it finally came to him that the person he had hitherto known as Lizardo Real was in fact a compound of several people – mayors, gamblers, generals, sorceresses, stationmasters' daughters – each with desires that changed. Their modified amalgam did not necessarily enjoy the same experience tomorrow as they had enjoyed today. Or yesterday.

Or was it a lot simpler? Was it merely that he discovered French women, among them the *femina destruens* who may have passed on the disease that was eventually to kill him?

In that month, Lizardo was to out-Melgarejo Melgarejo in his womanising, taste more strange spirits than Melgarejo's horse. Eyes widened at the money that flowed from him. Seeing those eyes, like the billiard-ball eyes of his China Supay mask, Lizardo's desire was to widen them further. His conscience wasn't ruffled by what he spent, not even on a portfolio of American railroad shares that promptly collapsed. The sums he lavished, he would recoup at the drop of one of his Borsalino hats.

Some weeks after the constriction in his throat, after three cancelled appointments with Monsieur Clémenceau, Lizardo paid another visit to the Banque de la Nation. It was a different man who walked from his hotel, not daring to spend a few coins on a cab. In walking, he bent like a stunted tree as if his legs, which now and then knocked together, were not strong enough to support the rest of him. His once confident moustache meandered over a face pinched with pain. The pain was caused by his fever, but his expression also owed something to what he had swallowed – a solution of mercury potassium iodide and opium.

He shuffled energetically into the bank. Someone – he didn't know if it was an attendant or a client – found him a chair. He produced his credentials and was given a metal badge with a number on it. A few minutes later, after experiencing initial difficulty in explaining what he wanted, he was brought the balance of the Oruro account.

Of the 115,000 francs owing to Monsiuer Clémenceau, less than half remained.

Lizardo walked out into the street. He needed fresh air. He needed time to think. Once more he consulted his diary, recording the appointment postponed from the previous week.

'11.00 a.m. M. Clémenceau. 115,000 fr,' read the bald entry. He loosened his amethyst cravat. He could taste grenadine on his lips. 115,000 francs. His memory was as furry as his tongue. He tried to think of his uncle, the gambler at cards who had once returned with a sheep under his arm and a finger across his lips saying, 'Don't ask . . .' He thought of his work as treasurer. One spectacular investment, that would save him. That was all he needed.

He was shuffling past the Salon des Indépendants when a man thrust a leaflet into his hand.

'Read it, *monsieur*.'

Lizardo read. The leaflet promoted the current exhibition, devoted to an important new movement, the Excessivists. Beneath the announcement was an extract from the Excessivist manifesto, printed the previous week in *Le Figaro*.

Excess in everything is strength. The sun is never too strong, the sky too green, the distant sea too red, darkness too thickly black.

'Where's the exhibition?' asked Lizardo.

'In there.'

The rooms were hung with canvases, crudely hammered onto large frames. They struck Lizardo as incomprehensible. The centrepiece was a painting depicting nothing on earth that Lizardo could recognise, except that the colours reminded him of his aunt's bezoar stone.

'It's a masterpiece,' pronounced a man in front of him, standing back for a better view and treading on Lizardo's toes. Lizardo hopped about the floor. The man apologised, then walked off, muttering about a confrontation of obsessions.

'You know who that was?' said someone. 'The great critic D——.'

Lizardo stood stiller than a pink flamingo in the lake of Pampas Aullagas. He cocked his head. His mind filled with the blankness of the wall above Marie's bed. His eyes lurched over the granular surface before him.

'I'll buy it,' he said.

A fortnight later, Lizardo lay in Marie's bed, holding a newspaper to the window. He was reading and rereading and reading again, as if he had missed the sense of it, an article in *Le Figaro*, which unveiled the Excessivists as hoaxers, sick of fauvists, symbolists and every other ist – and his 50,000 francs masterpiece the result of tying a brush to the tail of a donkey belonging to the owner of the Lapin Agile.

He threw the paper to the floor. He hurled the curtains together above him.

A donkey!

In his fever, he cursed the vile creature. He hadn't eaten for three days because of mouth ulcers. His frail body was sustained on a diet of hyssop and porridge. His mind was driven by mirages. He saw himself tied to a donkey in La Paz, the same pack animal on which Melgarejo had strapped the British Consul for not paying homage to Juana Sanchez. He saw himself galloped out of La Paz backwards, towards a furious English Queen who had famously responded to Melgarejo's insult by pouring ink over a map of Bolivia. He couldn't see her, only the diminishing figure of Melgarejo, but over the Hero of December's shoulder he heard Queen Victoria's voice declare that as of this moment Bolivia no longer existed.

Thinking of Melgarejo, he coughed. 'Donkeys must be in our destiny,' he said aloud. Someone moved in the kitchen. 'Juana?' he yelled, raising himself on an elbow. 'Juanita . . . ?'

Along the quai de Béthune during the third week of November 1910, a man in a dirty brown suit known as 'the Bolivian' began his market performance like this: 'Which is the journey not begun in hope, which is the *chicha* not mixed with tears, which is the cloth not woven with thorns, the bird that is not a vagabond . . . ?'

His French was halting and a woman soon bundled him away.

Early in December, two men disappeared up the same

stairs of the mansion block. When they reached the landing of the fourth floor they consulted a piece of paper. They knocked at a door. A moment went by. They knocked again, louder. The door opened, wide enough for the head of the woman who looked at them. She wore a loose dress stained with milk. Her face was empty of expression. She seemed exhausted.

'Where is he?'

The question was spoken in Spanish. She shook her head. She didn't understand. Behind her a child cried. '*J'arrive, j'arrive.*'

She hesitated. She looked from one to the other, registering their determination. She opened the door. The child screamed.

The room was as dark as a mine. It smelled stale and bitter, like flowers left too long in their water. The two men found Lizardo in bed, under his mother's blankets, beside a window with the curtains drawn. They pulled back the curtains. In the afternoon sun his face shone like a scrap of leather nailed to a bone, except the vermilion had disappeared from the blood and the skin was black, as if he had been hung in smoke. The eyes opened. Then closed. They opened again and narrowed deliriously on the two Bolivians standing over him.

'Soldiers of Liberty!' he greeted them.

He lay watching them search the room. They looked in the panelled sideboard, under the bed, behind a large garish canvas on the wall, in the wardrobe where they found a crumpled silk dress. In the wardrobe they also discovered a suit which contained in its pockets the correspondence between Guillermo Valencia and Monsieur Clémenceau, and a receipt for 50,000 francs. They returned to the bed.

'Where is it?'

'France is far, I hear you say!'

'Where is it?' One of them slapped the leather cheeks. 'Or have you spent it all?'

The voice rattled. '. . . which is why we must set off immediately.'

They dressed him from a pile of clothes on a chair by the door. The woman held her baby daughter in her arms, watching.

'Come on,' said one.

'*Vous l'emmenez où? Il est malade.*'

The door slammed.

They took him in a hansom cab to the avenue Béco. He said nothing for the whole journey. His head lolled from side to side as if it were not properly connected to his shoulders. His eyes had a diseased sheen. His jacket was spotted with leaves. They arrived at the foundry. One of the men dragged him into the building by his shirt collar. The other demanded a meeting with the *directeur général*.

Five minutes passed.

Clémenceau sent word he would see the gentlemen from Bolivia.

They abandoned Lizardo in a chair downstairs. A coughing attack made him too weak to walk. The doorman promised to attend to him. Impatiently, they climbed the stairs.

Clémenceau was not overjoyed by their arrival. They had interrupted an article he was writing for the *Revue de Métallurgie* on the property of binary alloys, with special reference to Pierre Martin whom he accused of sounding the death knell on the puddling furnace. Nevertheless, their arrival was something he had expected.

He replaced the top on his pen and sighed. From a drawer by his knee he slid out a folder. Then he walked round the desk to see how he could assist the two councilmen from Oruro.

'He cancelled me here. He cancelled me there.' His fingers played piano on the designs he laid out. 'He cancelled me everywhere.'

Not hearing a word for two months, Clémenceau contacted Monsieur Real's hotel. He had left.

'He still owed them money. If he can't pay his hotel bill, I thought, how can he pay us? I wrote to your Mayor, Monsieur . . .' He searched through the correspondence. 'There was the question of the deposit.'

He looked again at the artist's proof. 'Such a pity. A wonderful commission.'

'Oh, we still want a statue of General Melgarejo,' said one of the men. 'That's why we're here.'

That's why, popping with anger like an over-roasted

guinea pig, Valencia had sent them. That's why on the morning he received Clémenceau's letter, not waiting for his beard trim at the Hotel Terminus, he had marched up the Calle Bolívar coiling his moustaches into a tangled fleece that trailed in a single coil behind him, and burst without a knock into the house next door, staying only to apologise to Señor Mendoza, the Fricke Company accountant, for having disturbed the love he was making so energetically to his *chola* cook, then appearing at the right door to tell Juan Alonso, his vice-president, that he had to set off for Paris immediately, to find out what had happened to Lizardo, the protégé who had failed him so abysmally, and to bring back, as if his life depended on it, the town's monument to the Hero of December.

'But the deposit is all we have,' added the other, Juan Alsonso, now engaged to the stationmaster's daughter. 'What will it buy us?'

'Fifty thousand francs?' Clémenceau closed the folder. 'Less the artist's fee . . . not much.'

At that moment, a terrific shout penetrated the window behind the desk. It was accompanied by the clashing and clanging of metal. The hubbub rose from the square below. Clémenceau hurried over. He opened the window. His cheeks were pink.

'You'd better see for yourselves,' he said at last. The two men squeezed past his desk. They looked down on a small internal courtyard of rusting statues, cracked moulds and cast-offs: Cupids without bows, Venuses with twisted ligaments, negroes bearing bent sundials, broken vases, benches, street lamps – and in the middle of this cast-iron, copper, phosphor-bronze detritus, a large equestrian statue of Marshal Ney.

The shouts were Lizardo's. He was mounted behind the hero of Borodino. He was kicking the green sides of Ney's horse with the heels of an untied shoe. He was hugging the rider, seeing in the shape of Napoleon's general the general of his delirium, taking the *via dolorosa* of exile after the coup of 1871, which had left him without money, without uniforms, without medals, with just his horse Holofernes.

He was shouting his agonised shouts because he had just discovered that the Indians, made homeless by Melgarejo, had lopped off Holofernes's ears.

'Fifty thousand francs,' said Clémenceau, the perfectionist, ignoring the deranged figure of Lizardo stretching forward to staunch the bleeding bronze, and seeing the cast he had rejected because it contained too much zinc, 'might buy you that statue of Ney.'

By the time they reached the courtyard, Lizardo Real had slipped from his saddle for ever. He was buried in the Picpus cemetery, next to the guillotined body of a Carmelite nun. He was not yet thirty.

But his horse rode on, a slightly imperfect cast commissioned to celebrate the centenary of Borodino, the battle for which Marshal Ney, the red lion, the bravest of the brave, had won for himself the title Prince de la Moskova.

Transported with enormous difficulty to Bolivia – thirty stevedores had lowered it into the *Thuringia*'s hold – it was erected opposite Oruro's railway station to the rhapsodic squeal of a brass band and toasted by the whole community with *chicha*. The *chicha* soon flooded away Valencia's doubts, after he had jerked away the shroud at his third attempt, that General Melgarejo's features were somewhat finer than he remembered, his figure leaner, that he lacked a beard.

What could be the reason? Perhaps there was something about a clean chin, Valencia thought, searching for his own, concealed beneath its manicured tufts, and contemplating the bronze face above him. Maybe, after all, a beard was a little ageing. Maybe there was no end to what not wearing a beard could do . . .

In the end, men see what they want to see. Only Juan Alonso, who succeeded Valencia as Mayor a year later, knew the story behind the statue and Lizardo's dereliction. Nicanor Mendez, Lizardo's replacement as treasurer who had accompanied Ana's fiancé to Paris, took the secret to his grave in a field above Oruro where he had been able to purchase a small concession, a *pertenencia* of fifteen hectares, with the silence he sold to Alonso.

Lizardo's family, like the rest of Oruro, knew nothing of this, believing he had died of incipient uraemia in 1912. Once a year, on the last Sunday in April, there was a Mass said for him, attended by Lizardo's uncle, who always promised his wife that he would touch neither drop nor playing card until the next day; by the sorceress who preferred her own incantations to the priest's; and for the first years by Ana, until one year she failed to turn up, confessing she had been worn down by her husband's unaccountable irritation whenever Lizardo's name was mentioned.

Today, the monument still commands the square. On certain days, on feast days and for the four days of the Diablada, its massive neck is garlanded with flowers and little children are lifted onto the plinth to scuttle between the legs. On the benches in its shadow, new generations listen to old men repeat the story of its rider, caught at the very moment he sets out across the barren plain, followed by his soldiers.

No ceremony attends the identical statue in the rue Lapin, lost in the trees. But if you were born in Oruro and you emerged one lunchtime from the bistro called Jean dans le Désert (where they serve a whiting *en colère*, tail in mouth, as if doubled in rage), you might well rub your eyes in astonishment at the vision of General Mariano Melgarejo galloping towards you, having finally crossed the seas to liberate France.

The Orange-bellied Parrot

Alison had never liked her grandmother, who lived alone in a big overheated apartment in Zurich, and so when Helen went into hospital after a mild stroke and, rather than consent to enter a nursing home, elected for a 'self-determined death' with the tidy assistance of Swiss law, drawing stumps, as it were, on ninety-one years, Alison was pleased for Helen and relieved for herself.

The meaning of an act differs if it is performed by an old lady or a young boy, by an Australian or a Swiss, by a twice-widowed battleaxe or a divorced granddaughter. Upon learning of her grandmother's decision, Alison recognised how consistent it was with Helen's conservative and stubborn nature. It was the act of someone who refused to listen to anyone. 'I had a very difficult relation-ship with her,' Alison remembered her mother once explaining, 'because I would not let her dominate my life.' A characteristic which may have descended.

Alison was visiting London with Josh, her fourteen-year-old son, when she received the text message from Karl asking her to call him in Switzerland. Karl was Helen's only child from her second marriage. Alison's immediate response on speaking with him: she would make a detour to Zurich before flying back to Hobart. She and Josh were the last surviving members of the Australian side of Helen's family, and out of some superstition or instinct Alison felt impelled to take her son with her to say goodbye. Josh as a result had one of his tantrums. There seemed to Josh really very few things more boring than going to see an ancient relative you have not met and were certain never to meet again. Alison had had to bribe him with the promise of an excursion to Basel to look at a stuffed auk.

On their first afternoon in Switzerland, they visited Karl at his studio in Zollikon on Zurich's southern outskirts. Karl in black jeans and a black roll-neck jersey stepped out of his elaborate front door and gave Alison a crushing hug. Josh stared at something on the fence before shaking hands.

Alison's half-uncle was good-looking and aware of it. But not a man for horseplay. Fifteen years older than Alison, he seemed suspended half a generation away; neither sibling nor parent. Over a late lunch of cold meats and asparagus, he talked about his mother, her grandmother; and about the period following Helen's stroke.

Helen would have quietly died without treatment, he said in his accentless English. After a few days in hospital, she became clear in her head. It was obvious that she could not return to her apartment. But she did not find it pleasant to be hospitalised. In the course of thinking about where she would have to go ('I proposed a nursing home in Lavigny'), his mother resolved to contact Exit, an organisation which assisted those who, as Karl expressed it, 'wished to call it a day'. A man came to the hospital and explained what had to be done. Helen first needed to join Exit as a member, with a membership fee ('which I paid'). Then she had to fill out many forms ('which I never saw, basically declaring that what she was doing was her own decision, nobody was pressing her'). The man returned to pick up the forms; a date was set. The procedure could not have been more sensitive or diplomatic. His mother had one last document to sign – Karl would be taking it to her after Alison's visit. On Friday, an ambulance was booked to drive Helen to an apartment in Zurich where an official from Exit would terminate her life.

'I absolutely agree to the way she has chosen,' Karl said, plucking at the skin below his shiny round chin. 'Nobody has tried to stop her.'

It is well known that some people cheer up when their parents die, but the mourning-free manner in which Karl looked forward to his mother's end made Alison, now confronted with the clinical details, strangely uneasy – even though Helen had kept the family busy with her death, about which she had talked since she was sixty, when her Swiss second husband, Karl's father, passed away.

Josh, fidgety, asked if he might go into the garden.

Left alone with Alison, Karl wished to demonstrate how he had kept Helen's affairs in order. He ran around the room, talking to her and producing papers. 'Look, even her Australian passport is up to date!' In the same spirit, he had organised wreaths – white flowers, except for Alison's (she had requested orange and green). The will – who was going to get what. And her burial place.

Karl cleared a space on the table and spread out a map. 'The reason we stayed with this cemetery is that it's maintained like a park. No vandals and not near a river. We own this whole plot here.'

There were four places left, should Alison be interested.

One matter alone had troubled Karl: the gravestone. He produced a photograph of a rocket shape carved from black granite. Karl, being an architect, had wanted to design a monument. 'I tried hard, but the old girl wouldn't choose a bigger stone.'

'What does she want on it?'

'"Loved and blessed."'

Till we meet again, At home with Jesus and *She served the Swiss-Australian community with dignity* – his mother had rejected each of his suggestions.

'She really wants to die?'

Karl stepped back, arms folded. 'Oh God, yes.'

What smiled across at Alison from the other side of the dining-room table was still the discreet and polite efficiency of Europe; and the space it smiled across was broader than the Indian Ocean.

After some small talk about Tasmania, two perfunctory questions concerning Alison's work as a history teacher and the best way to get to Basel, plus another bear hug, they were on their way.

Only when they reached the street did Josh remember. He was abject. 'I think I put them on the windowsill,' he muttered. Furious, Alison marched back up the path. Is anything more fucking embarrassing, she thought, when you have gone through the ceremony of saying your thank-yous and farewells, than to discover you have left something behind?

Ding dong. Staring at the metal door. The network of bronze hexagons. And the glass circle in the centre which presently blurred with a face.

Karl's expression when he saw her again was confused, tense.

'I'm sorry. Josh forgot his binoculars.'

The following morning, they visited Helen in her hospital room. She had a bright melon scarf around her neck and sat in a wheelchair, with her back to a window overlooking the lake.

'You're thinner,' after Alison tried to kiss her.

When Alison began to introduce Josh, Helen's lips contracted and she gave Alison a questioning look: 'You've seen Karl?'

Alison nodded.

'I've changed my mind.'

Josh glanced at her, Alison too.

'About the words,' in the squashed-out drawl of someone trying to hide an accent. 'If I'm going to have a rock on my head, I don't want "Much loved!"'

'I thought it was "Loved and blessed."'

Helen seized on this as proof that her architect son planned unilaterally to replace her tombstone with something larger, with more words. His first suggestion had been: 'To live in hearts we leave behind is not to die.' She would not sign his document until she had seen a photograph showing the inscription.

'I just want my original family name, Helen Olderton, born in Hobart, died in Zurich, and the dates.'

In every other respect – it was clear to Alison, thinking about it later – Helen's mind was made up. Death to a woman who has resided fifty-one years in Zurich was too familiar an experience to excite either terror or regret. She had hung on to the branch long enough, outlived two husbands and a daughter. It was no big deal what she was about to do.

Already in London, Alison had decided that she would temper the occasion by taping some of Helen's memories. She wheeled over a trolley, explaining that she would like to ask a few questions – about her grandmother's childhood in Hobart, her first marriage. Nothing difficult. It was something she encouraged her pupils at her school in Taroona to do. 'It'll give Josh something to remember you by.'

'Josh?' And looked at her son as though Alison had launched the boy on the slide down the razor blade of life by naming him that.

But Josh was not paying attention.

'What is he looking at?'

'Josh?'

He turned from the window and trained his 'bins' on his mother – fumbling with her tape-recorder lead. Next, on Helen.

The old lady, caught in his unreflecting focus, straightened in the wheelchair. Her eyes flickered. She pressed her right hand into her cheek, then took it away, and the flesh, grey and puffy, stayed depressed for a few seconds and refilled like an old tennis ball.

He lowered the binoculars. 'You know you've got a collared dove nest in your Virginia creeper?'

'I'm just going to see if I can borrow a plug,' announced Alison.

Ten minutes later, Alison returned. The wheelchair faced the window. Helen leaned forward, an unnatural look in her eye, as if she was interested and didn't want to show it. 'Why was it on the lake, do you think?'

'Blown off course, probably,' Josh said. 'It went horribly overland the wrong way and got royally lost.'

And Alison, setting up the tape recorder (a receptionist

in Oncology had found her an adaptor), knew that he was talking about the bird they were going to see at the Naturhistorisches Museum. A long-billed murrelet. The first ever found in Europe – turning up drowned in a fishing net on Lake Zurich in December 1997 when it should have been in Japan.

'Hey, what's that?' asked Helen.

Josh tracked a large speck with his bins. 'Another little brown job.'

'Another little brown job . . .' Her laugh was less hard. She knew no more about birds than the man in the moon did.

'Most birds are brown and boring,' said Josh.

'Funny,' Helen reflected, 'I was never interested in birds.'

'Nor was I,' chirped Alison, inserting the cassette. She always thought that birds were stupid. There was nothing there. They were only dinosaurs. Feathery dinosaurs.

'They really are dinosaurs,' murmured her birder son. Who suddenly lowered his shoulders, as though preparing to take flight. Excited, he handed his bins to Helen. 'There – on the quarry face,' and bent over, adjusting the lens for her.

'What am I looking for? Oh, now I see,' came the grudging voice that was losing its solemnity. 'Red and grey, isn't it?'

'I'm pretty certain it's a wallcreeper,' Josh was telling them both. He'd seen one in his book. A delightful little bird, a resident of the Alps that in winter came to lower altitudes.

'Does it sing?' asked Helen.

'Only when defending its territory.'

The wallcreeper flew off. With reluctance, Helen returned the binoculars. A freckle on Josh's eyelid drew attention to his eyes. His face was smooth. 'What do you think drives you?' she asked.

Alison felt a pang for her son. He could never put it into words without sounding peculiar or awkward. At the same time, it was important that he try and describe it.

'Answer your great-grandmother, Josh.'

He held his bins against his chest, abstractedly twisting the focus wheel. 'Well . . . it takes you to some amazing places.'

His mother turned back the cloth on the trolley and laid the tape recorder on the glass underneath. 'Tell Helen about that parrot you want to go and see in the Tarkine.'

When, five days later, Alison tried to explain it to Karl, her grandmother's spontaneous explosion of lucidity, she recalled how during the interview Helen had begun to speak of Australia with a special quality in her voice.

'What the hell did you say to her? You must have said something. I simply can't . . .' On the other side of the world, Karl was swearing. 'She's cancelled everything. She's talking about some blasted parrot with an orange stomach. She says there are only thirty-five left and they all live in Tasmania and she has to go and see one.'

Not until she replayed the tape did Alison catch the vital note unheard at the time. Helen was discussing with Josh the definition of 'a credible sighting'.

'*If just you or me saw it, no,*' Josh said.

A pause. '*What if we both saw it?*'

'*Yeah, that would count.*'

A little word can be a clap of thunder. After a perpetual winter of being herself, Helen had woken on the morning following Josh's visit feeling invigorated. She had risen from her bed at the second attempt and shuffled in small steps over to the window, stared out, and informed Karl, when he turned up an hour later with the final document for her to sign, that she wished to look down on Hobart again, the city where she had been born by caesarean section ninety-one years before, the streets that were dyed in the green and orange colours of her youth.

On top of it all, she wanted to go with her great-grandson to the Tarkine.

Acknowledgements

Although inspired by events that took place in Broken Hill on New Year's Day 1915, *Oddfellows* is a work of fiction; the characters are, in large part, creatures of a novelist's imagination. Gül Mehmet and Molla Abdullah did exist, but little is known of their background, and what information has passed down to us remains uncertain and contradictory. I am grateful to Murray Bail for introducing me to their story and for taking me to Broken Hill; to Brian Tonkin, Archives Officer in the Broken Hill Council; to staff of the Broken Hill Library and Railway Museum; and to Felix Ogdon. I would also like to pay tribute to *Tin Mosques & Ghantowns: A History of Afghan Cameldrivers in Australia*, by Christine Stevens (Oxford University Press, Melbourne, 1989). The quote from the *Leipziger Volkszeitung* is taken from Steve Packer's article 'The odd angry shot', *Sydney Morning Herald*, 3 January 1998.

'The White Hole of Bombay' was first published in *Granta 100* (London/New York, Granta, 2007).

'The Princess of the Pampas' was first published in *New Writing 7*, ed. Carmen Callil and Craig Raine (London, British Council/Vintage, 1998).

'The Death of Marat' was first published in *Ox-Tales* (London, Profile, 2009).

'The Castle Morton Jerry' was first published in *The Children's Hours: Stories of Childhood*, ed. Richard Zimler and Raša Sekulovic (London, Arcadia, 2008).

'The Statue' was first published in *The Paris Review* (Paris/New York, 1991, Vol. 33, Issue 119). For his summary of General Melgarejo's life and achievement the author gratefully acknowledges the work of Max Daireaux in his book *Melgarejo* (Paris, Calmann Levy, 1945).

'The Orange-bellied Parrot' was first published in *The Monthly* (Melbourne, December 2011).